KILLER-BEAM DEATH

Sturgis saw O'Reilly cut in half by the red light-beam. Jesus, he'd never seen anything like it! A tank that flew—with a laser killer-beam!

The tank banked and came back for another strafe. Sturgis and a half-dozen of his men took aim and fired a stream of ammunition, but shells and bullets bounced harmlessly off the tank's hull. Grenades and Liquid-Plastic Fire did no damage, either. The damn thing was near invulnerable!

"Take cover!" Sturgis hollered over the radio.

But the tank's gunports had already opened, and with a thunderous *boom*, shells rained from the sky, scoring direct hits on two men, blowing them into tiny fragments . . .

ASHES
by William W. Johnstone

OUT OF THE ASHES   (1137, $3.50)

Ben Raines hadn't looked forward to the War, but he knew it was coming. After the balloons went up, Ben was one of the survivors, fighting his way across the country, searching for his family, and leading a band of new pioneers attempting to bring American OUT OF THE ASHES.

FIRE IN THE ASHES   (1310, $3.50)

It's 1999 and the world as we know it no longer exists. Ben Raines, leader of the Resistance, must regroup his rebels and prep them for bloody guerrilla war. But are they ready to face an even fiercer foe—the human mutants threatening to overpower the world!

ANARCHY IN THE ASHES   (1387, $3.50)

Out of the smoldering nuclear wreckage of World War III, Ben Raines has emerged as the strong leader the Resistance needs. When Sam Hartline, the mercenary, joins forces with an invading army of Russians, Ben and his people raise a bloody banner of defiance to defend earth's last bastion of freedom.

BLOOD IN THE ASHES   (1537, $3.50)

As Raines and his rugged band of followers search for land that has escaped radiation, the insidious group known as The Ninth Order rises up to destroy them. In a savage battle to the death, it is the fate of America itself that hangs in the balance!

ALONE IN THE ASHES   (1721, $3.50)

In this hellish new world there are human animals and Ben Raines—famed soldier and survival expert—soon becomes their hunted prey. He desperately tries to stay one step ahead of death, but no one can survive ALONE IN THE ASHES.

Available wherever paperbacks are sold, or order direct from the Publisher. Send cover price plus 50¢ per copy for mailing and handling to Zebra Books, Dept. 1993, 475 Park Avenue South, New York, N.Y. 10016. Residents of New York, New Jersey and Pennsylvania must include sales tax. DO NOT SEND CASH.

C.A.D.S. #4

#4 TECH STRIKE FORCE

BY JOHN SIEVERT

ZEBRA BOOKS
KENSINGTON PUBLISHING CORP.

ZEBRA BOOKS

are published by

Kensington Publishing Corp.
475 Park Avenue South
New York, NY 10016

First printing: February 1987

Printed in the United States of America

PROLOGUE

Colonel Dean Sturgis is leader of the C.A.D.S. Force, a special U.S. combined-services commando unit referred to by the Soviet occupiers of the East Coast of the U.S. as the Blacksuits. He's the one man that the Russians fear. He has time and again delayed their push westward, using his computerized attack/defense system-equipped high-tech battle force with daring against the best Soviet troops. Colonel Sturgis and his men have used every capability of the multi-million dollar C.A.D.S. suits and wished for more! Each suit is equipped with weapons built into them that can be fired through weapons tubes hung under the metal sleeves. These include machine guns, flame-throwers — and much much more.

Its huge mirror eye is actually a computer-activated viewscreen with many functions, or "modes." Sturgis and his nuke troopers can, by voice-command, call up a variety of sensor-enhanced depictions of their surroundings. "Blue mode" projects position and number of friendly forces; "Red mode" depicts enemy forces just as clearly. In addition, there is "Zoom Telescopic mode" and "Infrared mode" — capable of seeing in total darkness. Plus dozens of other capabilities. Each man has the firepower of an entire regular battalion of soldiers, easily defeating any conventional force.

Since the surprise Soviet nuke attack seven months earlier, on Christmas Eve, 1997, the C.A.D.S. Force—a few hundred men—have been all that stood in the way of the Russians.

But now the Russians have an outfit similar to the C.A.D.S. unit—the Graysuits. General Petrin, commander of the Graysuits, is determined to wipe out the Blacksuits. Sturgis and his men have just engaged the Graysuits with heavy losses. Nevertheless, the Americans accomplished their mission by destroying the Chesapeake Bay Bridge-Tunnel complex the Russians were using to move troops and supplies.

Sturgis and the survivors of his Tech strike force walked miles underwater in their heavy servomechanism-assisted suits to escape a closing iron ring of Soviet troops. The Reds didn't know the Blacksuits could be submerged; that probably had saved Sturgis and his men. The C.A.D.S. unit has now emerged from the waters of the Chesapeake Bay . . . It is up to Sturgis to regroup them, get them back to Refuge Island in the Okefenokee Swamp that the C.A.D.S. unit now calls home. But, first, they must reach their immediate destination—the Revengers' guerilla camp, 250 miles away. . . .

CHAPTER ONE

In the dim light of a low sun obscured by layers of dark clouds, the black metal figure rose from the waters and strode toward the sandy Virginia beach. The robotlike walker, rising like a demon of the deep, moved forward with strong certain strides trailing seaweed. The figure paused; its metal hands moved up and picked globs of kelp from its huge black head which bristled with pointy antennae. The foot-wide mirrorlike eye turned this way and that to observe the barren shore, looking for something.

It wasn't a robot, nor a diving suit, nor one of Neptune's darker companions. It was a high-tech armor suit. And inside that space-age marvel was a man — Colonel Dean Sturgis, leader of the Omega commandos. He anxiously counted the other similarly clad men he saw coming up out of the water down the beach — ten in all. Only ten.

"Blue mode," he voice-commanded the suit computer. Instantly the suit's big reflective eye that he peered through turned a deep glowing blue. The colonel saw a holographic depiction projected of a five-mile area around him. It was as if he were in some sort of video game. Twenty blinking blue dots appeared on the computer-generated grid. Twenty of his nuke troopers were shown to be still alive, ten in the water, ten ashore. The beach was depicted as a wavy yellow line.

He could on "Clear mode" see a figure identical to him walking down the beach. Soviet hellfire and water had eroded the identifying decals on the metal suit and his I.D. mode screen was out—so he asked over the radio, "Who's approaching?"

"It's me, Tranh, Colonel. So we made it! Rad level's okay according to my readout. . . . It smells lousy in this suit. I'm opening up."

As he came up Sturgis saw the Vietnamese-American's visor slide up, revealing his sweat-dampened sallow face. Sturgis too ordered "Visor up." His helmet's faceplate whined open. Warm air. Face to face with his trusted second-in-command, Sturgis said, "Eighteen others are near shore or out of the water—but my I.D. mode is out. Do you know who they are?"

"Checked I.D. mode a minute ago," Tranh said solemnly. "De Camp is still with us, Fuentes, Billings . . ." Tranh rattled the names off. Many of the veteran fighters in the colonel's command were missing, presumed dead. Sturgis got on the commlink and congratulated all the survivors of the mission. He ordered them to spread out along a twenty-mile-wide line and move inland as planned. There was too much danger if they clustered—this way, if one were spotted, the others would probably still make it.

"Tranh, I love your company, but . . ."

"I know—I'll move south one mile, keep in touch

8

by radio. Good luck!" Tranh closed his helmet and moved off.

Sturgis started walking alone over rolling sand dunes. He soon crossed an asphalt road, then made his way through the parking lot of a burned-out frozen custard stand. Skeletons still sat inside the doors of the blistered cars in the parking lot, other skeletons lay on the floor inside the shattered glass doors. Custard's Last Stand. Sturgis had seen it a hundred, a thousand times before. Americans suddenly caught in their humdrum rounds by the brilliant flash and heat of a nuke warhead detonation. These people had been lucky—the firestorm had brought instant death. Millions of others had died slowly, painfully, of radiation, their insides torn by pain for days as they retched their guts out slowly, screaming in pain as their skin blistered and parted exposing their raw flesh to a thousand rampant infections. And others had died of the bites of rabid animals or of plague spread by the rats and insects that swarmed through the dead cities of America.

Sturgis again tried to access his I.D. mode screen. Maybe now that the suit was dry, some of his minor malfunctions would cease. The light-pink grid flickered, then activated. Damn! It worked. All the blue dots that were his men within a five-mile range were there, and each was identified by a readout of the first four letters of their last name—alongside the dots.

Two miles north was FUEN, meaning that was Roberto Fuentes. He had been a New York City teen gangleader. Back when there was a New York City, not a gaping, miles-wide radioactive crater. He'd been fleeing a jail sentence when he joined the Air Force. His great intelligence and technical aptitude was recognized, and within a few years Fuentes was among the Omega commandos. It was Fuentes who had found the Refuge Island in the Okefenokee that the C.A.D.S. unit now called home.

Beyond Fuentes a mile or so was DECA. That was Dr. Sheila de Camp, the only woman in the C.A.D.S. Force. Though she and Sturgis were often at odds, she had assumed an unofficial place in the colonel's inner circle of officers . . . and friends. Then there was WENT, for Wentworth; HOLL, for Hollings. Good. They were spread far and wide. All fine men, good fighters.

Just at the farthest range his I.D. mode could pick up was FIRE. Sturgis smiled. That would be Joe Fireheels. The Indian recruit from north Arizona. Fireheels was the only survivor among all the fifty-five *new* men. The tawny dark-eyed youth gave a good accounting of himself in battle, just like a vet.

Immediately to his south was VANN—Tranh Van Noc.

If *he* personally didn't make it, he hoped Tranh would. His second-in-command, Trah Van Noc, could lead the men as well—or better—than he could. Tranh was an expert both in the C.A.D.S. suit and in military tactics. He'd served with Sturgis during the Indochina MIA rescues and had been a good friend since then. Since the unit had moved east from the Omega Base at White Sands, New Mexico, and set up forward operations in the Okefenokee Swamp, Tranh had several times already assumed command. That had been because Sturgis had biked into the hill

10

country searching for Robin, his wife. Sturgis hadn't found her, but he had found her note, telling him when and where she would be, begging him to meet her. Twenty days from today. If he could stay alive, if she could, they'd be together. But twenty days might be too much to ask in these times . . .

He kept on walking, temperature 102 degrees. The southeast had been above 100 degrees every day for two weeks now — all except the oceanfront. Their destination — the Revengers' guerilla camp was 250 miles away — and the Soviets would sooner or later figure out how they escaped. They would by now have caught up to heroic Lieutenant Grimes. Grimes had taken their tribikes, the low-slung three-wheeled speed cycles that had been the main transportation of the C.A.D.S. Force till recently, north on the highway with him to fool the Reds. The idea had been that the Reds would think the whole unit had gone with Grimes. But he'd be dead by now and the Soviets would soon be on their real trail again. But if they all could get into the mountains ahead — into the twisting, turning canyons and valleys of the Appalachians — maybe they'd make it to safety.

Walking to the Revengers' caves was the only choice. The hidden base was the only refuge within their range. The suits would not make it all the way back to the Okefenokee. The Revengers, mountain people who had lived all their lives along the Appalachians hunting and fishing, now were the main guerilla force acting against the Soviets. The Revengers would welcome the C.A.D.S. Force.

The C.A.D.S. unit, walking with power-assist, could make a constant twenty miles an hour — the fuel-cell power of the suits amplified the stride of a man's legs. *A twelve-hour walk lay ahead.*

Rolling dense fog with some low radioactivity started rapidly closing from the Bay around Sturgis like a wet blanket. The Reds would have trouble detecting the black C.A.D.S. suits against the charred soil of the area, and the radiation would play havoc with their helicopters. But Sturgis had no trouble seeing in I.R. mode. The scene before his eyes was clear. Every object was illuminated by the heat it threw off with the infrared ability of his sensors.

Suddenly a readout crawled across the bottom of his screen: WARNING — APPROACHING VEHICLES.

"G.I. mode," he shouted. The screen faded and a geometrically rearranged view of the area from a computer-calculated overhead perspective replaced his view. He stood still, looking at the blinking dots of green moving on the grid. CYCLES, said the readout. Could it be one of the many marauding biker gangs that terrorized post-nuke America? No, it wasn't. Next to each dot a positive computer analysis of the motors of the vehicles and their geometric shape gave their identity. TRIS! The tribikes. How the hell could they be here?

His channel 70 crackled to life. "Sturgis, Billy Dixon and Lieutenant Grimes reporting in. We got some transportation for y'all!"

"Billy," Sturgis responded. "You're alive — Grimes — how the hell did you make it? Come on up the hill."

He went back to I.R. mode, and after a bit saw the bikes coming. Two figures on the first low-slung cycle appeared, and then eighteen unmanned cycles, following

12

by remote control like baby ducks follow their mother.

Sturgis opened his visor and so did the approaching troopers. They dismounted and saluted. Then they shook hands and Sturgis patted them on their shoulders of steel. Billy Dixon, the young blond-haired Southerner, drawled out their story. Billy had trouble with his tribike during the battle. He had been attacked by a Mig, but had managed to meet up with Grimes and join in his diversionary move.

Grimes cut in. "Once ol' Billy joined me, we both took the tris north to draw fire. The Reds came at us with everything—helis, tanks, the works—but they had trouble firing at so many targets all moving up different roads. And they missed eighteen bikes—we were on two of the eighteen they missed. A fog rolled in—the same kind we're in now—thick! Our sensors are better than theirs. They lost us. We came around the long way—at high speed—and here we are."

"Well, you both are a welcome sight. It also gives me hope that Fenton and Rossiter somehow survived too—any sign of them?"

Billy frowned. "No, sir."

Sturgis sighed. It wasn't just two brave inner-circle men lost. The loss of the nuclear-powered "Rhino" battlewagon hurt a lot. The huge tear-shaped vehicle bristled with antiair weapons and contained the recharge battery. The C.A.D.S. suits needed a recharge after twenty-four hours of use. Otherwise the suits eventually would only be a burden, powerless. Each, loaded, weighed over four hundred pounds. Dead weight when the batteries died. They'd last, though, at least until the men reached the Revengers' caves. He'd figure out another way of charging them somehow.

Sturgis selected one of the less-battered tris. Then he told the two young fighters to take the rest of the tribikes to the other C.A.D.S. men. Some would have to double up. But before Billy and Grimes could move out, the Approach Warning Systems of all suits went off simultaneously. "Maybe it's the Revengers," the colonel said. He closed up his helmet and accessed I.D. model. PRED was printed next to each of twenty approaching red triangles three hundred meters to their left. Velocity 10 mph. "SPECIFY TYPE OF PREDATORS," Sturgis asked the computer. There was a pause and then the word PRED changed to CANI. Canines. A dog pack. Beginning in the first days after the nuking of America, rabid dog packs had been a problem.

In their metal armor, the dogs were little danger to the C.A.D.S. men. Still, Sturgis wanted to wipe them out, for the benefit of any Americans roaming this area not similarly protected. "They're about to come over that rise to my left," Sturgis radioed to Billy and Grimes. "They've got our scent—it's amazing. We must smell bad—just exposing our faces put 'em on to us."

Billy checked out his SMG mode, reported, "Let me have first shot—a few bursts of explosive 9 mm bullets should do it."

"Let them get close. Don't miss any."

"Close? Hell, let 'em try to bite us," the Southerner laughed.

"Billy, Grimes—move away from the tris. We want to attract them. The bikes might scare 'em off. Switch to Infrared mode."

14

On his I.R. screen, Sturgis watched the dogs half tumbling from the top of the debris-strewn hill. The twenty dogs appeared as glowing blotches. Their furry bodies glowed purple to red, but their hotter mouths, dripping saliva, appeared blue-white. Most startling was their black holes of eyes—staring like the pits of hell. The figures seemed the embodiment of all evil. Sturgis shuddered. There was something about the long, lanky movements of the skinny curs, something ominous in the way they walked. They were doomed creatures of a doomed world. Once, these had been domesticated suburban yard dogs that guarded the house and played with children. Now they had probably been infected with rabies by the raccoons and other wild creatures they ate, or worse—some dog packs spread the plague.

The dogs spread out, coming within visible range in the fog. Growls pierced the hot mists. "Switch to clear modes," Sturgis shouted. "Get ready . . . Here they come!"

They were coming on the run, big fellas, slavering, saliva-dripping mangy things, blood in their eyes. Sturgis faced them impassively. He thought the dogs might turn tail once they saw their C.A.D.S. outfits, but the curs seemed oblivious. They were all too ravenously hungry to turn around; too hungry to stop to think that *these* humans had something odd about their clothing. All they could think about was meat— human meat!

One big black dog—some sort of mutt that looked half St. Bernard, half Doberman, came first, heading for Billy. Billy raised his arm to fire.

"No," said Sturgis. "Let's waste them with our fists

and feet. No sense wasting good ammo."

"Yeah," agreed the Southerner. "Some karate chops."

Grimes said, "Okay by me, but —" The lead dog for some reason diverted from Billy and with a tremendous leap was biting into the steel neck of Grimes. The dog bounced off him as if it had crashed into a steel wall. He reached and grabbed the dog about the neck with his steel left glove and squeezed. There was a snap and the dog fell with his spine snapped. But two more dogs were on each of the three nuke troopers, and more snapping at their metal-clad legs. Sturgis delivered kick after kick, each blow caving in rib cages. Some of the dogs cringed and walked away, tails lowered, their teeth drooling blood — their own, not that of their prey. But they were hungry, driven. They came again. The noise was deafening, barks and whelps and death rattles.

A scruffy brown collie streaked with oil seemed to take the lead now. He led a run against Sturgis with two smaller dogs snapping at his feet while the big bad cousin of Lassie made for his throat. Again teeth clanged against hard alloy steel, again rib cages and canine windpipes were caved in by carefully aimed hands and feet.

Suddenly there were sparks from Sturgis's suit — a malfunction in his electrical systems. He had to get out of his suit or toast like a marshmallow — he had just minutes. "Kill 'em off, SMG fire," he yelled as he opened up his helmet's visor. Instantly the collie saw the opening and headed in a tremendous leap from a boulder at Sturgis's face — only to be met in midair by a hail of bullets from Billy's right-arm tube.

16

"Thanks," yelled Sturgis. "Keep it up."

He blew the seals on his thorax piece and on the leg seals as well. It was up to his buddies now to protect him against the six or seven remaining pack dogs. Bullets flew right and left as Sturgis, now with his disassembled suit lying next to him, pulled out from the enormous traction boots. The firing died down. "Got 'em all," said Billy. Indeed, there were mounds of smoking carcasses around the three troopers. The parched ground was sucking up the spilt blood. Senseless eyes stared vacantly into the morose black clouds above. "I guess you have," said Sturgis. "Well, that was closer than—"

"Lookout!" yelled Grimes. A dog had appeared on a high boulder ten feet to Sturgis's right. Snarling, and with a tremendous leap, its foam-flecked jaws made for the Tech Commando's jugular. But again Billy's submachine gun spoke death. Still, Sturgis had to dive to the side to avoid the dog, even in death slamming its jaws into his neck.

"Shit," Sturgis said, "Check the screen for any more, quick."

There weren't any. Sturgis rose, brushed off the dust-covered black coveralls. "Now all I have to do is fix the suit. At least the fire-control system worked— it isn't burned up . . ."

"Well, I'm the best fixer in the unit except for Rossiter," Billy said. "I have some spare fuses in my utility belt, and if that's not enough, I'm good at scavenging. My systems are all up. I can spare some parts."

Sturgis thanked the Southerner, and ordered Grimes to do the tribike resupply alone.

17

CHAPTER TWO

An hour later . . .

"NPN silicon high-voltage diode, check . . ." said Sturgis.

"Check," Billy responded.

The two men were sitting on rocks in a steep-walled valley dotted with pines. The valley contained a lazy stream, just yards away. An assortment of circuits and computer chips lay strewn about on a broad flat rock between them. Sturgis had his C.A.D.S. suit disassembled; part of the computer board was in his lap. His task at hand—to find out what shorted his suit. Billy still wore his C.A.D.S. suit, using his computer to analyze each move.

A billowing pinkish fog clung to the sheer walls of the defile, cloaking their position. Nevertheless, Sturgis had Billy keep an eye on his visor screen while they ran the problems down.

"Annular memory driver, fast switch . . . check."

"Check, skip," replied Billy. "That's all the inverters and capacitators. Must be something in the D.G. field generator, or the saturators for the weapons relays."

"That means I need a diag-light for the next check."

"Got it here, skip." Billy retrieved the tool from the repair kit on his tribike, parked a few feet away. The colonel placed the tester light in the dual gate circuit.

"*Here* it is," the colonel said. "It's the damn D.G. field diode. You got a spare?"

"No way. Those babies aren't supposed to break."

"All right," said Sturgis, exasperated. "We'll try a bypass, or a substitute. Ask your computer which would be better."

"Computer — dual-gate field gen for bypass or substitute — recommendation," Billy queried through his voice-activated programmer.

WORKING . . . his computer responded. USE MPF820 CHIP.

"What are consequences for using my MPF820 chip as dual-gate field gen substitute for donor suit and receiver suit."

WORKING, Billy's computer responded.

"Here it comes, skip," Billy said as the data flowed across his visorscreen. "We'll both be on half weapons, plus we lose, let's see, gas chromotography capability. No big deal. But fuel consumption increases."

"And we're both already low on power. I don't know, Billy. Maybe you'd better go on a—"

"Aw c'mon, skip. Don't even say it. You know we're better off staying together. Working as a team. C'mon. Let's make the switch. We still got the tris. We'll be outta here in no time, and once we meet up with the team we can straighten everything out."

"All right. Break it out. We'll chance it."

Dixon released the vacuum clamps on his C.A.D.S. suit and extricated himself from the armored gauntlets. Once free, he stretched and limbered his aching muscles. "Oh, wow! It feels so good to get outta that sardine can. Skip, you mind if I take a quick dip in the stream while you make the connection? I'm beginning to smell a bit ripe."

"Sure, pal," Sturgis said, already busy with his tools. "But check the rad level of the water first. In fact, if it's okay, I'll join you as soon as I'm done."

Billy removed the hand-held Geiger counter from the utility belt on his suit and eased along the broken slate base of the valley, slipping and sliding on the sleek, wet stones. Colonel Sturgis watched until he disappeared into the fog. He soon heard the young buck yipping and splashing in the chilly pool not thirty feet away. Sturgis lifted the microchip from Dixon's C.A.D.S. suit with tweezers. He deftly flash-soldered it into place in his own suit with the circuit welder. "There!"

"C'mon in, Skip," Billy shouted. "The water's fine."

Chunka chunka chunka chunka chunk . . . The distant sound of post-nuke reality echoed through the valley. Sturgis froze and cocked his ears, hoping he wasn't hearing anything but the valley's trick winds.

Chunka chunka chunka chunka chunka . . . The sound grew louder.

There was no mistaking it now. "Choppers," Sturgis yelled. "C'mon in, Billy! There are—"

"I hear. I'm on my way!" Billy jumped into his

21

coveralls, scrambled up the bank, and soon emerged through the fog. Sturgis was already suiting up as Billy hurriedly joined him in the time-consuming task.

The C.A.D.S. suits transformed them from ordinary soldiers into fierce warrior-gods. Like the ancient Roman legionnaire sheathing his broad sword, or the Plains Indian streaking red ocher across his face to strike terror in the hearts of his enemies, the nuke troopers donning their C.A.D.S. suits were but another link in mankind's endless saga of warfare.

Sturgis was seconds behind Billy in sealing his suit and turning systems on. "Ready now," Dean said as he lowered his visor. "Be sure to activate your overrides and bypass the master relays."

"Copy, Sturg," Though just twenty years old, Dixon was a hardened fighter. Resolve, not fear, showed on his face as he lowered the visor on his helmet of alloy steel.

"I'm operative," Sturgis said over the intercom, "thanks to you. What's your ammo situation?"

"Skip, my Liquid-Plastic Fire is out. I have one E-ball left, but its firing system is jammed. I'll work on it. I got a few 9mm rounds, and a half-dozen impact darts. Servo-systems are working."

"Good." Sturgis replied. "Let's—"

Chunka chunka chunka chunka chunka . . .

"—Use the tris. Get some cover!"

They clambered back along the shattered rocks, mounted their tribikes, and burned rubber. The steel-rubber tires of the tris enabled them to speed along the broken gravel of the stream bank as if it were a

22

highway. As they sped along at 90 mph Sturgis ordered his dull-purple radar screen up, then reported, "I got a bead on 'em. They're big helis. Computer indicates ten to twelve of them. Three and a half miles north by northeast, moving at eighty knots. They must be powerful turkeys if we heard them this far off."

"We must be within missile range already, skip. They couldn't have spotted us yet," said Billy, setting the pace along the twisting valley.

"The sheer walls of the valley might be shielding us."

"Yeah, and this fog," added Billy. "Rad fog does havoc to most radar."

"Right—Hey—look at the configurations on the Geometric I.D. mode!"

Sturgis had accessed the G.I. mode's luminescent turquoise grid on the lower part of his screen—keeping clear screen on the upper view. He saw twelve squares in a V pattern at grid mark 500 feet. The word UNKN was printed next to each square. "*Strange.* The computer says 'unknown—they don't read like any of the regular commie choppers. Their mass is way too high, like nothing on our programs."

"Could be a glitch in the G.I. mode," Billy suggested.

"I'm gonna ride up on the hill," Sturgis said, "and get a direct look-see with Zoom mode. You keep moving, Billy. I'll catch up."

One dozen coal-black choppers, with giant hammers and sickles framing a skull and crossbones emblazoned on the bottom of each craft, flew at 500 feet in a tight wedge formation. It was two hours and twenty minutes since they'd left the flight deck of the aircraft carrier *Mockba* in the Atlantic to join the flagging search for the Blacksuits. Called "fat geese with big red noses" by the Russian peasants near their home field, they were really nothing to be laughed at. The twelve helicopters winging in pursuit of the Blacksuits had been tagged "Groznys"—literally, "Terrible Thunder." The Groznys were the deadliest helis in the Russian air command. They were equipped with special long-range rad-fog penetration radar. They had searchlights and boom-microphone systems. In addition to conventional weapons—four armor-piercing machine-gun/grenade-launch turrets—each carried two canister eject-tubes, fore and aft. Canisters filled with special unconsciousness-producing SP-3 gas. Of the twelve machines lumbering above the fogged-in Virginia landscape, six transported fifty fully-equipped shock troops each. Each of the other six contained two tons of SP-3 gas. In the lead chopper, his dark eyes glued to the radar-probe screen, was swarthy Air Commander Betrov.

Betrov had been ordered to find the U.S. commandos that had devastated the Chesapeake Bay Bridge-Tunnel hours before. The Air Commander had decided to go further over Virginia than the other searchers. Absolutely no one believed the U.S. commandoes could have gotten that far—so Betrov suspected that's where the sneaky devils were!

He scanned methodically for the raiders. He had never believed the wild stories told by survivors of other encounters with these metal U.S. commandos.

24

The Blacksuits had, it was told, *never* lost a battle, never failed to achieve their objective. And death and destruction on an unbelievable scale was supposedly left in their wake. Now a whole unit of Petrin's Graysuits had failed to stop the U.S. commandos. And the Premier had ordered all Groznys up to search for the U.S. super-squad and engage them. *Could the stories be true?* The possibility made Betrov quake.

Betrov reasoned that the feeling in his gut was justified. Why shouldn't he be afraid? Any *rational* man would be!

Yuri Betrov, a 42-year-old career officer, was gambling, prolonging the search, extending it further than ordered. He was sure at least one Blacksuit could be captured with the Grozny's SP-3 sleep gas. If he could do what Petrin had failed to do, he might even replace General Petrin. And Betrov's ambition was even greater than his fear!

Sturgis stopped his cycle at the summit of a bare thousand-foot hill. He scanned ahead on I.R. He turned his face to the bearing indicated for the helis.

"Zoom mode, two hundred power," he ordered. His visor fuzzed over gray for a moment, then cleared. His zoom mode focused on the helicopter attack wing. They looked like twelve dragonflies, red and orange with heat traces in the infrared spectrum.

"Computer, plot probable courses of enemy helis."

WORKING . . . replied the ever-slowing brain tool. COMPLEX PATTERN OF FLIGHT, POSSIBLY RANDOM IN NATURE.

"Identify intruders," Sturgis ordered.

HELICOPTERS. TWELVE, replied the weary computer.

"I can see that, damn it! Specify type!"

NOT IN FILE. ELECTROMAGNETIC DISPLACEMENT SUGGESTS SEARCH RADAR ABOARD CRAFT.

"You monitor that?" Sturgis radioed Dixon, now about three quarters of a mile ahead up the stream.

"Roger, skip. Radar searchers! We're in for it, I suppose. Better catch up with me! What's ahead? — I'm reading two hundred rems."

"Hold on a second."

Sturgis scanned ahead with a combination of modes, then reported. "The going is rough for six miles, lots of high-rad earthquake-tossed land. But twelve miles ahead the sensors show structures, apparently intact. My map grid of this area indicates it's in the location of one of those historic towns — Williamsburg."

"If they spot us, maybe we can lose them there. Or should we engage them?"

"Negative, Billy. We're low on ammo and power. I'd just as soon avoid tanglin' with 'em. Be kinda like two flies taking on twelve sumo wrestlers. You keep moving. I'm on my way."

Sturgis slid his tri back down the slope and roared along the stream, racing through the "hot" area at 120 mph.

The thunder of the Soviet helicopters filled the air like a storm rolling in off an angry sea. The tribikes raced across tumbled and tossed rock. The terrain was crosshatched with even-larger fissures, some emitting steam from far below. Avoiding them made the going slow. Meanwhile, radar mode showed the choppers break formation and stretch out into an elongated arc.

Sturgis noted the change in their position. "It looks ominous. The computer is predicting choppers over us in eight minutes—they've spotted us! I sure hope Grimes delivered the tris to the men, and that they're far the hell away from here. We won't make it easy for the bastards, Billy. We'll do our best to trick them. How about the old Trojan Horse routine?"

"Sounds like fun. Leave one of the Tris. Right?"

"Check. When the Reds land to have a look-see— *boom*!"

In a few more minutes they pulled under a charred trunk of what once was a sizable spruce tree. A wood-rail fence ran off in either direction down a long dirt road coursing between two ash-covered fields. In the near distance stood a roofless barn, the ribs of its burned silo framing the horizon. Sturgis dismounted his tribike. Quickly and expertly, the colonel unpacked a handful of plastic explosives from his tri's supply case, and stuck it underneath its chassis in the hollow of a fuse box. He nudged the long metal detonator into it and connected the circuit to the bike's time clock.

"Ten minutes," said Sturgis. "Maybe we'll catch a Trojan."

"Let's hope they haven't read Homer."

"If they don't take our bait, Billy, we blow the tri up anyway, from a distance."

Sturgis leaped onto Billy's bike, holding onto Billy. They ripped across the burned field sending up a cloud of dust. Scanning his computer-generated area map, the commander picked their destination. "Williamsburg dead ahead, Billy. We hole up there, and wait!"

Betrov's beady eager eyes watched the two Blacksuits through his heli's telescopic viewscreen. The radar had picked them up from four miles off, and at three miles he could clearly see the men on the strange motorcycles as they raced across the ground. There were only two. No other Blacksuits were in his scanning area. Could they be separated from the others — fallen behind? Or — could they possibly be the only two survivors? That thought brought a wicked gleam to his eye. Maybe they weren't so invincible after all. Maybe they had paid a terrible price for their victory at Chesapeake Bay. In any case, *two* should be easy prey for the Groznys.

What were they doing now? They left one vehicle and the both of them went off on the other. Perhaps there had been a malfunction of one of the odd vehicles? This was an unexpected opportunity to be able to examine one of these motorbikes.

It would be a prize worth pausing for!

Betrov ordered his wingman, Grozny 4, to bank off and pick up the strange low-slung three-wheeled motorcycle. "Proceed with caution," he added prophetically.

The remainder of the wing he ordered to toil onward. "Don't gain on the Blacksuits. Just keep them in view. And above all — don't shoot. I want them alive!" Without their other motorcycle the

Blacksuits would be at a disadvantage. Doubling up on the vehicle would slow them down.

The Grozny landed and six men jumped out and quickly loaded its prize inside, right over its fuel tanks. Then it headed off, back toward the main group. It was at 1200 feet and climbing, doing 85 knots, when it blew. In a few more seconds it would have reached the squadron, would have destroyed them all, perhaps.

Commander Betrov cursed a blue streak when he saw the cherry-red explosion. Damn! He fell for a trick! The way he felt now, he wished he could make a few holes in the Blacksuits to teach them a lesson. But they were valuable—too valuable to kill. The sleep gas would be used to prevent the two Blacksuits heading across the land below from enjoying their joke. But first he'd see whether the Americans would lead him to their friends.

Sturgis and Billy were about seven miles from Williamsburg when their "Trojan Horse" blew. They could detect the explosion only as a dim glow on their screens. "One down, eleven to go!" Billy shouted exultantly. Sturgis didn't smile. The odds were still against them. They roared off the rutted tobacco field onto U.S. 60, heading west. They were soon rewarded with a bright green sign that read "Colonial Williamsburg Information Center Exit—one mile."

"I remember being told by White Sands that the Premier of Russia once visited Williamsburg," said Sturgis. "He liked it so much that he instructed his missile command to spare it. He supposedly wants to use it as his colonial capital, like the British did when they controlled the States."

"What makes this place so special?" Billy asked as they turned down the exit. "According to the computer it's only a historic amusement center."

"Where's your sense of history, boy? Don't you realize that this is the place where George Washington, Thomas Jefferson, and Patrick Henry initiated the call for independence? The place where the Virginia Convention passed a resolution to declare the Colonies free and independent? That this was the colonial capital of the United States? Besides, it's pretty."

"How do you know so much about it?" asked Billy.

"I wish I could say it was from hitting the book," Sturgis replied. "But in truth, I came here back in the early seventies when I was a boy — with my parents and my Uncle Bob and Aunt Edna. I'm betting the commander of the choppers won't want to waste this town and offend the Premier. They'll have to come at us on foot — rather than strafing. That will give us a chance."

They raced up the road past the visitor's parking lot to the big, modern red-brick building. "Let's see, if memory serves me correctly, the little shuttle buses leave from the other side of that wall — they didn't allow private vehicles past this information center. There's a big lot for cars to the left of the road. We'll break the rules — turn right, Billy." They passed a row of rusty buses waiting for visitors who would never come. The sign read, "Buses leave every five minutes. Be sure to see the *Story of a Patriot* now showing continuously."

"We'll catch the movie later."

The road was now its true historic muddy self.

They rode through streams that interrupted the roadway, bumping over fallen rocks in a narrow ravine. Suddenly the tri was throwing up gray-white dust along a street lined with many white clapboard houses. They were in Williamsburg — an untouched eighteenth-century American colonial city perfect in every detail — picket fences, formal gardens, the works.

"Damn. Williamsburg ain't been touched a bit except it looks like it snowed here," said Billy.

"That's not snow," said Sturgis. "I'm getting a reading — low-rad ash — probably fallout from Richmond." They rode past taverns, apothecary shops, the signs of the golden ball, the smithy, the barber's and wigmaker's shops. The neat little town covered by the layer of ash looked like one of those Lionel train sets depicting winter — only it was rad ash, not white snow, that decorated the diorama.

They passed the octagonal building known as "the Magazine on Market Square."

"That's an arsenal, Billy, but it's full of replicas of flintlocks — I doubt any really fire, and even if they did, they wouldn't help much. Stop at the church ahead on the right. Drive the tri right into it. It's made of brick; the radar will lose us. Those choppers can't be too far behind. We need cover, and a good view. Bruton Parish Church will do handily."

There was a low brick wall around the church. Billy drove the tribike up three steps into the open gate, and then up some more low slate steps. He banged the huge front tire of steel and rubber against the white-painted double door. Whatever lock was holding it closed burst, and they roared into the church

31

and screeched to a halt on the chancel floor of the wide main aisle.

The interior was a wonder; soft luminous light sifted through the tall casement windows on either side of them. Everything was painted oyster white. A balcony ran halfway up all along both sides of the nave. The royal governor's velveteen box pew was up front, set away from the commoners' pews. A simple altar fill with dry flowers and a plain gold cross in the center stood in the apse, which had a magnificent crystal-glass chandelier hanging over it. The pulpit was set at least ten feet above all, with dark wood stairs leading up to it.

"I'll get up on the balcony and check the western sky—they should come that way. Billy, disassemble your weapons tube and fix the damned firing mechanism that's on the blink, if you can—we need that E-ball!"

"Will do," Billy said as Sturgis rushed to the balcony stairs. The young Southerner sat down in a forward pew, opened his visor, and took out a screwdriver from his utility belt. He started removing his left weapons firing tube from the left arm assembly. He paused for a second and said, "Excuse me, Lord, for this repair job here, but, Lord, there's a mess of commie atheists after us, and so I'd like to ask your help, O, Lord, in this here repair, *amen*." Then he spread out the tools from his utility pack and focused the bright beam of his helmet light, a steady two hundred watts, on his work.

Sturgis took up position looking out the western casement window, scanning the sky for signs of the big choppers. It wasn't long before he picked them up on I.R. mode. "How you doing?"

"I think I've got it, skip—*yes*, I do!"

"Well, for God's sake, get it together. They're coming."

In a second or two, Billy said, "E-ball systems *go*, Skip," and leaving the tools scattered on the pew seat, he rushed up to join the colonel.

Sturgis heaved a sigh of relief. "*One* E-ball; better than none! Wait till I give the signal. First I'll knock out the windowpane." This he did with his left metal fist. He computer-tracked the flight of the big helis which could now be heard buzzing like angry flies. They were above some white frame buildings to the west.

"Now, skip?" Billy asked, lifting his left arm at the wide hole in the window, pointing it at the distant dots in the sky.

"No. Wait till I give the signal. Gotta get as many as possible!"

The tension mounted. Finally Sturgis said, "Use your Zoom. Fire at the chopper with the number three on it—see it?"

"Fire!" the Southerner commanded. The E-ball sailed up in a computer-calculated arc from Billy's weapons tube.

The electro-ball, an apple-sized explosive shell with shimmering blue electricity coating its surface, was the most powerful weapon a C.A.D.S. suit had— capable of destroying by concussion alone for a range of 250 meters from point of detonation. Sturgis had picked the centermost of the choppers, the one painted with the number three, for the E-ball, knowing that anything near it would be destroyed also.

Chopper three evaporated in a blinding flash of intense heat. The E-ball sent screaming debris out to four more choppers and they burst into flames and descended wildly, dripping bodies with flailing arms — *men* trying to be *birds*. Five choppers were no more. The sound of the five explosions as they hit the ground was music to the American's ears.

"Yahooooo!" Billy shouted. "That'll teach 'em. See, the rest of them are turning tail. They're going away."

"I doubt it," said Sturgis. "They'll come back maybe with reinforcements. In any case, they'll land this time. They have computers too. Even if they didn't see, the computers will figure out where the shot came from. Let's get up into the bell tower, before they come back. If I were the Red commander, I'd come in low, land well off from here — maybe on the far end of the green — and come at us with troops. Assuming, of course, still, that he doesn't want to blow this magnificent architectural monument in his Premier's future colonial capitol to bits."

"Yeah, assuming . . ." Billy said.

They went through a narrow door and began climbing a circular wooden staircase that led to the bell tower. Sturgis stopped Billy at the second level and peered out the window facing the green. "Don't see 'em yet." The bell rope hung down the space in the stairs. Sturgis pointed up. "That's the Liberty Bell up there, like the one in Philadelphia, Billy — except it isn't cracked. It was rung when the Declaration of Independence was signed."

"Maybe we should get up there — it's higher."

"No, the view's good from here — and we can hear

better in case someone slips into the church below."

"Whatever you say, Colonel. But I hope you got more bullets than I've got—six."

"I've got ten."

Just as the colonel had predicted, the Red helis came in low, and landed and started discharging soldiers—lots of them—at the far end of the green. Three hundred meters away.

"Should we pick off a few? I think they're in range."

"No, Billy. That'll give us away. They're splitting up, see? Gonna search the whole town. Each squad has two RPGs. *Shit*. And notice there's one chopper missing. I bet their fearless leader is in the one that stayed up."

They watched as a group of ten soldiers armed with submachine guns ran toward the church and entered below. In a matter of moments there were sounds of men coming through the nave, and then footfalls on the staircase.

"This is it, Billy. Let's make each shot count. Don't fire until you see the whites of their eyes."

"Yeah," the Southerner said grimly.

But the footfalls ceased, frozen in place as a voice boomed out of the sky, a voice in heavily-Russian-accented English.

"*Citizens of New Russia,*" the voice called on a mike from the chopper. "*There is no purpose in further resistance. The fighting is over. It is time to rise from the nightmare of the past and to march boldly into the new dawn of the future. The workers alone can rebuild your land. We want to help you. We are workers also. We shall work together . . ."*

"This guy sounds like a lot of *work*," Sturgis said over the suit's intercom. His signal was picked up, men redirected.

In a matter of seconds the Russian troops poured out of every street, across the square, and soon boots resounded on the stairs. The brutal fanatics stormed up the stairwell at the Americans. They leaned out into the stair opening, firing their submachine guns. Billy's return fire dropped five. They fell spurting blood. More Soviets took their places. A hundred 7.2mm slugs chipped away the banister.

More Reds came into position outside. The one helicopter still aloft began circling the church, opening up on the granite edifice with strange, cigar-shaped canisters that bounced harmlessly against the structure. Sturgis fired at the metal dragonfly with the last of his bullets, without effect. Billy pinned the staircase Reds down with his last darts. The colonel's viewscreen turned black. He was out of ammo and suit power, inside a dead suit — what good would that do? He removed it, dragged the suit to the top of the belfry while Billy covered him. There, next to the Liberty Bell, he set the suit for detonation upon approach by anyone without the code. As soon as Billy's suit was out of ammo he too popped his clamps and carried his suit up next to Sturgis's. He set it for detonation too. Now all they had were their regulation .45's. They went back down one flight and hunkered low on the circular staircase. Sturgis took his .45 out and took up position on the stairwell, expecting he could take a few more Reds down before he died. Billy did likewise.

"Looks like the Redcoats won this round," Billy commented.

"Guess so," Sturgis acknowledged. "But they won't get us, or the suits — and the bike's set to blow in a few minutes unless I give the code to disarm."

The two men couldn't help clutching each other's shoulders in a soldier's embrace. Then they resumed their stance, holding guns ahead, wondering when the soldiers would again brave the attack.

But their death, at least at that moment, was not to be. A private in Betrov's Grozny hovering outside zeroed in on the tower's casement window with his sighting scope. He unleashed six canisters of SP-3 knockout gas on Betrov's order. The air commander watched as the canisters soared downward toward the holed-up enemy and smashed the glass. A perfect bull's-eye!

Sturgis and Billy heard the pop, and saw the gas pouring up the stairwell of the sanctuary. Before either could so much as move, they were in a cloud of oblivion. They gasped, clutching at their constricted throats. Then blackness overcame them.

The Soviet troop just below their position quickly donned gas masks and moved up to the fallen commandos.

Betrov ordered continued firing until the whole church was fogged in with the thick gas. Then he waited for thirty minutes. Finally deciding he was safe from unpleasant surprises, he ordered the pilot to land far from the church along the edge of the green. He got out of his chopper and walked to the historic edifice, entered. He moved quickly past the odd motorcycle.

Led by an eager sergeant, Betrov went to the stairwell and began ascending toward the bell. He soon came to the two Americans who lay sprawled out cold from the gas.

"Sergeant, make sure they're really asleep!"

The sergeant walked up to the bodies, and with the point of his boot turned each commando over on his back. Betrov took out the description he had been given when the search began.

"Hmmmph," he snorted. "That one's *Sturgis*. Good. Put them on my command ship!"

As he watched the two being carried out, he reflected on the battle. Six of the new Groznys destroyed, twenty-six men killed, some wounded. But the knockout gas had worked perfectly. Betrov mentally rewrote the report: *Mission completed, without a single casualty!*

He'd be a hero of the Soviet Union now. A promotion was certain. Just deliver the two Americans, and their metal suits—which must be *somewhere*. Betrov smiled. He had really shown up Petrin. Now to just find the suits and deliver the whole package to Veloshnikov!

Betrov supervised the airmen who carried the Americans back to his chopper, and he boarded it with his prisoners. Some of his other men searched for the suits.

He was looking toward the building when the Liberty Bell tower exploded. A shower of debris billowed out the windows. Then there was a second explosion, and the church's door blew halfway across the dust-covered square.

"Damn," Betrov snarled, his fist hitting the arm of his flight seat. "Incompetent fools have blundered again."

Swearing and gesticulating wildly, Betrov ordered his heli to take off immediately. He told the pilot to radio ahead to base that he had captured the Americans, and was bringing them to Veloshinikov, the Supreme Marshal.

"But—" said the pilot, "General Veloshnikov is at sea, aboard the submarine *Lenin*."

"Radio ahead, then, to prepare a ship for transport of the prisoners to him. Make sure he knows it was I, Betrov, who did this magnificent capture."

CHAPTER THREE

The dawn mists rose like steam from a gray Atlantic Ocean. The ship, an American destroyer escort that was now under the command of Soviet forces, sped away from Virginia Beach out to sea, to a rendezvous with the Russian giant nuclear-missile sub, the *Lenin*, which cruised the waters near the mouth of Chesapeake Bay. The nimble escort carried extremely important cargo that would be transferred to the sub by small craft. The cargo was human — two American prisoners of war, officers of the C.A.D.S. Commando Force.

Sturgis, along with Dixon, stood on the bridge of the ship — an unlikely place for prisoners of war, but Betrov had ordered it, so that they would be awed by the sight of the mighty *Lenin*. The Americans posed no threat to the Soviet crew. They were manacled and hobbled with steel chains, and no matter which direction they turned, they faced the muzzle of a machine gun trained on them by a guard.

The captured commandos weren't going anywhere, except straight into the waiting arms of a vengeful General Veloshnikov, Supreme Marshal of the Soviet war forces.

As Dixon caught sight of the Russian sub, he let out a long whistle. "*Jee*-sus! Either I'm hallucinating, or that's one helluva boomer."

Before them, the mists were parting to reveal an unbelievably enormous black hulk thrusting up from the water. Only part of the *Lenin* was visible—the conning tower and the top half of the hull. This was the sight Betrov had wanted the Americans to see: Russian power and surpremacy, personified in a single, intimidating war machine.

"That's no vision—she's for real," Sturgis said. He kept his gaze on the vessel ahead, watching it expand as they drew closer. God knew what was in store for them aboard—interrogation, torture, perhaps death. He had been captured once before by the Russians, shortly after the war started, and had been tortured with hot pokers before he escaped. He had the scars on his face to show for it. But that had taken place in a makeshift prison on land—not in a nuclear missile sub that could descend far below the surface of the ocean, making escape impossible.

As far as Sturgis knew, Dixon had never been faced with torture. Torture could put fear in the hearts of even the strongest men. He glanced at Dixon, who stood with his athlete's body straight and stiff, a resolute look upon his face. He had every confidence the young man would stand American proud, no matter what the Russians dished out.

"Hey, Dixon," Dean spoke up, "the opera isn't over until the fat lady sings, and I reckon there's a hell of a lot of singing to be done before *this* show is over."

Dixon grinned. "I never was good at carrying a tune, but I sure can make a racket."

The escort slowed and began a wide starboard turn

as it approached the *Lenin*. Sturgis jangled his hand-cuffs to catch the attention of the sullen Russian soldier before him. He wanted a smoke, but didn't want to make a move that would elicit a blast of machine-gun fire. "Hey, *soldat*." He held up his hands, made a V with two right fingers, which he put to his lips. "Cigarette? *Mozhna?*"

The soldier nodded. Sturgis awkwardly drew one out of the pack Petrin had allowed him to keep in his breast pocket. He stuck the unfiltered end in his mouth and stuck another one in Billy's, and waited for a guard to step forward and light them.

"*Spaseeba*," he said in thanks when that was done. He indicated the Russians could join them in a smoke—he knew Russians preferred American ciga-rettes to their own harsh native brands—but they refused with obvious disdain. They were conquerors, and were not interested in gifts from the conquered, no matter how small. If they wanted something, they would take it—by force.

"Since when did you speak Russian?" Dixon said between puffs, keeping one eye on the maneuvers that were bringing their ship alongside the sub.

Sturgis shrugged. "I don't really speak it—I know only a little. A long time ago, when I was still in the regular Air Force, before I joined up with Omega, I took one of those cram courses the government gives—*gave*—to military and diplomatic personnel who were going to be sent overseas. I had it in the back of my mind that I should understand the language of our main enemy—in case I needed it someday." He blew out a thick stream of smoke. "I never really thought I would. Hell, it certainly never crossed my mind that one day I'd be a prisoner of war in my *own* country, and have to speak Russian to get a smoke." He inhaled deeply and held the smoke in his lungs. "I'm pretty rusty, but some of it's coming back to me, the more I hear and the more of it I read."

Dixon grimaced. "I hate to think of Russian as becoming the new language of the United States of America."

"Like I said, Billy, the fat lady hasn't sung yet."

The telephone in the bridge sounded, and the Russian captain picked it up. He listened briefly and then said, *"Da, da."* As he replaced the receiver, he turned his cold eyes on the American prisoners, and switched to a heavily accented English: "You will prepare to board the *Lenin*."

Supreme Marshal Mikhail Nicholaevich Veloshnikov sat humped over his desk in his private quarters aboard the *Lenin*, trying to control his temper. He was not succeeding. His eyes were closed, but his hands were white-knuckled fists, pressed into his face as he leaned on his elbows. He was a volcano on the verge of exploding.

For decades, he had harbored his hatred of America, ever since that black day when he was stationed in Hanoi during the Vietnam war, when an American B-52 bomber had killed his wife and children.

For decades, he had stalked an enemy that was thousands of miles out of reach, vowing to destroy it. With great satisfaction, he had ordered the nuclear missiles launched six months ago that had devastated this strutting peacock of a country, America. He had been ashore to witness first-hand the death and destruction of its perverted, capitalistic masses.

But the murder of millions was not enough to satisfy him. The millions who'd died knew nothing of his personal loss. Veloshnikov realized that the fire would not be quelled until he could look an American in the eye and say, "*You* were there! You and your fellow soldiers destroyed my family! And now *you* will pay for that crime!"

That "now" might have arrived at last. There were two American prisoners in a cell a few dozen meters from him. They were military officers, leaders of this Blacksuit brigade that was giving the Russian victory forces more grief than it should. Well, that would come to an end! The capture of the commanding officer and his sergeant dealt the Blacksuits a crippling blow.

But more than that, the prisoners symbolized the reason for his hatred. Symbolically, these two Americans could be held accountable for *everything*. If he discovered they were veterans of Vietnam — no matter where they had been on that fatal day — he would be especially pleased to watch them die slowly.

A knock sounded on his door, and he grunted permission to enter. He opened his eyes and looked up. A tall, muscular figure in a black and red uniform stood before him — Lt. Vladimir Pavelovich Revin, of the KGB. Revin's eyes were narrow, and had the color and warmth of steel. His lips had an odd shape, having been brutally smashed in a furious fistfight. That was a long time ago; now Revin was the one who did the smashing. He was a master at interrogation.

"The American prisoners are in the interview room," Revin announced.

Veloshnikov nodded and rose. The interview room. Every Russian vessel had one, not only in case prisoners of war were taken, but to discipline errant Russian sailors as well.

Revin went on. "In accordance with your orders, sir, I have done nothing yet. They are lucid and fit for your questioning."

"Very good, Lieutenant. You will remain present while I speak with them. When I am done, you may follow standard procedures."

Revin's damaged lips curled.

Veloshnikov picked up the intraship telephone and stabbed his index finger on a button on the control panel. "Conn, Guriev here," a voice said in his ear.

"Captain, take her down to four hundred meters. Maintain present speed and course." The *Lenin* was cutting a wide circle off Chesapeake Bay and the Virginia coastline, to be maintained pending interrogation of the prisoners.

"Diving to four hundred meters," confirmed Guriev. Within moments, the sounds of the ballast tanks filling with water reverberated through the sub's titanium hull.

Veloshnikov strode down the narrow corridor of the sub, Revin following on his heels. The admiral straightened the tunic of his uniform, which was heavy with medals and decorations of his long and illustrious military career. He exploded through the hatchway of the interview room.

There before him were the Americans, stripped of their clothing and their dignity, shackled like sheep,

46

forced to stand beneath two hot spotlights, the only light in a pitch-dark room. They turned as the light from the open hatchway spilled into the room, creating a tunnel on the floor; but no sooner had their heads swiveled than a sharp command came from the darkness — from an armed guard — and they faced front again.

Veloshnikov stepped inside, and Revin slipped into the room and moved off to the side. The admiral shut the hatch door, cutting off the tunnel of corridor light. He stared at the naked Americans, letting his eyes adjust to the blackness and the sharp, bright pools of spotlight. He saw immediately that one of them was too young to have fought in Vietnam; he was uncertain about the other. He walked slowly around the perimeter of the room, examining them from all sides, taking pleasure in the knowledge that he could see them clearly while they could barely, if at all, see him. But they could hear him, hear his shoes scuffing the metal floor; they knew they were under a microscope. Revin took up a post in a corner and remained silent.

Well done, Commander Betrov, Veloshnikov thought. Well done! A fine capture, no ordinary two Americans, but perhaps the most important Americans next to the President — if the President is still alive. Betrov, you have certainly repaid your previous errors — perhaps even earned yourself a medal!

Veloshnikov eyed Sturgis and sized him up quickly as a formidable opponent. Tough, unafraid, hard, with scars all over him, including one from a gash across his chest, prominent because the hair had refused to grow back there.

The Supreme Marshal passed Revin and shot a look in his direction, discerning in the shadows the intensity of the interrogator's expression. Revin's gaze was riveted on the younger one, the one with a head of unruly blond hair and a muscular and smooth but hairless chest. He knew immediately what thoughts were in Revin's head. Inside the Soviet Union, men were jailed for such thoughts. But, this was not the Soviet Union, this was a captive enemy in a state of war. Revin could do as he pleased.

Veloshnikov continued his slow tour around the room, staying in the shadows, letting himself be heard but not seen. Get nervous, Americans, he thought. Feel the powerful presence of your enemy. Wonder what he is like, what he will do to you. *Pray* to your God, your God who's abandoned you.

I want to savor this moment forever, thought Veloshnikov. How helpless they look. They are America, the enemy. They are the killers of my family. And they and their wretched Blacksuits are the only thing standing between the Motherland and total victory!

Veloshnikov cleared his throat and announced in excellent English, "The interview will begin."

Sturgis nearly sighed with relief at the words that came out of the darkness behind him. The tension in the room was unbearable. The light shining in his face blinded him. He had heard the ballast tanks lose air and the hull pop with the descent, knowing that every foot it dropped in the Atlantic lessened their chance of escape.

There *had* to be an escape; he refused to accept otherwise.

The voice went on, "Colonel Dean Sturgis and

48

Sergeant Billy Dixon. Yes, I know who you are, so we can dispense with your foolish ritual of name, rank, and serial number."

Two sets of footsteps circled to the front of him and Dixon. Suddenly bodies and faces materialized. Sturgis squinted. A young KGB officer in a trim black and red uniform, and an older officer whose naval uniform was draped in military decorations. Both men had eyes of chipped ice.

"I am General Mikail Nicholaevich Veloshnikov, Supreme Marshal of the Soviet military forces," said the older man. He sat on the edge of the only furniture in the room, a table. There was an ashtray on the table; that was it. "And this is Lieutenant Vladimir Pavelovich Revin. We have some questions to ask you; let me warn you that Lieutenant Revin likes to get answers, and he has my permission to do whatever he feels is necessary to get them." At this, Revin smirked.

"You might as well save your energy and kill us now, Marshal," said Sturgis. "You already know everything we're going to tell you—name, rank, and serial number."

Veloshnikov laughed curtly. "You try hard to be courageous, Americans, but it is impossible for men stripped naked to be anything but totally humiliated."

Sturgis felt his skin prickle; he bit back a retort. Dixon shifted uncomfortably on his feet.

Veloshnikov drew out a long Cuban cigar. Revin stepped forward and lit it for him. As Revin turned his body away from the Americans, Sturgis noticed the black leather whip coiled and tucked into a pouch on his belt on his right side.

"So," Veloshnikov said, enjoying the cigar, "tell me, Colonel, about this army of Blacksuits you command. How many are there, and where are they now? What are your supplies?"

Sturgis was silent.

"Why did your men not come to rescue their illustrious leader? Have they abandoned you? Are they cowards?"

"You'll find Americans far from cowardly, sir."

"Where is your base, your command center?"

Sturgis gave no answer. He swallowed hard; his throat was becoming dry.

The Russian's voice rose. "Who gives you your orders, Colonel? Is there a political center left in this dying country? Is the President still alive? Or are you on your own, a renegade making a last but useless stand?"

Veloshnikov stood and approached Sturgis. The Russian was a big man, over six feet, equal in size to the C.A.D.S. commander. His dark eyes bored into Sturgis. "I don't have much patience, Colonel. It would be better for you and your sergeant if Lieutenant Revin does not take over this interview."

"I don't have answers to your questions," Sturgis said.

Veloshnikov turned away from him and looked at Dixon. "Perhaps your sergeant does." He stepped over to Billy, who refused to look at him until the Russian's face filled his vision. "Have you ever had your fingers broken one by one, Dixon? I understand it is a most exquisite pain."

Billy stuck out his jaw. "Name, rank, serial number—that's all you get."

Veloshnikov gave a flick of his hand to Revin. The KGB officer seized Dixon by the wrists and yanked him forward, causing Billy to fall onto his knees. Revin pulled Dixon's manacled hands onto the table, grabbed the little finger of his left hand, and quickly forced it backward.

There was an audible crack as the finger broke at the knuckle. Billy let out a cry of pain.

Sturgis gritted his teeth. He did not want to see Dixon tortured—he would rather take the punishment himself. He could endure whatever they subjected him to physically, but he was not certain he could endure witnessing the escalating torture of one of his own men—torture that Sturgis could end by giving in.

He realized that was exactly what Veloshnikov hoped to achieve. He stifled his reaction to Billy's pain, knowing he could not afford to show any weakness.

Veloshnikov addressed Sturgis. "Perhaps you were hoping we would give you both beatings. Beatings merely render one senseless and are not as effective as broken fingers—and other methods. Do you know what the strappado is, Colonel Sturgis? It was popular in Europe during the barbaric Dark Ages, and it found new popularity in Stalin's gulags. Russian interrogators are still trained to use it. The victim's wrists are tied together by a rope. The rope is tied to the ceiling, and the victim is dropped over and over again. Perhaps you can guess that the severity of the jerk eventually pulls the arms out of their sockets." The Russian paused. "In a submarine this size, we have some high-ceilinged room that do nicely for the strappado. I shall ask again, Colonel Sturgis: the location and strength of your unit?"

Sturgis shook his head. Immediately Revin grabbed Dixon's left ring finger and broke it.

Billy let out a cry that turned into a moan. Revin allowed him to drop his hands from the table. He crouched on the floor, his good hand clutching his left, wincing and stifling the groans that rose in his throat.

"He has three good fingers left on that hand," said Veloshnikov. He smoked his cigar. "Plus five on the other. Or, maybe you'd rather we saved his fingers and shattered his kneecaps instead. The choice, Colonel, is yours."

Billy looked up at Sturgis, his eyes pleading. "Don't tell them anything, Sturg," he said between gasps. "They can break—every bone in my body."

Veloshnikov grunted derisively. "What admirable sacrifice. What will it be, Colonel Sturgis—fingers or kneecaps?"

Sturgis was full of anguish. He could not stand to see Billy suffer at his expense; nor could he make such a horrible choice. "Kill him," he said softly.

"Kill him?"

"That's right." Sturgis spoke more emphatically. "I don't give a damn about him, so you're wasting your time. He doesn't have the information you want, anyway. You might as well kill him. He is not a friend of mine—just another soldier."

Veloshnikov peered into the commander's face. "I don't believe you. Your eyes betray you."

Sturgis tried to shrug carelessly. "The only fingers and kneecaps that matter to me are *mine*. You make it easy on me by torturing him. You won't get anything out of him — he knows nothing."

"You are a very bad liar, Colonel." Veloshnikov pointed down at Billy. *"Palets,"* he said to Revin, indicating Dixon's fingers.

Revin pulled Dixon's hands back up on the table. The sergeant grimaced. His two broken fingers stuck out at odd angles from his hand, which already was red and swollen. Revin took hold of the middle finger.

"You can spare your man further pain, Sturgis," Veloshnikov said.

"You underestimate both of us. This is futile exercise, Admiral. I can only assume you proceed out of sheer perversity and brutality."

Veloshnikov gave Revin a signal. Billy cried out as the middle finger broke. He slumped back to the floor, eyes glazed with pain.

Sturgis shut his eyes. For God's sake, they were going to take Billy apart bit by bit. He had expected to be tortured himself; this was far worse. In a blind moment, he nearly hurled himself at the Russian admiral, to get in one solid, last punch before the bullets from the guards cut him down. *Bastard!*

"He'll be lucky to use that hand again," said Veloshnikov. He paused. "We could make a deal, you know."

"A deal for what?" Sturgis did not want to show signs of capitulation, but he wanted to forestall more torture for Dixon as long as possible.

Veloshnikov paced a small circle by the side of the table. "The surrender, Colonel, of your entire command. And the negotiation of the surrender of whatever resisting government remains in America."

Sturgis started to swear, but Veloshnikov cut him off. "It's only a matter of time before we hunt you down and destroy every one of you. You must know that, Sturgis. You are outnumbered and outgunned, dying even as we speak. You prove nothing by resisting. Surrender your Blacksuits to me, Colonel, and reveal any known strongholds of resistance."

"In exchange for what?"

"In return, I will not torture or execute any of you. You and all your men will be allowed to live out your radiation-shortened lives in your own country— under our supervision, of course. You will have food, women. Your last days will be comfortable."

Sturgis's reply was heavy with sarcasm. "Doesn't that sound peachy. The benevolent Soviet state. You don't know Americans and you don't know my men, Veloshnikov. We'll fight for our freedom until our last breath. Not one of us will ever, *ever* betray his country!"

Veloshnikov arched an eyebrow. "A passionate speech, Colonel. You have thirty seconds to consider my offer before Lieutenant Revin breaks your sergeant's kneecaps."

Oh, God, thought Sturgis. Oh, my God. Forgive me, Billy.

Dixon, humped over his damaged hand, slowly straightened. "Break them," he whispered.

Sturgis's throat was full and aching. "Billy . . ." His voice trailed off.

Revin disappeared into the shadows and remerged with an iron bar. He laid it on the table with a clank.

Sturgis saw a look pass between the KGB officer

and the marshal; it was silent communication. Veloshnikov grunted and nodded. He moved off into the darkness; his voice carried out.

"Lieutenant Revin wishes something else first. I must grant his request, as a man with shattered kneecaps can do nothing but lie on his back. Guards."

The two soldiers who had been training their machine guns on the Americans shouldered their weapons and came behind Billy, each grasping an arm. Sturgis's heart thumped in his chest. He had a feeling of what was coming, hoping he was wrong.

Veloshnikov came out of the darkness to peer into Sturgis's face. "You will excuse me for a while, Colonel. One last question before I go: Did you serve in the Vietnam War?"

The question took Sturgis aback, it was so out of left field. He searched the Russian's face for clues as to why such information was of importance, but found none.

"No," he said. "I did not."

Veloshnikov nodded to himself. Some of the fire burning behind his eyes seemed to die. He slipped back into the darkness. "Carry on, Lieutenant," he said to Revin. The door to the room opened. Light spilled in, then the door closed.

Sturgis looked at Revin, horror and revulsion filling him. The KGB officer ordered Billy to lie with his legs spread. He opened his belt and unzipped his pants.

Sturgis was forced from the room, leaving Dixon to his fate.

CHAPTER FOUR

Sturgis came out of his haze. He was prone on his stomach on something cold and hard, and his back was on fire. He wanted to turn over and extinguish the fire on the cold slab beneath him, but movement was excruciating. He didn't know where he was, or why his body should be such a mass of pain. He heard the hums and throbs of distant, unknown machinery.

Then it came back to him, in flashes and pieces. He opened his eyes and took in a tiny, dark room. He was lying on a floor, nothing but a thin garment and equally thin blanket between him and the metal. He remembered. The nuclear sub *Lenin* . . . Veloshnikov . . . Revin . . .

Revin.

Dean's back was on fire because Revin's leather whip had lacerated every square inch of flesh. That came after the KGB officer had returned from torturing Dixon.

Good God, Billy!

"Billy!" Sturgis called. His voice was hoarse. With great effort, he rolled himself up to a sitting position.

57

His entire body screamed in agony. Barely formed scabs split all across his back, bleeding anew. He was clothed in a sacklike garment the Russians had put on him, and the blood caused it to stick to his wounds.

Sturgis saw the young sergeant's body on the other side of the small room, also clothed in a shapeless gray garment, curled into a fetal position facing into the wall. "Billy!"

Dixon made no response.

Sturgis crawled on his hands and knees. "Billy, are you all right? Talk to me!" He reached out, half afraid he would touch a stone-cold corpse instead of Billy, the man.

The flesh was warm; Dixon was alive, but unconscious.

Sturgis gently uncurled his limbs. He was enormously relieved to see Dixon's legs undamaged; the KGB lieutenant had not carried out the threat to smash his kneecaps with the iron bar. Sturgis didn't know why—perhaps Revin had decided to save it for the next round—but he thanked God Billy had been spared. He never would have walked again.

Billy's entire left hand was swollen and grotesque, the three broken fingers splayed out from the knuckles. Sturgis shook him, mindful of tender and bruised spots from the beating he had taken from Revin. "Billy!"

Dixon opened his eyes, stared unseeing at Sturgis for a few moments, then recognition spread across his face. He groaned. "Sturg, oh, God. What's going on?"

Sturgis helped him sit up. Billy yelped in pain as he hit his left hand against the wall. He stared at the

58

balloon-shaped paw as if it didn't belong to him. Billy worked his jaw, testing it. "That bastard . . . really did a number on me." He looked at Sturgis, his blue eyes conveying everything he could not bring himself to put into words. Dean understood. There would be no reference to the sexual humiliation Billy had suffered, though it was in Billy's eyes.

"Yeah, they gave us a hell of an opening number," he answered Billy. "At least we're alive and no parts are missing."

"If anything was missing, I wouldn't know it. I'm numb."

Sturgis helped Billy position himself so that his back was propped up by the wall.

"Hell, Sturg, you've got blood all over your face."

Sturgis ran his fingers over his face. On top of the dirt, dried sweat, and stubble of whiskers was a cake of dried blood that came from a slash on his right cheek. The slash must have been the work of Revin's whip. He didn't remember getting hit there; he must have been unconscious by then. He felt his other cheek, which bore the scar from his previous encounter with Russian captors. Matching scars courtesy of the Reds, he thought grimly. He said, "Shit."

Dixon drew in a long breath and cleared his throat. "So what now? They come back and work us over again? If I see that fucking bastard KGB thug again, I'm going to smash his ugly face in with my good hand—and they can fill me with lead."

"Here, let's see those fingers." Sturgis gingerly took Billy's injured hand. "I'll have to try to set these, Billy, or you're going to risk losing the use of them."

"Trouble is," said Billy, "there's nothing to use for a

59

splint."

Sturgis looked around the cramped room. It was bare—not a shelf or a container or even a loose rivet. "We'll have to make do with tight bandages. It'll be better than nothing." He grabbed his garment and ripped off a wide, long strip from the bottom. He positioned Billy's left hand palm-side down on the palm of his own left hand. "This is gonna hurt, kid."

"I'm ready." Billy shut his eyes and gritted his teeth.

Sturgis began with the middle finger, taking hold of it and then pulling straight out with a hard jerk.

"Annnhhh!" cried Billy.

Sturgis did the same with the other two broken fingers. Then he wrapped the cloth strip around the entire hand, tight enough to keep the fingers as immobile as possible but not so tight that circulation would be cut off. He split the ends of the bandage and tied a knot. Dixon slipped off into a fog of pain.

Sturgis dragged himself to his feet, moving in agonizing slow motion. No windows on a sub—no dropped ceiling like the time he'd escaped captivity before. The steel door to the room was—no surprise—firmly locked shut.

He was about to bang on the door when it opened. Two armed Russian guards grabbed him and pulled him out into the corridor. They slammed the door shut, leaving Billy inside.

"Where are you taking me?" Sturgis demanded. He got no answer. The guards pulled and pushed him down the narrow walkway. Once again, Sturgis was reminded of the enormous size of the nuclear beast. *Somehow we are going to survive this*, he vowed to himself, *and then we will blast this crate and every-*

thing in it to hell.

He was taken back to the interview room.

The guards took off his gown and made him stand, spread-eagled, facing into a wall. He stood that way so long he lost track of time.

Presently, he heard the door open and footsteps enter. He was not allowed to turn around; he did not speak.

Nor did the visitor. The only noise Sturgis heard was the sound of leather unrolling.

Crack! Revin's whip came down across his buttocks, snaking around his thigh. Sturgis gasped at the shock.

Crack! Another blow.

Jesus, he thought, they didn't even ask me a question. I didn't even have the privilege of saying no.

"No!" he cried out loud. The whip came down again.

Blood dribbled down his legs to pool on the floor by the time the hatch door opened again, and Sturgis recognized the heavy, measured footsteps of Veloshnikov. "Enough," the Supreme Marshal said. Sturgis's gown was flung at his backside. "Put it on," Veloshnikov ordered, "and come with me."

Sturgis did as he was told, moving slowly because of the pain. "Come where?"

Veloshnikov smiled grimly; his obsidian eyes were hard and shiny. "I will show you the defeat of America. Like fools, you and your sergeant are willing to be tortured to death. You believe there is hope for America. There *is* no hope. I will convince you, and you will change your mind about joining the winning side."

Veloshnikov spun on his heel and went out the door. Sturgis followed, groaning with the effort, Revin making certain he did not lag. They passed through a long, tubelike corridor. The *Lenin*'s nuclear powerhouse hummed and throbbed around them. Russian sailors they passed eyed Sturgis coldly. The American tried to take in as much detail as possible — it would be useful later. He was still determined to break free.

They descended a steel staircase to another level. At a closed hatchway, Veloshnikov paused before turning the handle to open it. "What do you think of our little ship here, Colonel?"

"I'm an Air Force man — I don't know much about subs."

"The *Lenin* is an example of Russia's superior technology. It is bigger and faster than anything you Americans have built — nearly three hundred meters, with a sustained top speed of fifty knots, armed with twenty of our biggest nuclear warheads. The *Lenin* is one of the reasons why you lost our brief nuclear war."

"That's strange, I don't recall us surrendering," said Sturgis.

Veloshnikov snickered. "Your defeat is de facto, Colonel Sturgis." He spun the wheel that unlocked the hatch, and pushed the door open. "After I show you some of the *Lenin*, you will see no reason to cling to your dying nation."

Sturgis saw that the compartment that lay ahead of them was much different than the surroundings they'd passed through. The gray of steel and alloys gave way to white paint, so bright it was almost dazzling. Running along the white walls were stainless-steel counters, and the paraphernalia of a lab — beakers, Bunsen burners, test tubes, and boxy equipment for which Sturgis could not guess the purpose. The personnel were dressed in white smocks, like medical technicians.

"This is our newest section, added just before the Christmas Day strike," Veloshnikov said with obvious pride in his voice. "It is our sick bay and dispensary, and it is fully equipped to combat radiation poisoning. While you Americans sicken and die, *we* survive."

"How is that so?" said Sturgis, trying not to sound disgusted.

Veloshnikov pointed to the door along one wall. "Behind that is a freezer stocked with liver tissue from hundreds of miscarried and aborted fetuses. As you probably know, Colonel, fetal liver — "

" — is injected to help repair bone marrow damaged by radiation," Sturgis finished. "The question is, Veloshnikov, how many babies did you murder so that your troops can survive and go on killing?"

"No insolence from you!" roared Veloshnikov. "Or I'll have Lieutenant Revin take you back for interrogation!" The Russian let his words sink in, then continued, "The point, Colonel, is that the *Lenin* carries enough liver supplies to sustain thousands of fighting men through the worst of the fallout. We dock, and the men who have been ashore and exposed come for treatment. Soon, the radiation will fall to nonlethal levels. In the meantime, we can keep on fighting with full strength."

Veloshnikov pushed Sturgis back out the hatch.

Revin stepped aside and brought up the rear again. The Supreme Marshal set a fast pace. They went down a length of corridor and down a ladder to yet another level.

"The War Command Room—the nerve center," said Veloshnikov, ushering Sturgis into a round room filled with computer and electronic gear, and colored grid maps that flashed on giant screens on the wall.

Sturgis took it in quickly, astonished at what he saw. If his guess was right, the Russians could tell at a glance the exact position of every military unit of major size *all over the globe*. What other countries besides America had been hit?

But Veloshnikov, entering commands at a computer keyboard, turned off the global map before Sturgis could answer his own question. The world map was replaced by one of the United States.

"Look closely, Sturgis, They gray areas are those places that won't sustain life for a thousand years."

Sturgis felt his stomach turn. The Eastern seaboard, the power nexus of the nation, was *half* gray. Further south and inland, the gray became more scattered—except Texas and Illinois, which had suffered a heavy dose of death, due to unfortunate winds the first two days after the nuke hits. All these months, he had been holding on to the hope that some parts of America had escaped unscathed. But if Veloshnikov's map was correct, just about seventy percent of the U.S. had been subjected to a dose of fallout that meant centuries of death.

"Fucking barbarians," he cursed under his breath.

Veloshnikov picked up on his distress. "You see, America is beaten. Our land troops are spreading through the country, destroying what little pockets of resistance are left. Why doom yourself to a useless defense, Colonel? There is plenty of room for you in the service of the Motherland. I assure you that you and any of your men you bring with you will be treated with all respect."

Sturgis would have spat, but he had no saliva. He said, "That'll be a cold day in hell, Veloshnikov."

"You'll regret those words, Sturgis."

"Not as much as I'd regret selling out. How much of the rest of the world have you blitzed with your bombs?"

Veloshnikov crooked a hard smile. "That's classified, Sturgis. You've seen enough in here."

Outside the command room, Veloshnikov led the way through a steel tunnel to a ladder. They were going to ascend. The far end of the tunnel was sealed off and marked with the symbol that indicated radiation hazard.

Sturgis stopped. He was creating a mental map of the sub. "Is that where your reactor is?"

"Yes," said Veloshnikov.

"But there's no hatch. How do your men get back to service and run it?"

"We have a crew sealed in there."

"What! But that's a virtual death sentence, unless you've got extraordinary shielding."

Veloshnikov shrugged. "The shielding is adequate. The men are paid double what their counterparts earn. After their tour of duty, they come out and are decontaminated and treated."

Sturgis didn't answer. There were no words for such barbarism. No amount of decontamination could

65

help men exposed to a nuclear reactor like that. But, then, life had always been cheap in Russia.

On their way up, threading through corridors, the three men passed by a gauge which Sturgis recognized as a radiation meter—and it was recording significant levels, right in the *Lenin*. He pointed this out to Veloshnikov.

"Despite your fetal liver, you've got a serious radiation problem on your hands," the American said. "You can't escape what's happening to the rest of the world—which *you* polluted. We have reports that your own people in Russia are dying from the fallout spreading over the globe."

"We anticipated the winds," Veloshnikov said testily. "You could not possibly know of anything outside the United States."

"You're killing everybody. What did you think you had to gain by pushing the button?"

"Do not lecture me," Veloshnikov said angrily. "Ours was a preemptive strike. You were building your war machine, getting ready for your own offensive. It was you or us!"

Dean shook his head. "How wrong you are," he said softly. It was then that he noticed a black mole on the side of the Russian commander's neck. The skin around it was red; the mole look festered. It was one of the first signs of skin cancer. He said nothing.

Next Sturgis was taken to a luxurious suite decorated in plush blue fabrics, with oil paintings hung on the walls and furniture that looked invitingly comfortable. "My Blue Room," Veloshnikov explained. "I had it done in a reproduction of the Rainbow Room in the old czar's summer mansion outside Leningrad.

Loyal servants of the state are well rewarded. A room like this could be yours somewhere."

"In Russia," Sturgis said sarcastically.

"No, here in America. If you join us, we will set you up well. Even your well-known clergyman Reverend Jeeters joined us a while back. His defection to us serves as a *model* for other Americans." Veloshnikov turned and looked Sturgis straight in the eye. "This is your last chance, Sturgis. Will you join us?"

Sturgis met the Russian's gaze with defiance. "Never. And I speak for Sergeant Dixon and the rest of my men." It was hard for Sturgis not to betray a smile at the reference to Jeeters. The Reverend was using his "traitor's" role to pass intelligence to the guerrilla forces of the United States!

Veloshnikov's mouth twitched as he struggled to control his anger. "Then, you and your sergeant will be shot. As soon as we anchor in Norfolk for minor repairs. That's in five hours—think about it till then!"

The nighttime approach of the *Lenin* to the Norfolk harbor was monitored by the watchful eyes of Tranh, Fireheels, Grimes, and Fuentes, who were hidden in an empty warehouse on one of the piers. Their black C.A.D.S. suits gave them good camouflage in the darkness, allowing them to slip into the Red-held area.

They were here because Betrov had made one fatal mistake—communicating with the *Lenin* on a supposedly scrambled radio channel that the C.A.D.S. men monitored and unscrambled. Then the Russian-language-translator function typed out the message that Sturgis and Dixon were being taken aboard the *Lenin*. So sure was Betrov that the American couldn't decode his commlink that his casual talk gave away the fact that the sub would anchor at Norfolk! They'd brought two extra C.A.D.S. suits along on their tribikes and stashed them in the empty warehouse.

Using infrared and zoom vision, Tranh now tracked the movement of the shape through the carbon-colored ocean. "Mode Blue," he commanded, and got an instant analysis readout on the inside of his visor.

"It's the *Lenin* all right," Tranh said, "and she's surfaced and is coming in. I guess it's like Veloshnikov told Betrov—she needs maintenance, a reactor core repair of some sort. They won't attempt to start loading on the repair crews while it's dark."

Fuentes shivered inside his suit. "Let's hope so. It depends on how confident they are that this port is secure. My guess is that you're right—they'll wait till dawn."

"Only one way to find out," said Fireheels. He checked his suit's magazines of machine-gun ammunition, darts, and the occasionally malfunctioning E-ball system.

Van Noc studied the readout on his visor that gave the *Lenin*'s specs, speed, and course. "Our best shot is to get her the minute she drops anchor. By full daylight the vodka-heads who are half asleep around here will be crawling all over the damned thing to do the maintenance."

"I know just the way," Grimes spoke up. "Those coracles we saw stashed in the next pier."

The coracles were little boats made of hoops of wire covered with stretched and oiled tarpaulin. They probably had been used in survival exercises. They were ideal to float out on the waves as bits of flotsam—with C.A.D.S. raiders flattened on the bottoms.

The four men took three coracles and sneaked out to the edge of an unguarded pier. "She's a big ship," said Van Noc, "but I have a feeling I'll know where to hit. Maintain radio silence and follow my signals." Quickly, he outlined the attack plan.

They slipped quietly into the water, and floated out to the submarine, which had cut engines and was idle in the water. "Four A.M.—Now dawn is 6:06 this morning," said Fireheels.

Van Noc found himself holding his breath. Everything hinged on the *Lenin*'s radarman passing off the coracles—if he spotted them at all—as debris.

What seemed like an eternity later, they were in the path of the oncoming sub. It would slide by them. There would be only one moment to strike, and Van Noc knew he damn well better pick the right one.

The dark shape of the hull loomed before them like a great whale. Grimes lashed the three coracles together with nylon rope and gave the leader to Fireheels.

Now, thought Tranh, and gave the signal.

With a simultaneous scream of jetpacks, Van Noc, Fuentes, and Fireheels jumped for the flat-topped deck of the hull. They hit aft of the conning tower with dull thuds, scrambling for holds, Fireheels anchoring the rope to the steel railing. Grimes stayed behind in a coracle, using his jetpack to propel the boats alongside the sub so that they would not be torn to pieces.

Almost simultaneously, alarms went off inside the *Lenin*, the screech reverberating through the hull. They had seconds to act before the sub dived beneath the waves. Tranh let his gut instinct guide him. He picked a spot on the hull and sent an electro-ball searing into it. The three commandos smashed into the smoking, damaged metal with all the power they could call forth from their suits, ripping a gigantic hole clean through the titanium. The *Lenin* would not dive now!

"Okay, let's move it!" shouted Tranh. They jumped down through the ragged hole.

The whoop of the sirens going off jolted Sturgis and Dixon awake. Their tiny cell was almost pitch-dark, save for a sliver of light that showed around the hatch door. Despite the pain, Sturgis jumped up and hobbled to the hatch.

"What's happening?" said Dixon.

Sturgis pounded on the door. "I don't know — an emergency — maybe something malfunctioned." He caught faint sounds of shouting.

Sturgis groped frantically around the cell. There was chaos aboard the *Lenin*, and that meant opportunity for escape. If he could only find something — anything — to help them get out of here! He knew there was nothing in the cell, but he searched anyway, hoping for a miracle.

Suddenly a white-hot ball burst through the hatch and smashed into the back wall of the cell, sending a shower of sizzling sparks all over Sturgis and Dixon. Sturgis yelped. If he had been still standing at the door, he would have been cut in half.

There was the sound of rending metal, and then the dark silhouette of a C.A.D.S. suit stepped through the hole, illuminated by light from the corridor behind.

"Hello, boys," said a familiar voice.

"Tranh!" Sturgis exclaimed. "How—?"

"Don't ask now—just follow me!" Van Noc reached out with his powerful arms and grabbed Dixon and Sturgis, shoving them through the blasted door. "Come on! Fuentes and Fireheels won't be able to hold them off much longer!"

CHAPTER FIVE

Chaos was everywhere inside the *Lenin*. Sturgis and Dixon squinted as bright light exploded around them. The two guards by their cell lay dead on the floor, twisted lumps of bloody flesh.

"This way!" Tranh shouted, prodding the two with sharp jabs. Sounds of machine-gun fire and screaming came from other parts of the sub. The far end of the corridor had been blasted by another E-ball, sealing it off from the Russians in one direction.

Sturgis and Dixon stumbled along in their blood-encrusted, oversized tunics, their bare feet cold on the metal. They clambered up a ladder. Behind them, Van Noc let out a burst of machine-gun fire, cutting down an armed sailor who came at them from the open end of the corridor. "Move it!" Van Noc screamed as he pushed up.

The scabs of Sturgis's wounds split open again, bleeding afresh, but he didn't care. He could no longer feel pain. He had one thought, one goal: to get out.

They came out at the armored feet of Fireheels who grinned through his visor. "Sorry for dropping in without calling first," he quipped. "This way, sir!"

A chatter of machine-gun bullets zinged at them from one end of the corridor. Fireheels stepped in front of Sturgis and Dixon, shielding them with his suit. The bullets ricocheted off harmlessly. He raised his right arm and sent off a hail of bullets. The Russians died screaming as the bullets pierced their lungs and hearts.

Fireheels shoved the prisoners up another ladder. "One more flight!" He and Van Noc brought up the rear.

Fuentes, who was guarding the next level, was caught in a crossfire of enemy bullets. Sturgis ducked back down as bullets sang over his head. It took Feuntes a few minutes to silence the fire; then he alternately pulled and pushed Sturgis and Dixon to the hole punched in the top of the *Lenin*.

"I can't believe you guys! If Uncle Sam still has medals to give out, you guys will get a chestful!"

The icy night air and the salt spray of the waves rushed at them as they clambered out to the deck. The *Lenin* had gone dead in the water. No doubt, thought Sturgis, Veloshnikov was somewhere deep inside, trying to figure out what in the hell was going on.

He saw the coracles, and Grimes waving. He didn't think twice. He slid down the hull, metal tearing at his reopened wounds. Grimes caught him and jammed him to the bottom of the boat. "Don't move," Grimes said. "I'll cover you. We're gonna go like hell!"

Fuentes got Billy into one of the other coracles. Fireheels unlashed the tie and was the last to jump in the third craft. The three suited commandos fired up their jetpacks, turning the coracles into makeshift speedboats.

Behind them, Russian sailors poured through the hatch fore of the conning tower, firing at the departing boats with machine guns. Bullets bit the water around them and pinged off the suits.

As he steered the coracle, Grimes turned up his external audio and shouted to Sturgis above the roar. "We brought tribikes and two extra suits! I hope to hell that they're still there."

Sturgis shouted back, his words snatched away by the wind. "We'll make it," he yelled.

The weary nuke troopers on the low-slung bikes watched as a pale sun rose through sickly gray-green over the North Carolina countryside. Once lush and verdant, this part of the South was succumbing to the ravages of radiation. Their tribikes tore through the withered, dying land, heading for the Revengers' crystal-caves hideaway in the wilds of the Appalachians.

Sturgis, back in a C.A.D.S. suit, felt fused to his bike. To move meant breaking open wounds.

Dixon was also back in his suit, having managed to get his swollen hand in the large glove. He could not move the broken fingers, but he could use the other two like pincers, and he could still operate the weapons systems.

The whole daring rescue mission had only been possible, Sturgis learned, because Fireheels had been monitoring all Soviet communications channels. He did that on a hunch. He heard snatches of Betrov's message to the *Lenin*, telling of the capture of two American "Blacksuits." By the time he and some other troopers came to the town, the colonel and Billy had been spirited away.

Van Noc filled Sturgis in. He, as commander in Sturgis's absence, had ordered the rest of the force to continue on toward the guerilla base.

"Good thinking, Tranh. You all did well. This is the first time I'd ever thought there was really no chance for me to live. And you guys proved me wrong—by God, you did!"

"Yeah, we gave those Russians something to think about," Tranh muttered, embarrassed by the compliment.

"Busted their sub up—half-creamed the pride of their force, and shot several dozen Reds. I'm only sorry we didn't have a chance to scuttle that sucker, skip," Billy added, his voice filled with anger.

"Next time," said Sturgis. "There'll be one for sure."

After a long, hard ride to catch up to the other C.A.D.S. men waiting in a concealed valley, Sturgis, Billy, and their rescuers received a tremendous welcome. The colonel quickly moved the unit. Soon they were riding single file along a narrow mountain trail that Sturgis knew led to the general area of the Revengers' cave.

The distinctive sound of 9mm fire brought the column to a halt. Sturgis, using his Audio mode analyzer, located the direction and distance of the echoing shots. They came from six miles to their northwest.

The colonel rode his tri up the steep slope and used his Telescopic mode at full two hundred power. He could see a waterfall in the distance, at the bearing the shots came from. And near that tumbling stream of mountain water were men in uniforms. Soviet uniforms. Sturgis announced over his radio, "I can see sixty, maybe seventy Red troops. They have six civilians — and a donkey — pinned down. Let's go and help the poor bastards before the Reds overwhelm them."

Sturgis decided to bring his troopers along the left flank of the Russians who were so happily pounding their poorly armed opponents. The nuke troopers kept to the high ground.

The Soviets engaged in the fire-fight failed to notice the new arrivals on the heights. They had the Revenger squad trapped like rats. The six local militiamen were on one of the many cliff-ways that ringed the region and provided the only means of cross-country travel. The small band of Revengers had been caught spying on a new chopper base, and the Reds had pinned them down for hours, toying with them, machine guns and mortars against squirrel shot and two .22 rifles. Each hour the Reds had picked one Revenger off.

The Revengers had created a piled-stone redoubt, and were prepared to fight to the death. They would welcome it, rather than being captured and tortured. If capture seemed inevitable, they planned to shoot

77

themselves, so as not to give away the location of the Revenger headquarters.

Sturgis could now see the small chopper base. Five P-11s. He saw Soviet crews putting cases of ammo into the open doors.

Sturgis worked feverishly with his computer, reading in a series of commands and instructions to determine range of enemy forces, variations in terrain, status of each man's suit, and then issued his orders.

"Tranh and Billy, hover to the trapped Revengers. Stay with them and cover them. Roberto, neutralize the force on the hill. Grimes, you and I take the chopper base."

"What about me?" Fireheels asked.

"Wait here, watch the Tris, and monitor everything. You're reserve. Go where you're needed. C'mon, Grimes—those choppers are almost loaded and airborne."

The C.A.D.S. warriors leaped from the precipice into the thousand-foot chasm, on the attack, screaming out *"Victory!"*

A frustrated Joe Fireheels could only watch the proceedings, his mind weighed heavy with anger that he, of all of them, should be left behind. But orders, understandable or not, were orders. Maybe it was because he was the newest man. "Frig it."

"What'd he say?" asked Sturgis.

"He's mumbling about being left," replied Grimes as they descended from the heights in vertical position, their jet packs slowly lowering them, giving in bit by bit to the forces of gravity. They stabilized at about four hundred feet. Then, swooping up in a wide arch, they alighted on the slope of a hill just two hundred yards from the chopper and began directing their submachine-gun fire at the Reds, who looked up in amazement.

Sturgis saw that Roberto headed straight over the hill to the Russian forces on the far side, while Tranh and Billy were over the civvies, helping their cause greatly.

The C.A.D.S. warriors struck with precision and aplomb, surprising the poorly deployed Russian troops in simultaneous deadly attack. Underdog became master in a matter of seconds!

Roberto fell on the main body in a leap from overhead, hovering over the clearing and dishing out a double-barrel dose of 9mm hot steel, ripping the Russians to shreds like fish in a barrel. The carnage was total. The civvies who had been pinned down cheered as bodies fell in piles. The confused Reds scattered like frightened ants under the hammerlike strafing.

Sturgis and Grimes jetted to the barbed-wire perimeter fence containing the makeshift chopper base just as two of the craft were lifting off. They marched straight through the fence, impervious to the small-arms fire raking them from the wooden guard towers planted around the field. Powerful bursts of armor-piercing shells shot from the C.A.D.S. arm cannons into the fuel tanks of the choppers.

Several Red soldiers dove from the whirlybirds in horror as the terrible C.A.D.S. troopers advanced spitting fire. But they were too late. The ships erupted in dual all-consuming infernos, sending shrapnel everywhere—hot smoldering metal sprinkled with meat and charred bone.

Next they turned and trained their deadly weapons on the towers. The Soviets inside the flimsy structures quickly tossed their weapons out and put their hands on their heads. Suddenly, from all around, troops were coming forward, surrendering to the awesome robotlike warriors.

Sturgis walked his seven prisoners to Tranh's position. Tranh reported, "Everything okay up here. Including the donkey. All of the Russkies on the ledges ran like rabbits when they saw us moving in. Billy's out rounding them up. Oh, I think that there's a few familiar faces in the bunch we rescued."

"*How you doin', Sturgis, you old hound dog!* And that ain't no donkey. Nellie Belle's a *mule*. Her mare was a champion quarterhorse," a rangy old coot stepped forward and said.

"*Jake?* Jake McCoy?" Sturgis opened his visor and stared at the dirt-encrusted beard and the wrinkled tan face hidden in it. The colonel cracked a smile. He had only met Jake once before, when the squad had passed through the Revengers' secret cliff tunnel fortress on their first real counterpunch against the Russians. Sturgis was thunderstruck. He had rescued a friend, a dear friend, and hadn't even been aware of it.

"How you doin', partner?" the cocky old man said.

"Just fine, you old badger. I'm glad we could help you out."

"Warn't no sense in you boys gettin' involved, we coulda handled 'em. But I guess you men comin' along saved time. We hear you boys been given the Russky commie bastards fits up and down the coast."

"We do our small part," admitted Sturgis. "And you? It looks like you and your boys are still full of spit and vinegar." Sturgis eyed the motley crew of five other mountain men.

"We still control the hills, if that's what you mean. But we spend a tolerable amount of time and energy a-doin' it! Saved us a bit of time, your boys did, and I thank ya."

"Don't mention it again, Jake, old boy. But we'll talk later. Back at your camp. That is, if we're invited."

"Why a'course y'are! I'd be mighty offended if ye didn't stay a spell. I tell ye what, we'll burn the barn down for ye!"

"That won't be necessary," laughed Sturgis.

Lieutenant Grimes, after a few things were squared away, used one of the intact Soviet helis to fly the exhausted Revengers back to their cavern base; Jake called ahead so they wouldn't get shot out of the sky. The prisoners had been rounded up into the confines of the palisade, and had to be dealt with.

An officer stepped forward from their ranks. He was a young, clean-shaven major with short-cropped blond hair and chiseled features, a powerfully built man with a proud and haughty bearing. He said he spoke English. He began a running translation of Sturgis's words as the colonel spoke. Three Revengers had died at the Soviets' hands, and Sturgis was mad. "As official representative of the United States government and military governor of a region under martial law, I hereby charge you men with crimes against humanity. By operating in the invasion of America you have proved yourselves the agents of the regime that perpetrated the greatest crime in history—unprovoked nuclear attack. Have you anything to say in your defense?"

The English-speaking Red officer, who turned out to be the major in charge, said, "Yes, I do, American swine. You in your godlike manner accuse us of crimes. What crimes? Exactly *what* is the truth of the matter? Are we not mere humble soldiers pressed into the service of our country?"

"Don't give me any fancy double talk, mister," intoned Sturgis. "That old story about 'just following orders' went out with Hitler and his bunch."

"But, surely, we have the right of some appeal. What about the honor of American law, the sanctity of human rights? Surely these proud principles still burn in your heart?" The Red was sneering slightly, thought Sturgis.

"Your attack has brought martial law to my country," Sturgis explained in his iciest tone.

"That means we drop the formalities and play hardball. Now, back to business. You punks are members of the gang of social misfits that did the maddest slaughter of all time. Killed lots of civilians. Killed the law. Made yourselves . . . undesirables."

"Undesirables, are we? Such an un-Soviet word. Are you ashamed of what you say? If not, at least let us see the face of the man that condemns us. Or are you afraid to face the men you condemn?"

"All right," interjected Roberto, "that's enough!"

He had been listening in angrily. He stepped between Sturgis and the Russians, his weapons readied. "Enough talk. *No prisoners!*" He raised his arm to fire.

"No, wait!" snapped Sturgis.

The Red colonel smiled. "Change of heart?"

The C.A.D.S. commander released his vacuum seals and lifted the helmet from his shoulders. "Now you see me—I am military governor of this area by presidential edict. In time of martial law I must decide the disposition of *all* prisoners on this sovereign American territory. I will hear pleas of clemency from you and your men—"

Just then the Red colonel produced a small silver pistol that he had concealed under his arm. He fired. The bullet struck Sturgis under the chin, passed through his palate, and lodged in his left part of his jaw. Roberto returned fire, killing all the Reds, the shooter first.

A pinpoint glow flickered in the darkness like a diamond. He fenced with the light. A candle? A tunnel? A star? Cyclops? What was it?

"Unnh."

Slowly the outlines of familiar faces came into focus, but the background still glistened and sparkled. Finally Sturgis came to realize the walls were of crystal.

"Camp X . . ." he whispered in a dry voice, a pain shooting through his jaw as he spoke.

"You got it, skip." It was Billy, all smiles, leaning over him. At the foot of the bed stood Grimes. There were others too. Tranh—and Roberto.

"What—what happened?"

"What's the last thing you remember?" asked Billy.

"I was talking to the Soviet colonel, then—then—I don't know." Sturgis felt a pain in his jaw. He lifted his hand to it and touched a thick bandage.

"Wha—what happened?"

"It's a bullet wound," said Tranh. "You're okay. But the Sov that shot you up isn't."

Sturgis smiled as Jake McCoy came up to the bedside. Then he saw the beautiful young strawberry blonde with him. She had sparkling turquoise eyes. He couldn't get a good look at her, as she stood half hidden in the crowd of men. Her hair was tightly drawn back, and was long and shiny. His mind felt like lead. Who was she?

"I guess I've been out of it for quite a while . . ."

"Bingo," exclaimed Billy. "Three days. And this pretty little gal's been with you all that time." The blonde with tied-back hair approached. "Cat!" Sturgis exclaimed.

Billy nudged Cat Curie forward, prodded her to speak.

"Hi, Dean. Remember me?" she asked coyly.

Sturgis said, "And how!" bringing a chorus of laughs from the company. She was radiant in a sparkly silver clinging robe.

"Anyway," Cat continued as she blushed, "they brought you in by helicopter, for treatment after removal of the slug."

"That's right, skip," Billy ran in, impatient with the pace. "After that Red running dog plugged you, we rushed you here in one of the Russky choppers. Jake here explained how Cat's become a regular Ben Casey. Seems she's got a natural touch for medicine."

Sturgis's jaw dropped. "You mean Cat operated on me?"

"Hell, no," Jake cut in. "Cat is postoperative care, that's all. Your Doctor de Camp did the surgery. Now she is busy with our other patients. Damned busy. We've got a hundred, if a one."

"I see," Sturgis remarked. "When do I get to stand up?"

"Plenty of time for exercise later," said Cat. "Let the colonel get some rest for now," she said to those gathered.

Sturgis protested, but it was obvious that Cat's word was law in the medical ward.

"You're a very lucky man," Cat said with a smile once the others had left. She touched his lips with hers, which led to a series of kisses.

"I have had that very same thought, and now more so than ever," Sturgis said, his heart pounding. He wanted to continue their kissing, to move it on, but she demurred, stressing his condition.

"We'll get to that later," she offered.

The last time Sturgis had seen Cat she had been a brazen young country gal interested in having sexual desires satisfied. There was a lot of that going around just then. She was desperate to be comforted, like so many others. Camp X had been nothing but a primitive wilderness cave community held up by sheer guts at that time. Now his room was small but quite clean and comfortable, outfitted like a prewar hospital room. Impressive. But these physical changes were dwarfed by the human ones. Cat Curie seemed so poised and confident, sophisticated. Her whole being exuded confidence, a glow. But her *outfit* . . . Sturgis asked, "The silvery robe you wear, Cat. Does it have any significance?"

"Medical garb," she said tersely. "Any other questions?"

"No need to get steamed. As a matter of fact, yes. Why do you tie back your lovely hair?"

"I want to be more womanly. A lot of things have changed . . ."

"Tell me about those changes, Cat."

"I'll do better than that, Dean Sturgis. I'll show you. But first you need a rest." With that Cat swung a violet-colored crystal globe over Sturgis's head.

"What's that for?"

"Rest now. Talk later," said Cat, giving him a warm peck on the cheek. He noted someone had been shaving him over the last three days as he drank in her sweet perfume and lost himself in her. He opened his mouth to speak.

"Shhhh," she cautioned, finger to her lips, crossing to the door. She turned a glowing dial and violet light illuminated the crystal globe. Soothing. Sturgis willingly drifted to sleep.

Some hours later, Billy Dixon raced into the colonel's room. "Colonel Sturgis! Great news! Fenton and Rossiter *made it!* They're here, safe and sound, brought the Rhino battlewagon too," shouted the excited Southerner.

"Tell them to come here," Sturgis demanded. "Right away!" That had sure woken him up in a hurry. Imagine. They were alive!

Billy departed, and in a few moments the tall, bulky Fenton MacLeish and the chubby, short Mickey Rossiter came in the door. Their black coveralls were sweaty and dirty.

"Reporting for duty!" they said simultaneously, saluting.

After the colonel gave them a salute and shook their hands, the pair of fighters inquired about Sturgis's condition.

"I'm fine—but how the hell did you get away from the Russians, anyhow? Damn, last I saw of you guys you were surrounded, doing the hero bit."

"Wasn't easy. The gist of it is, we created a six-way crackup with our Rhino and some of their tanks and pursuit vehicles. We knew the Rhino's giant spherical wheels could roll over them like they were V.W.'s. And with all their big stuff crumpled up, they had nothing to chase us with—then there was the fog . . . Tell you in greater detail sometime," Fenton finished. "The gorgeous doctor said you need more rest. We'll see you later; get well soon. We'll party."

A brown-robed male orderly brought Sturgis some solid food. Scrambled eggs and bacon. Plus some fresh salad. He ate heartily. To his surprise, his jaw felt almost natural. Cat and Jake came in, stood watching him devour fresh sprouts and cherry tomatoes mixed in a salad seasoned with basil, olive oil, and vinegar. Sturgis even thought he tasted a hint of lemon in the roughage. Sturgis had so many questions, he didn't know where to begin. Involuntarily his hand reached up and scratched at the bandaged underside of his chin where the bullet had entered.

"It's healing nicely," said Cat. "A very small caliber. She held the tiny lead slug up between thumb and forefinger for him to see. "I thought you might want to keep it."

"Naw," Sturgis laughed. "I don't get sentimental about those kind of things."

"Well, if you don't mind, then, I'll keep it."

"Suit yourself . . . Say, listen, Cat . . . I've been meaning to ask you something. It's about your new role here at the camp." Sturgis had a perplexed look on his face. "I seem to remember—now, you stop me if I'm wrong, Cat."

"Will do."

"Weren't you a kitchen worker the last time I passed through? Isn't it, well, a drastic occupational change to become a doctor?"

"Lots of opportunities are open to women now to advance," Cat said in a rather haughty manner. The atmosphere grew charged.

"Well," Dean said finally, breaking the momentary silence, "it's about time I had a look-see at what's been going on around here." He glanced back at Cat. "Okay with you—Doctor?"

She paused. "Well . . . I guess so. But you've got to take it slow. You really have been through a lot."

"Oh, I believe it. How about that tour you promised me? Can you spare some time right now?" he asked, wheeling his legs over the side of the bed.

"Good idea," enjoined Jake. "Take Colonel Sturgis here on the grand tour of the place. Show him everything. Why don't you meet us in the war room

88

at, say, 1400 hours. I'll get all our intelligence reports together and give you a full rundown on our operations since you last visited us."

"Sounds good, Jake, old timer," said Sturgis, noting the man had assumed quite an air of command over the months. "Tranh, Fenton, we'll meet in the war room at 1400 hours. Tell Billy, Roberto, and Rossiter to join us." Then he leaned over and whispered something private to Jake.

Sturgis and his private duty nurse soon were walking through the hallway outside his room. Doors lined the long white corridor.

"These are private rooms, for serious or . . . special cases," explained Cat as they passed the rows of doors leading to cubicles like the one Sturgis had occupied. "The general ward's out here."

They entered a low but expansive cavern at the end of the hall. Stone benches ringed the walls, and medical staffers, easily recognized by the white robes they wore, scurried about wheeling patients and moving equipment.

"This is basically outpatient work here. We provide everyone with vitamins and minerals. We grow fresh kelp in the pools and make iodine capsules for the mild rad cases. Of course, the whole thing is experimental, but with rad burns we've had *some* success using a variety of holistic, natural remedies. We've been flooded with 'wanderers' lately. Those are wander-in radiation victims. We treat them now, and some recover. Before, all we could do was watch them die in agony."

Dean noted two Revengers guarding the entrance to one of the many tunnels that fed into the general ward. The armed militiamen were the only persons not dressed in robes of one color or another.

"What's with the robes?"

"Oh," laughed Cat. "One of our real problems right off was clothing. We fashioned these robes and dyed them according to our service. It seemed to add order and meaning at the time, so we continue the custom. It's not so strange, Dean. You're watching a culture develop. A better, more natural one."

"What's down there?" he asked, indicating the guarded tunnel.

"Critcal ward. Nothing there for you."

"I want to see."

"Why, Dean? Don't you see enough on the outside? Give yourself a break."

"No," replied Sturgis. "I have to see it all. It keeps alive my will to fight."

They passed the guards and Cat used a large iron key to unlock the latch to the door of the ward. The passage led downward, and seemed smaller than that leading through his wing. After about sixty feet they came to a door with three clipboards hanging outside. "The man is a bit—wild. They are 'Wanderers,' rad cases," she intoned. "A family . . . father, wife, and their eight-year-old daughter. They were on vacation when it hit. Camping out. The men found them wandering in the woods about a week ago. They're all blind."

Sturgis turned the door handle and went into the whitewashed room. It was only slightly larger than his cubicle, the three beds lined up in a row, father, mother, and daughter. The smell of death hung in the room, though a ribbon on the small air vent showed movement. Someone was weeping quietly.

The victims wore sunglasses even in the darkened room, and ugly red scars ranged across their cracked yellow skin like craters on the moon. Only the woman showed any trace of hair: a limp strand hung from her left temple which she stroked endlessly with her long bony fingers.

"Who's there!" the man demanded irately.

"Easy, partner. My name's Sturgis. Colonel Dean Sturgis."

"Well, Colonel, come to gape? It's a little late for the cavalry, isn't it? Excuse the dimness of the room—the red glow is part of the treatment, they say. As if it will do any good. As if you coming here will do any good!"

"Look, mister. Don't go off half-cocked. I didn't order up any misery for anyone. I'm here as a friend."

"Yeah, well, I don't need any fr—"

"Sam! Please!" interposed the man's wife, extending her hand in the dim glow emanating from the rose-crystal ceiling lights.

"I'm Irene Dodsworth. This is my husband, Sam, my daughter, Amelia." The girl was asleep, so Sturgis lowered his voice.

"Pleased, ma'am," replied Sturgis, softly grasping her cool limp hand.

The husband pulled her hand away, and snarled out, "Well, you've had your show, Colonel. I suppose you watched the war from some secret bomb shelter somewhere; I suppose you officers built plenty of bombs and nice shelters for yourselves. Milked the taxpayers dry. Billions of dollars. Most powerful nation on earth. Then the Russians give a war and you don't show up. Stay home and watch the fire-works on TV. Yeah, my wife might not be willing to admit it. But you military men killed us all. The blame's on *you*, Colonel. *Colonel.* Humph. I'd be ashamed to call myself a colonel nowadays. Now go away. Leave me and my family alone. You make me sick."

The girl started crying as he finished his tirade.

"Dean, perhaps we'd better . . ." said Cat.

Sturgis took a good look at each of the afflicted, then followed Cat out of the room.

"Enough?"

"You're right," he said. "It's a sad story."

"C'mon. I'll show you our gardens and agriculture projects. It's much nicer there."

CHAPTER SIX

They continued the pleasanter side of the tour. The colonel felt more like he was in a shopping mall than a postwar underground hideaway. The corridors were wide and well-lit.

"I know a lot of the Revengers were miners, but how have you managed all this expansion?" asked Sturgis.

"A lot of the wings are the result of finding more natural caves revealed by our constant probing of the stone around here. But you'll want to now see the valley. That's another story."

They passed through another tunnel and exited into a brilliantly bright valley carpeted with an assortment of crops in varying stages of development. Green-robed laborers worked the fields, which stretched for a mile in either direction, although nowhere was the space more than a hundred yards wide.

As Sturgis perused the scene, a voice boomed out.

"Why, Sturgis, you old hound dog," said the robed man coming up the path. A big hand the size of a catcher's mitt slapped the colonel across his back, sending him forward a step.

"Anson? Is that you?"

"One and the same."

"But you're . . . you're . . ."

"Alive?"

"Well . . . to speak plainly . . . Yes! Anse, the last time I saw you, you were a real meltdown case!"

Sturgis saw that although the man had lost his hair, and his teeth had been replaced by a set of obviously artificial ones, he seemed healthy as an ox. The radiation scars that had plagued his skin were gone, and he no longer covered his eye with reflective sunglasses. His eyes seemed clear and sharp.

"Anson was one of the most remarkable turn-arounds," said Cat. "Of course, his original robust condition helped."

"I feel pretty good now, most of the time," said Anson as he rolled up a sleeve. He created a bicep that would have pleased a wrestler. "I see," said Sturgis, "that you have changed to all-green."

"Yes," said Anson. "I'm not with the militia any-more. This is the robe of an agri-technologist, friend. I work in the fields. I manage the water reserves and the kelp pools."

"He really has a green thumb," said Cat. "He's also carved several of the beautiful sculptures you see here in the garden."

"I'm on my way to the Guild quarter. These chompers still ain't quite right," he said, indicating his false teeth by grabbing his jaw and shaking it. "Care to join me?"

"Go with him, Dean," said Cat, rushing off. "I really *must* get back to the ward now."

"But, Cat! . . ."

"I'll see you . . . Tonight!" She winked and sped

off.

Sturgis joined the monklike Anson who seemed so relaxed and contemplative in his new role. When they first met, months ago, he had been near blind, ragged, a rad-scarred nuke warrior with a missile launcher slung over his bear-sized shoulders. Violent. Now, as they walked along, Sturgis noted that Anson seemed at peace with himself, and with everything. What a change!

They passed by Rossiter, who was looking around on his own. He joined their little tour. Rossiter was gaining weight, that the colonel could readily see. "Think you can get into your C.A.D.S. suit now, Mickey?" he joked. "You'd better cut down."

"Aw, Colonel, I just haven't had any good food for months. So maybe I gained *one* pound!"

They were in a long sinewy section of the crystal caves, well lit by overhead lights. A score of khaki-clad men and women sat in some open stalls they came upon. They saw utensils and tools displayed at the stalls. Some "patrons" ambled from shop to shop asking questions and contemplating wares.

Sturgis was startled by the sight of one of the C.A.D.S. suits stretched out on a table in a tinker's stall. Fireheels was standing next to it, speaking to a short red-haired man.

"Colonel. Good to see you up and about."

"What goes on here, Fireheels?" Sturgis asked.

"This guy's a genius, sir. We couldn't get the pneumatic pump that feeds the portside servomechanisms going on my suit. I thought I'd have to scuttle the system. But this character fashioned a replacement part and it works like new!"

"We do fine with the base metals," said the red-head. "Copper, lead, even iron. And there's enough raw material to serve our needs for the present. There's also gold and silversmiths, and armorers who manufacture ammunition for the militia and keep their guns in repair."

Anson found the shop that did work on teeth, and while he did his business inside it, Sturgis drifted next door. He watched in amazement as a craftsman fused crystals together with hot blown glass. The result was a crystal healing globe. He was told they came in blue—like this one—or violet, rose, or smoky.

Anson returned and they continued their tour. The men passed into another spacious cavern crowded with people in all colors of robes as well as with militia men in their now distinctive "uniforms" of the old everyday clothing.

Anson continued a running commentary. It was not without pride that he said, "We're at the old center of the complex. As you can see, fifty newly dug wings emanate from here. This was once a combination barracks, workroom, kitchen, *everything*. Now we use it mainly as a meeting area, and of course the punishment stocks are here too, in the old kitchen area."

"Stocks?" asked Sturgis craning his neck to see in the dim light. He saw men playing checkers at the tables and racks of books lining one wall.

"This way," said Anson, leading him around a low-hanging outcropping from the ceiling.

The prisoners, six of them, were set, head, hands, and feet, in massive oak stocks on a ledge overlooking the far end of the room.

"We do have our share of malefactors," Anson explained. "Mostly minor offenders, new arrivals usually who have trouble readjusting to civilization. There have been one or two serious incidents, but those men are kept in a security cell. There's a rotating panel of judges who set punishments. Usually a couple days in the stock, or extra labor.

"In the stocks they are condemned to silence. If they speak, they must serve another day. Their crimes are clearly indicated."

Sturgis saw that each wrongdoer had a cardboard placard dangling from their entrapped necks. He moved in for a closer look.

"LOAFING," "PUBLIC NUISANCE," "SPAM SNATCHER."

"Spam snatching!" laughed Sturgis.

Anson encouraged him to move in closer and have a good laugh. "It's a serious crime now," he explained. "They have to learn not to pilfer our small supply of canned goods."

"I don't know, pal," Sturgis yelled. "I been pretty hungry, but I think I'd rather starve to death than risk getting caught stealing a can of *Spam*. A man has to have *some* dignity!"

The perpetrator steamed violet but held his tongue. He'd already served two extra days and wasn't about to get tagged for another. Anson checked his watch, said, "Time for your meeting." They moved on past dart throwers and story tellers to the tunnel leading down into the war room. Sturgis knew the way instinctively. The passageway was still cramped, crude, and irregular like the old meeting room. The Revenger community had decided to leave the older sections of the complex in their original condition.

They were deep underground now and the air was especially cool and damp. The war room itself had been slightly expanded to make room for radio equipment and files, and more electric lighting had been added. Otherwise it was unchanged. The same rough-hewn log table stretched from end to end cluttered with maps and reports.

"Welcome, Colonel," said Jake, looking up from the table and coming around to greet his friend as he entered. The war room had the same serious, almost sacred atmosphere Sturgis remembered. Despite all the changes at Camp X, it retained its character and functions. The soldier class that gathered there wore the ordinary clothing of the mountain men. Since their activities took them outside frequently, and they didn't want the Russians to link them to an organized community, it was decided they would wear frayed Sears-type hunting jackets, denims, mechanic's coveralls, and the like. The Revengers themselves were professional soldiers. They worked at nothing else, but they had to look like the other ragtag survivors of the Christmas Eve nuke attack.

I'd like to go over your complete operations," said Sturgis. "Deployment, contact with the enemy—the works."

Jake, as always, lugged his long trusty nickel-plated squirrel gun with the black walnut stock. The gunsmith had modified the relic to pack a higher caliber and had added a quick-load forty-shot magazine, but the weapon retained its rustic appearance and was legendary among the clan, having belonged to Jake's great-great granddaddy in the Civil War.

"Here's our status," the leader said, pointing to a

chart on the wall with the stem of of his corncob pipe.

"We got 386 actives here in residence. Of course, anyone could handle a gun in an emergency, and we got plenty of small arms, but these are our regulars.

"The engineer corps is up in Mountain City, here." he said, indicating a town about ninety miles north of Camp X.

"That's a hundred men, all ex-miners. They're militia too, but they don't patrol like us. They plan the tunneling operations and supervise the work. They're up there with a bunch of coal miners from West Virginia working on a new dig. We're overcrowded here now, as you can see, and we figured it'd be better to colonize somewheres else than to keep expanding. Our biggest worry is to keep our location hidden from the Reds. We have to restrict everyone but militia to the complex usually. If they discovered us it'd be the end.

"There's two other groups sprung up on their own. We're in touch with 'em and we've cooperated on two raids. All told, we can muster almost two thousand fully equipped troops.

"We don't bother keeping many vehicles. The roads are pretty much useless. We have a dozen motorcycles and a couple pickup trucks we keep hidden in the woods in case we need 'em. Those helis we captured from the Reds'll come in handy. Tranh and Grimes have been training a couple of our boys to pilot 'em, and we brought over the fuel reserves from the outpost you guys knocked out. We figured we'd set up an air wing on one of the mountains in the area."

"Good idea," said Sturgis. "Chopper support

would be vital against a full-scale attack."

"So far we've held our own," replied Jake. "The Russians have been trying to infiltrate by establishing chopper bases throughout the mountains. You remember my brother Bart?"

"Sure," said Dean. "I've been wondering—"

"Dead. Same with Duke Hatfield. They took a lot of Reds with them, died real heroes. Two weeks ago we attacked the Soviets' base outside Mountain City. Getting too close to our works. Quite a brush fire. We lost sixteen men but blew the place to high heaven. Duke and Bart . . . you'd a been proud of 'em, Sturgis."

Sturgis examined maps and reports. He quickly recognized that a strong front line was already established along the Appalachians. The underground fortresses, together with the natural barriers created by the mountains and earthquake activity, had coalesced into a central spine of resistance against the invaders.

"Central command at White Sands had hoped to make the Appalachians our first line of defense," said Sturgis. "And I see now you men have checked the enemy further east than we'd dare ever hope," Sturgis praised. "Jake, the time has come to officially recognize your achievements and leadership here." He signaled to Fenton who brought him a small blue box. Sturgis opened it and pulled out a set of gold stars. "These I've been holding a long time.

"Jake McCoy, under the powers granted me by the President of the United States of America, I hereby commission you Brevet Lieutenant General in the U.S. Army. As such, you will also carry the title of Military Governor of the Appalachian Redoubt, with full judicial and administrative powers as prescribed by martial law."

Jake's jaw dropped and the corncob pipe hit the floor as his trembling hands accepted the insignia of his new rank. The men, Revengers and C.A.D.S. troops together, crowded around the general and offered heartfelt congratulations, patting the blushing old codger on his scrawny shoulders and helping him pin the stars to his collar.

"But . . . I don't get it, Sturgis. How can a colonel appoint me a general? Is it legal?"

"The President has given me leave to appoint appropriate military governors as I see fit," replied Sturgis. "This region has become the front line in our defense against invasion, and we need a permanent authority in the area. You already command the main fortress, and exercise considerable influence at the other posts on the line. I'm simply formalizing your role, Jake, and thanking you, for your country."

"And I thankee, Colonel. I'll wear 'em proudly. A *general*! My great-great granddaddy served under Jeb Stuart and thar warn't none finer. I hope I'm half the man he was! A *general*! Wee dogeee! This calls for a celebration. *Zeke!*" he called, addressing one of his men, "call the musicians, order a feast. We're havin' a celebration."

Jake led the party of military men back through the tunnel, past the old meeting room, and out into a clearing covered by camouflage net. Its circular floor measured a hundred feet wide. On Jake's express

101

order, the whole clearing was strung with dozens of Chinese lanterns in a matter of minutes. It was getting dark out. Sturgis excused himself to take a shower, and to check on his men, tell them of the shindig.

At about nine o'clock that evening, Sturgis returned to the clearing. Billy, Rossiter, Fenton, and Roberto came with him. The platinum-haired young Billy had a gal on his arm—a pretty one. The others hoped to find something as good at the party.

De Camp appeared, dressed in a taken-up red robe. The first time Sturgis had ever seen the woman doc dressed up so pretty. She even wore gold earrings. But she had such a scowl, he avoided her.

The fiddle players were already warming up when the Revenger chiefs arrived, and tables were being set with food and beverage, including jugs of the infamous "dead bear" moonshine.

Jake immediately shouldered one of the heavy brown jugs, yanked the cork with his teeth, let it fly, and swallowed a long draught of the potent fluid.

"Ahhhhh . . ." he wheezed, coughing up a lung. "Smooth as silk." He passed it to Sturgis, who sipped it cautiously.

Sometime after his first drink, Sturgis cornered Cat Curie at a table. They sat in a secluded corner, sipping highballs and picking at their sliced turkey and potatoes.

Cat had let her hair down, it cascaded over her tan shoulders. Also she had put a dab of mascara on her eyes, highlighting their beauty.

"I like the glow of the lanterns reflected in your blue eyes," Sturgis complimented. "And the blue dress is sensational."

"I thought you might like it. You certainly don't like my medical robe!" Her nostrils flared.

"The robe isn't that bad. But royal blue looks good on you."

Another change—Cat smoked. She took out a pack and matches. The colonel took them out of her long and lovely slender hands, lighting two and passing one back.

"I'm sorry, Dean," she whispered through a stiff shank of smoke. "I can't be a simple, homespun sexpot anymore."

"What's on your mind, Cat? Talk to me. Level with me. Why are you so—so *irritable*. Did I do something wrong? What gives?"

"It's the new me, Dean, that's all." She was fingering a charm on a silver chain. He reached to have a look. It was the tiny bullet she had removed from his jaw.

"I'm trying to be rational, Dean. But I had the silversmith set your little bullet. So you see, even though I've changed a lot—I still care for you."

"So why do I feel shut out from you, Cat? You still care for me. And I care for *you*. Look—can we take a walk to that little cove we visited last time I was here?"

"That's a laundry room now. That's just the point, Dean! *Everything's* different now. Then, there was nothing . . . Now, maybe I'm a fool, but I have hope!"

"And that's bad? That changes things?"

"In a way it *does*. It makes everything more . . . well . . . meaningful. There *is* a tomorrow now. But there's more to it than that, Dean. Mankind—me, you, everyone—has to change. We all have to stop being so—immature. I want you, more than ever. But the whole reason is bigger now. You might not like what I'm going to ask you."

Cat paused, bit her lip, and then more words poured out. "We've got to abandon old ways. For one thing, the way we think of sex. Love, caring, even *lust*, can no longer govern whether people get married to one another. Because so many people have radiation-damaged genes. You don't know the number of babies we've had to kill the moment they were born. Hideous things, some with scales, some without brains, or with fins instead of arms—it's sickening.

"I've heard."

"Dean, you are one of the healthy males. One of the *few* males left who are not harboring radiation-altered hereditary material. Men like you are scarce. We might have to go to polygamy, abolish two-people marriages, in order to save the human race. There is research going on here. We may seem like a bunch of hicks to you, Dean, but there are lots of talented people among us. Some have only recently arrived. Knowledgeable people. People who, if they were listened to, could have saved the world this tragedy of nuclear war.

"These men and women have discovered that the female human egg is less likely to be affected by radiation. Mutated babies are *primarily* the result of the father's bad genes. Lots of the women who are new arrivals have been raped before they found us. We've given them abortions. I've been against those things, but that's what we *do* now, because the babies wouldn't be—human." Cat looked down, swallowed hard. "Dean, I am going to have your baby."

"What?"

She stared him straight in the eye. "For humanity. And because I love you."

Sturgis took her in his arms, kissed her tension away.

"When does all this procreating happen," he said at last.

"Few more months . . . Dean, come, make love to me." She took his hand and led him from the celebration.

Owing to the fact that Cat slept in a dormitory facility, they elected to go to Sturgis's hospital room for their privacy. They had been there for a half-hour, making love in the white-sheeted bed, when there was a commotion in the corridor. Raised voices. Sturgis pulled away from Cat's sensual body and reached for the sheets. He had just managed to pull them up over him and Cat when the door, lockless as hospital doors are, burst open. It was Sheila de Camp.

The woman doctor froze in the doorway. "Oh! I'm—I'm sorry. I thought . . ." She glared at Cat, who returned her look. "Hello, miss. Nice to meet you."

"Pleasure's mine," Cat replied. "Good-bye."

"I can take a hint," de Camp said. "I'll see you later, Colonel. I have a report about the *so-called* medicine being practiced—"

"Yes, *later*, de Camp," Sturgis said forcefully. The door slammed shut; there was the sound of high heels rapidly moving down the corridor.

Cat smiled at Dean. "Girlfriend?"

Sturgis frowned. "No. Our doctor. Seems she has a report . . ."

"Yeah. Well, where were we?"

Later Sturgis and Cat sat having a cup of coffee in a corner of the cafeteria section. Most of the cavern dwellers were up in the clearing at the dance. "Cat," Sturgis asked, "you are one of the people in charge of medicine here, right?"

"Right."

"What do you think de Camp was so steamed up about?"

"Dean, if I read her right, she's very—conservative."

"Well, you're right, now that you mention it. Why?"

"Don't you know that our crystal-elixir therapy and the other things we do here for rad victims and the injured and sick are very unorthodox?"

"So? It worked on me. My jaw feels like new. Hardly would know I was shot. Even your passionate kisses didn't hurt."

"Right. But it's not AMA—American Medical Association—type therapy. For decades they've been pushing one sort of medicine. Most doctors have been convinced any other way of treatment is, well, mumbo jumbo or worse."

"Well, I don't know much about these crystal elixirs. What are they? I have the feeling I'm going to be forced to defend your treatment, and I'd like to know what I'm defending."

Cat sighed. "It goes to the heart of a person's philosophy of life. We believe that man is a part of the universe, and health is harmony with that universe—physical and mental. Balance is health. Imbalance can lead to sickness—or collectively—war. Restoring balance is our goal. It's a *spiritual* response, as opposed to an AMA-type *physical* response to sickness. Understand me?"

"Perfect sense to me."

"There's hope for you yet, macho man! Well, to continue, nature, not a chemical factory, should make us well, restore balance naturally. Crystals come in many types; all natural curative crystals contain vibrations, colors, naturally attuned to vibrations in the human body. We take fluorite crystals, which are purple, and put them in cave water, then let them be exposed to sunlight. Then, after a month or so, the jars are unsealed and the water, which have become elixirs, are used against the rad sickness. The patient drinks it, or it's injected. I and the others learned this from a very old mountain man. He came here a few months ago. He showed us the various crystals that we had never thought of as more than decorations. He was an old hermit, lived alone for years, learned these things from books and from just sitting silent, listening, he said, to the universe. He sensed the disturbance in the collective mind of humanity that would bring the war. That's what he said, anyway. He sought out these caves, was surprised and happy to find us here. He taught us."

"Is he here?"

"He died. But he taught us a lot first. Name was Mel. Just Mel. Taught me rose quartz is used for a mood elevator; clear quartz crystal for opening psychic centers of the brain for self-directed healing, smoky quartz for—"

"Hold on. I'll take your word for it. Proof's in the pudding. In my recovery, for instance."

"De Camp wouldn't believe it if she herself was cured. The old way of thinking, unnatural, totally materialistic thinking, got mankind into the big trouble that ended in World War Three. It was caused by this stubborn belief in purely physical systems."

Sturgis was exasperated. He had told Cat that de Camp would understand the new treatments if Cat could just show her the statistics, the before-after pictures and charts of patients treated with the crystal elixirs.

But de Camp didn't want to hear of it. She wanted Sturgis to talk to Jake and the others and get them to stop the new treatment, and instead go back to antibiotics and other traditional ways.

Sturgis refused to do this. And when de Camp said she would speak to Jake herself, the colonel forbade it. And he ordered the doctor to take along some samples of the crystal medicines and other cures Cat had told him about when they left Camp X. He had been so impressed that he wanted the president to hear of the treatments. Especially the antiradiation treatments.

The colonel could only shake his head after his talk with the doctor. He suspected it wasn't just medical considerations that had drawn the line between Cat and Sheila. It was jealousy. De Camp was jealous of Cat. Which must mean, he concluded, that Sheila de Camp had designs on him.

After two more days, once all the suits and tribikes were recharged, the C.A.D.S. warriors straddled their tribikes, helmets in hand. The morning of their departure had arrived.

"We move south now," Sturgis told Anson, shaking his beefy hand, "on to Okefenokee. I want to be in a position to move east or west. From the reports you've been getting, the Reds might try to make a thrust up the Mississippi. If not, we'll still be in position to hit the coast. In any case, we have to leave now. We can't operate from your base. We'll just blow your cover."

They had formed up on a brief stone plaza outside the cavernous main entrance to the camp. Billy's fingers were healing in casts; Rossiter wrestled with his suit, the extra ten pounds he'd gained setting off servomechanisms left and right. Finally, General Jake McCoy appeared in his new uniform, a full general's outfit sewed together by the Crafts Guild. The stars twinkled on his collar and he clutched his trusty squirrel rifle. After he reviewed the long line of C.A.D.S. troopers astride their well-polished tribikes General Jake McCoy approached Sturgis at the head of the column. "Hope you've enjoyed your stay."

"Seven days' R&R. Thank you, sir," said Sturgis

with a salute.

Jake saluted sharply. "Any time, Colonel. You have a fine bunch of men here, and with you on our side, I know America will soon be free." There was wild applause from the spectators.

Sturgis thanked the general, then turned to the task at hand.

"All right, men," he said, "Seal the suits and check systems."

The vacuum seals clicked along the column and a dull whirr built as the suits powered up. Before Sturgis sealed, Cat ran over. He gave her a peck on the cheek. She winked, rubbed her belly.

"I'll be back," he said, slipping the heavy visor into place over his head. Call him Charlie, after my father, if it's a boy."

"I'll be waiting, Dean," she replied. "But if it's a girl?"

But Sturgis's attention was on moving his men out. He was regearing his mind to be, not a man, not a lover, but a hardened nuke warrior.

With a wave of the colonel's steel-encased arm, the C.A.D.S. men on their tribikes, followed by the Rhino battlewagon, raced off into the twisting canyon.

CHAPTER SEVEN

The trip back to the swamp base was swift and uneventful. The tribike riders set a punishing pace for the Rhino, but all were anxious to get back while heavy fog covered the east.

They rode through a parched Georgia grassland. "It's looking worse than the burning summer of '86 — I wonder if it'll ever rain here," Billy commented as he rode alongside the colonel.

"The animals are dying, too," Sturgis said, pointing to the rotting carcass of a doe alongside the road. "We've been seeing more and more of that." He didn't add the rest of his thoughts—that map of the U.S. aboard the *Lenin*—showing the huge gray areas of death.

The state of the land gradually improved the further south they went, but Sturgis suspected that the weather patterns had changed. The U.S. was drying up. Soon there would be no Okefenokee Swamp — there would be just parched desert — and they would be forced to find a new hiding place, like animals themselves, chased from one nest to another.

The Okefenokee Swamp was soon reached. It was

still alive with life. The waters still meandered through thickets of sawgrass and moss-covered cypress and palmetto trees; birds still sang; insects still rustled and clicked. It was a deceptively normal summer in the swamplands.

The pace of their travel slowed as the way became wetter. The C.A.D.S. unit eased their water-capable tribikes into the murky waters. The big tires' deep treads acted like paddlewheels. Sturgis knew the swamp well now. Awaiting the troopers were a group of women once held captive by a band of marauding swamp creeps. Months ago Sturgis had managed to set them free. Now these "swampwomen" took care of Okefenokee Base. They aided the nuke troopers, helped increase the fortifications, and guarded the place when the men were gone. Sturgis would sooner have these women on his team than a lot of male soldiers he had seen in his day.

It was only natural that the leader of the women, Dieter, should come into his bed. In their passionate unions, they had sought to assuage the bottomless pain that had filled every day since the bombs fell.*

Sturgis was looking forward to seeing the long, leggy Dieter. Thoughts of the times they had made love filled him with desire. Guilt rushed in on top of the longing. He was reminded of an old song that advised that if you couldn't be with the one you love, you should love the one you're with. He had certainly been doing *that* lately!

That was the situation he found himself in, over

See C.A.D.S. #3

and over. Robin, his wife, his one true love, remained out of reach. But there was the comfort of other women, wonderful, beautiful women. Like Dieter, at Okefenokee Base.

He pushed his bike faster, having reached more-open lake waters.

The base consisted of the ruins of an old runaway slave hideout. A few crumbling huts had been reconstructed and a primitive plumbing system installed. Deep in the swamp, it was accessible only by boat — or tribike.

When the C.A.D.S. band neared the base, they knew instantly that something was terribly, dreadfully wrong. Callie, the far lookout, signaled them from a rooty outcropping. "Go away," she said, waving at them to retreat. "If you value your lives, leave immediately. The swamp fever is back!" Her black hair was tangled, her dark eyes wild, panicky.

"What's happened?" Sturgis called to her.

"It's spreading — many dead — more dying —"

Alarmed, Sturgis surged ahead, ordering sealed suits to all following. Callie disappeared in the heavy growth of cypress and Spanish moss, heading to the base overland.

De Camp's voice came over the open radio channel in the suits. "The fever must have mutated, Colonel. We had those few cases — I'd hoped everyone else would respond to the vaccine I administered three weeks ago.*

Sturgis negotiated around a cypress log in the

See C.A.D.S. #3

narrow channel. "Do we have any medicine you can treat it with?"

"Negative," Sheila said. "Except, of course, the crystal elixirs you made me pack at the Revenger caves."

"Then, use those—that's an *order*, Doc."

Sturgis felt his stomach doing flip-flops. Dieter! Oh, God, she couldn't be dead! Not Dieter!

He rodded his bike up onto the base's green island, jumped off, and took giant, bounding leaps through the underbrush until he reached the cluster of huts.

The base looked like a ghost town. It was quiet—too quiet. He opened his visor and undid his suit as fast as he could. The air had the smell of death in it.

A skeletal, haggard face ravaged by disease appeared in the doorway of a hut. "Colonel," the sick woman rasped. "You shouldn't have come back."

He ran to the woman, shouting, "Dieter! Where is Dieter!"

The woman pointed a bony finger toward the hut that had been designated sick bay. With dread spreading through him, Sturgis ran to the hut and burst through the door.

"Oh, my God!"

A withered form lay limply on one of the straw pallets, racked with fever, breathing a ragged wheeze. Dieter, once so beautiful, so vital, was barely recognizable. Her long auburn hair was damp and stringy; her once-rosy complexion was a pasty gray. She wasn't conscious.

"De Camp! Come here."

Sheila de Camp arrived on the run. She reluctantly took a vial of crystal essences "for fevers," and let

Dieter swallow the droplets. After taking Dieter's pulse Sheila drew Sturgis aside. She shook her head slowly, for it was clear the sick woman was beyond help. "I'm sorry, Colonel." Then the doc left.

Sturgis knelt by Dieter's side and took her hand. The flesh was hot and moist. "Dieter," he called to her. She didn't respond to his voice, nor to his gentle shaking.

Fenton came in and sat down on a wicker chair while Sturgis stoked Dieter's sweat-beaded face. In a low voice the Brit reported, "They say it hit fast — they couldn't even keep up with burying the dead."

Sturgis stood up, whispered, "Take the bodies to the old slave cemetery. The bodies could spread the disease." He grabbed Fenton's arm.

"How many?" asked Sturgis in a thick voice.

Fenton shook his head. "Twenty, maybe more." Half of them, I'd say. I searched the supplies here but I couldn't find anything useful."

Sturgis shook his head. "We used it up. How long has Dieter been like this? Did anyone say?"

"Since last Tuesday. One of the girls told me the victims go into a coma that can last anywhere from a few hours to a few days. They slip in and out of consciousness."

Sheila de Camp, out of her suit, against orders, was abruptly inside the door. "How is she?" de Camp asked.

Despite the fact that he himself had unsealed, the colonel said, "I thought I ordered sealed suits!"

De Camp sighed. "The virus will be in everything — the food, water, even the air around here. We found that out last time it hit. We would have to de-suit soon for recharge, for new air, so why not now?"

"You're right. It doesn't matter . . . Could I be alone with her?"

"We're on our way out," the Englishman said. "I'll see that you're not disturbed, Colonel." He escorted de Camp through the door, leaving Sturgis and Dieter in a soft semidarkness. The colonel bent down over Dieter, kissed her. He rubbed her cold hands, said, "Dieter, can you hear me?"

In a few moments she roused, eyes opening slowly, unseeing at first. Then she recognized him and made a weak smile. "Dean, it's you, isn't it?"

"Yes." He tried to sound light. "This is a hell of a welcome."

Dieter gave a stuttering laugh that went into a cough. "When I felt myself getting sick, I prayed . . . you would come back before . . . before—"

He put his fingers to her dry, cracked lips to still them. There was no point in denying the truth, but no point in acknowledging it, either.

The effort to talk seemed to drain her. Sturgis drew her up and shifted his position, so that he could sit with his back to the wooden wall and cradle her head in his lap. She didn't have much longer—he could nearly feel the life slipping out of her.

"I'm here," he said. "I'm not leaving." He stroked her hair. "We didn't have any antibiotics, but gave you something . . ."

Dieter opened her eyes again. She began to speak again, the words coming haltingly. "After the war, and I lost my husband, Wayne, and my unborn baby, I thought I didn't want to live anymore. There was no reason, no hope."

"I know — we've all suffered, Dieter."

"But you gave me hope."

"We gave each other hope."

"That day I first saw you — when the swamp Indians brought you as prisoner to their village — you looked half savage yourself. I was afraid of you."

Sturgis smiled.

"You're as hard as steel on the outside, Dean," Dieter went on. "But I sense something deep inside you — something beautiful — it's there for Robin, no one else. I hope you find her."

She reached out to him, not having the strength to caress his face. He took her hand and pressed it to his cheek. She felt the healing cut from the Russian whip. She frowned. "You're hurt."

"It's nothing."

The frown dissolved. "You won — your fight."

Sturgis gritted his teeth. "Yes, we wasted them."

Dieter fell silent for several minutes, as though she needed to recharge her strength in order to speak again. Then she said, "Thank you, Dean, for the hope, the love. For everything."

"It's you who should be thanked. You and the others —" Sturgis broke off.

"Maybe where I'm going, I'll be with Wayne again. Maybe even meet the soul of the unborn child I lost." Her eyes were bright and shining. "You must keep fighting, never give up — for all the other unborn children who will come into this world."

Dieter smiled, and a long, rattling sigh escaped her lips.

"Dieter!" Sturgis cried out, shaking her. But she was already gone.

He closed her eyes and then sat unmoving for a long time, watching death settle into her face. Outside, the sun set, and darkness fell.

At last Sturgis rose and gathered Dieter in his arms. He carried her out beyond the cluster of huts to the old slave cemetery, where, under the moonlight that filtered through the trees, he dug a grave and buried her.

He cut and stripped two cypress boughs and tied them into a crude cross with palm fronds. He stuck the cross into the fresh, damp earth. He sat down by the grave and listened to the sounds of the night around him.

God, he thought, why? Why did someone like Dieter have to die? Why did millions like her have to perish? Why did the nuke war have to happen? *Why?*

Nobody wanted it, he thought. *Nobody!* There were billions of people on the planet, trying to live out their lives and fulfill their destinies as best possible, hoping to God that a few power-mad maniacs wouldn't do it. And according to Veloshnikov, they'd done it out of fear we'd do it first!

That's the way it had been ever since the dawn of civilization. Innocent lives were destroyed time and time again so that rulers could keep their little fiefdoms. Soldiers were sent into the living hells of battle so that generals could play their gruesome chess games. And as the centuries progressed, the killing and warfare became more sophisticated, more far-reaching — and easier.

Now, reflected Sturgis, mankind had finally done itself in with its own technology. What good were all the stockpiles of nuclear warheads in the name of "defense"? All it took was one person to unleash them in fear—and then nothing mattered anymore.

The grief that was tearing Sturgis apart inside began to turn to rage. So the Russians had launched their nukes thinking they'd get by—but they weren't—they were dying like right here—if not disease, then radiation, starvation, stalked everyone.

Nobody had won. The computers might say the Soviets had won, but the computers didn't love, didn't care. Didn't—cry.

And Sturgis wept now.

CHAPTER EIGHT

Dieter was the last of the ill swampwomen to die. The less-advanced cases responded well to Cat's "crystal elixirs." All of the swampwomen who were sick with the early stages of the fever recovered, bringing great joy and relief to everyone else in the camp. Two C.A.D.S. men also got sick and recovered. The deadly threat was over—unless the virus mutated again.

Doctor de Camp doubted that would happen. "I think the virus is defeated. I'm much amazed," she told Sturgis. "I want to get on the radio and tell White Sands about the essences. I think they might keep us all immune to the viruses, and there's more essence left. Lots. We must get some to White Sands somehow."

For Sturgis, it was bittersweet news. Why had the fever had to claim Dieter? Why couldn't she have been among the ones who recovered? She had held everything together, in her quiet, strong way. God! What was he going to do without her?

In the nights that followed, Dean found himself stumbling out to her grave, where he would sit, mute and morose, for hours. The realization of how close he'd gotten to her upset him almost as much as did her death. They had come together out of desperate selfishness, not caring to hide the fact that they were using one another. But somewhere along the line, the balance shifted ever so delicately, and they had begun to truly need each other.

Dieter had loved him; he knew that was true. And he felt all the more guilty because, as much as he cared for her, he could never love her, not really; his love belonged to his lost wife, Robin.

But Dieter had known that. She had not asked him for his love in return. She had simply loved him selflessly.

And now she was gone.

Characteristically, Sturgis said nothing of his inner turmoil. If anyone knew of his nocturnal ramblings, nothing was said. Gradually, he pulled his grief and confused feelings into a tight little ball and pushed it into the back of his mind.

The Rhino's balky satellite-link radio was used to inform the President in White Sands of all that had occurred. President Williamson was keenly interested in every detail that Sturgis — and Billy — could remember of the *Lenin*. This giant Soviet-command submarine had given the Soviets the edge in the nuke war that had devastated the U.S. last Christmas Eve. "It is vital that we at White Sands know all about Veloshnikov and the sub," the President insisted.

Sturgis reported what he had burned into his memory — the map of the Soviet Union's war damage, and the map assessing U.S. damage and its fallout zones. It was the greatest intelligence coup since the nuke war, and Sturgis proudly reported it all. First he told all he remembered of the U.S. map. Then he said, "Mr. President, the war-damage map on the *Lenin* shows Moscow is intact and has also been spared by the winds. Moscow has about the level of radioactivity right now that Kiev suffered in the Chernobyl nuclear-plant disaster back in 1986. But Leningrad is no more—it was taken out by one of our bombers, and a giant plume of fallout reaches up to the gulag from the former location of Leningrad. Also Riga is gone, and Pinsk, and Murmansk. Ditto Omsk and Odessa."

The President was silent for a long time, then he said, "Sturgis, do you know what this means? They've failed to get off with minimal damage. They blew it. They lost *too*."

The President had Sturgis draw what he remembered of both maps—including the oval-shaped gray rad areas—on maps of the U.S. and the Soviet Union. Then Sturgis transmitted them. The President had Sturgis's maps in seconds. He whistled. "They will need every available able-bodied person they have back in Russia to turn the soil, decontaminate, work to restore the crippled services and food chain."

Gridley, the science adviser back in White Sands, added, "And if we got Odessa and the fallout plume is as large as you've drawn, they have to develop whole new areas of Siberia to raise food. They can't do it here—the sad fact is that very little of the U.S. is suitable."

Sturgis said, "So now we can understand their

intense campaign to enlist American surrogates. They want a U.S. traitor force—those motorcycle gangs I reported last month. It's obvious now why they are placing such great emphasis on recruiting America's lowlifes. They will leave Soviet advisers to run them. They'll use the motorcycle gangs to keep the U.S. off balance, so that we're not a threat for years. Then the main Sov force will withdraw. But Veloshnikov, in my estimate, will keep his men here until C.A.D.S. is destroyed. He knows that the C.A.D.S. Force *alone* could wipe out the cyclists. Also, I'm sure many cycle gangs *won't* take the Soviet bribes of food and supplies. They won't *all* turn traitor. Give me a hundred more trained C.A.D.S.—"

The President cut Sturgis off. "Dean, we can't supply any more C.A.D.S. suits for a long while. Our fabricators are in need of extensive repair; our power supply is such that it would tax us too greatly. You have no idea of the electrical problems we have here. If some of your men die, and their suits are usable, we can drop you some new men . . . But no suits. Sorry."

About two weeks after the C.A.D.S. unit had reached Okefenokee, an airdrop occurred. Spare parts and ammo. Period.

Among the supplies was a new Telos communications antenna for tuning into the satellite that linked Okefenokee with White Sands. The old dish antenna was a battered mess as a result of the battles the Rhino had endured.

Sturgis wasted no time in having the dish installed;

nothing was more important as maintaining a link with White Sands. With Dixon, Van Noc, and MacLeish listening in, he quickly tested the new antenna. They soon heard President Williamson deliver some very bad news about a man named Pinky Ellis.

"You mean *the* Pinky Ellis, a.k.a. Morris Ellis?" asked Sturgis.

The President's voice crackled over the new connection. "That's right, I believe you've met him. He was the head of Exrell, the world's largest military contractor. Now he's contacted the Russians. He's planning to deliver classified technology secrets to them — including everything related to C.A.D.S. suits, weapons, and support equipment."

Sturgis, seated at the console and flanked by Van Noc and Dixon, unleashed a violent string of expletives. Their job was tough enough without some obscene, traitorous American giving the Reds a helping hand. "I should have killed the fat bastard when I had the chance!"

"When was that?" Williamson said.

"Right after N-Day, when we were heading east. We ran into his armored caravan. He picked a fight, and we took apart everything but the Rolls Royce he got away in."

Williamson's reply was lost in static.

"Shit," mumbled Sturgis. He fiddled with the dials. "Repeat," he said as he improved the connection. "I didn't copy that last statement."

"Do you know where his base is?"

"Negative. He said he'd come from Philadelphia. He was heading west. Looked like he was packing everything he had with him. We recovered enough gold bars to refill Fort Knox."

"You've got to stop him from delivering those secrets, Colonel."

"Affirmative. Give me the details. What's your source?"

"A woman named Morgana Pinter," Williamson said. "We found her wandering in the desert near here, half-dead from heat and dehydration. She claims to be a society girl from Philadelphia—says Pinky kidnapped her and forced her to be a sex slave."

"Christ," Sturgis muttered. He could well imagine the kind of perverse abominations a man like Pinky Ellis would force on a woman.

"She managed to get free of him and started running blindly into the desert. She expected to be either captured or shot. She was very good at hiding. Found an old dirt-covered root cellar. Pinky's searchers walked right over her several times. They finally gave up. Then she waited a long time, got out, and one of our patrols found her near death in the desert. Oh, one thing," Williamson added, "she was wearing a dog collar around her neck when we found her."

Sturgis grimaced. "You sure her information is valid?"

"Morgana says Ellis never let her out of his sight. She heard all his conversations, witnessed everything he did."

"What's his plan?"

"He's arranged to meet the Russians in New Orleans approximately three weeks from today. The Reds are coming in by sub—one of their little diesel

126

numbers, a Zulu Cargo class. I'll feed you map of area, best sub-disembark spots."

"What's Pinky getting out of this?"

"He's asked for and had been granted safe transport to the nuclear-free zone in the Pacific. He's going to take millions of dollars of gold with him and set up shop in New Zealand—where he will no doubt continue subversive work for the Russians, undermining the free zone until it, too, becomes a Red satellite."

"No, he won't—he'll never get out of America alive," Sturgis said. "Not if I have anything to say about it."

Tranh spoke up so that Williamson could hear. "What armed support does Ellis have now?"

"What?" said the President as the link faded.

Sturgis answered. "We destroyed Pinky's little band of thugs. Does he have new recruits?"

"Yes, according to Morgana. There's been no shortage of willing recruits—thieves and killers desperate to survive at any costs. Pinky promises survival."

"How many?"

"Morgana says she's very bad at numbers, but guesses about one hundred. Maybe more. Who knows; at the rate things are going out there, he could have thousands by now."

Shit, thought Sturgis. There were only twenty of his own men. With their superior suits and weaponry, the C.A.D.S. men should have no trouble taking on whatever motley army Pinky Ellis had managed to recruit, though. What worried Sturgis was the waste of time and ammunition. They should be spending both to repel the Russians, not to neutralize some cretinous, opportunistic traitor.

There was muffled noise in the background on the White Sands end of the satellite transmission. Williamson left the microphone and then came back on and said, "Morgana Pinter wants to speak with you, Sturgis."

A soft female voice came over the speaker. "Colonel? Is this Colonel Dean Sturgis?"

"Affirmative."

"I remember you—the men in those strange black moon suits! I was in Pinky's Rolls that day you had the battle."

"If I'd had any idea, Miss Pinter—"

"Please, don't apologize," Morgana broke in. "You couldn't have known. You were plenty busy with Pinky and his boys."

"He shouldn't have gotten away."

"Yes, but you cost him. You blew up his tank, killed his best men, and worst of all, confiscated his gold—which he stole, by the way, from a federal reserve depository." Morgana gave a bitter little laugh. "Pinky's mad as hell at you, Colonel. He swears he's going to get you at any cost. Why, it took him months to steal enough money and gold to replace everything he lost. You've *got* to stop him!"

"I plan to," Sturgis answered calmly. "When I find him, he won't be mad anymore—he'll be dead."

"There's more than just the classified blueprints, Colonel."

"What do you mean?"

"There's this tank—"

"You mean Pinky stole another tank to replace the

one we destroyed?"

"Not exactly. He created one."

Pinky Ellis *created* a tank? It would make sense if these were normal times, thought Sturgis. Pinky's empire, Exrell Incorporated, manufactured all kinds of weapons and equipment for the military. But there was no way to build a tank now. Even if a production plant were still intact somewhere, there was no electricity to operate it with, let alone anyone to run the machinery.

"Explain, Miss Pinter," Sturgis said.

"When we were in west Texas, we went to this cave. It was camouflaged—Pinky said no one knew about it but him and his key men. He said one of his subsidiaries had used this cave to hide super-secret equipment developed for the Army. We went there because an experimental tank was supposed to be in the cave."

"What do you mean, *experimental* tank?"

"It's a new design, I guess, that's supposed to be more powerful than anything the Army had ever had. Well, Pinky went into the cave—he made me stay in the Rolls. He was in there forever, and I was hoping maybe he'd gotten stuck or lost, or had an accident, you know, because he's so fat—"

"Did he find the tank, Miss Pinter?"

"He finally came out, puffing and wheezing and sweating like a pig. It was disgusting! Every time he put those fat, sweaty hands on me—"

Sturgis interrupted again. Morgana seemed engrossed in her revulsion of her former captor. "The tank, Morgana."

"Right. When he came out, he was all happy. His

'creation' was still in there, he said, and he was going to dig it out and sell it to the Russians."

"What! Where is this cave?"

Williamson's voice came back on, resigned. "We already found it, Colonel, in the mountains near El Paso. It was empty. Whatever was there, Pinky already got."

"Morgana, you've *got* to tell me more about this tank," Sturgis said. "It's vitally important that I know what it does, what makes it different from other tanks. It could make the difference between life and death."

"I don't know anything more." The woman's voice was a whimper. "He told me about it, but I didn't understand all that technical military jargon. All I know is, Pinky said there was nothing on earth like it, or as powerful. He said not even those 'bastards in the black spacesuits' could stop it." Little sobs and moans welled up from her throat, sounding, by the time they were garbled and distorted by the satellite transmission, like an animal's groans of pain.

"Morgana . . ." Sturgis coaxed.

"I'm sorry, Colonel." Morgana sniffed. Then came a sound like she was blowing her nose. "I feel like such a failure. I can't give you what you want. Pinky's going to win, after all!"

"Pinky is *not* going to win anything but a one-way ticket to hell," Sturgis said emphatically. "Listen, let me ask you some questions that may help jog your memory. You probably can remember more than you think — you don't have to understand what you've heard — I will interpret it."

"All right."

A burst of static came over the speaker.

"Damn," muttered Sturgis. "We lost it." He picked up a set of headphones and put one side to his ear while he turned dials on the control console, trying to tune into White Sands again. "Omega One calling Delta Four-Seven he called, using the transmission code. "Come in, Delta Four-Seven, do you copy?"

He got nothing but static.

"Must be atmospheric disturbances," said Tranh. "The air currents have been tricky ever since the war. The bombs seem to have upset the ionosphere badly."

Sturgis kept turning the dials. For a brief moment, he caught garble, then lost it again.

"Try the alternate frequency," suggested Van Noc.

Sturgis flipped a switch and called out the transmission code, but got no response. He flipped back to the main frequency.

"—you there, Sturgis?" it was Williamson's voice.

"Copy, Sturgis here. Communications temporarily lost, now restored."

"You're coming in loud and clear on this end."

"Read you fine now. Is Morgana still available?"

"Affirmative. Here she is."

"Morgana," Sturgis began, "let's be quick. I don't know how long this connection will hold. Did Pinky say what was unusual about the tank? Is it faster, bigger? Have different weapons?"

There was a silence from the other end, and for a moment, Sturgis thought he'd lost the link again.

"Gosh, I'm not sure, but I suppose so. Pinky said the Russians would be so ecstatic over the tank that they'd, ah, shit gold bricks for him."

Sturgis made an exasperated noise. It looked like he

wasn't going to get much detail out of Morgana.

She said, "You don't understand, Colonel. Pinky chattered at me all the time. Most of it was, well, quite demeaning—things he was going to do to me. I got so that I shut out what he said whenever possible. That's why I don't recall details. They've even tried hypnosis here, but—"

"I see. Miss Pinter, you've been a big help just the same. I'd like to speak to the President, please."

"Of course. Oh—Colonel?"

"Yes?"

"I hope I get to meet you sometime. You're an incredibly brave man."

"Thanks," Sturgis grunted as politely as possible, while Dixon and MacLeish snickered. They were leaning on the Rhino's open rear door. Billy did a fair imitation of a swooning maiden: *"Oh, Colonel!"* he sighed in falsetto, fluttering his eyelids, *"You're an incredibly brave mannnnn."*

Sturgis turned down the volume on the mike and turned to Billy. "Straighten up, Sergeant, before I bust you to buck private." The men guffawed. They knew he wasn't serious. But that shut up Billy.

Sturgis resumed his satellite communications. "Mr. President?"

"Here, Colonel."

"No one at White Sands has any knowledge of this experimental tank?"

"Negative. The project must have been classified top secret—need-to-know basis."

"All right . . . We'll take it as it comes. We'll push out immediately for the target destination, route undisclosed for security purposes."

132

"Copy." More static. "The connection's fading, Colonel, so here's science adviser Gridley. He wants to tell you about the lathe that was airdropped in one of the crates . . ."

"What's it for?" asked Sturgis. "Is this White Sands' way of telling us we have to manufacture our own parts now?" Sturgis was only half-serious, and he was surprised when Gridley answered in the affirmative.

"In a way, Colonel," Gridley's voice came on. "White Sands has an increasingly limited ability to respond to your needs — you're going to have to use what you can find of Soviet shells, that is. The lathe, plus the crates of parts and raw materials, will enable you to do two critical things: modify the Rhino to increase its speed, and modify the suits for VSF, Variable Shell Firing, since you have used the last of the E-balls. We don't have the wherewithall to manufacture more."

"I'm not sure *we* have the technical expertise to modify the weapons tubes and storage magazine for captured Red shells!"

"The modifications are *not* complicated — any car mechanic can do them. The Rhino shouldn't take more than half a day, and the suits less. At the end of our transmission, we will send all the data via high speed to the Rhino's computer."

MacLeish spoke up. "How fast are we talking for the Rhino, sir?"

"On the straight and smooth, it should be able to do about ninety miles an hour."

MacLeish whistled. "That'll be a good advantage, sir."

"What'll the suits be able to handle with VSF?" said Sturgis. "I'll sure miss the hellfire of the E-balls!"

"Anything from a fifty-caliber slug to a four-inch shell."

Dean grinned. "Great. We can use just about any ammunition we can scavenge, then."

"Affirmative . . . Colonel? One more thing—Dr. Van Patten wants to speak to you about the LWA . . ."

Sturgis started. That was unexpected news. He'd almost given up on the LWA, the Liquid Wave Amplifier gun developed by Van Patten. One step beyond lasers, the LWA had enormous destroying power, the ability to blast boulders into bits of molten rubble. It also had enormous defects, the most serious of which was an overheating problem that caused the gun to explode, killing its user and every other living thing nearby. Van Patten, Sturgis knew, was working furiously to correct the defects and get the weapons out in the field, where they would add a significant advantage to any encounter with enemy forces.

But old man Gridley's voice was fading into a crackle of static. Sturgis slipped on the headset over both ears and worked the dials and switches. "Omega One to Delta Four-Seven. Losing you, Delta, do you copy?" Static filled his headset. "Delta Four-Seven, come in, please. Omega One to Delta Four-Seven. Mr. President? Van Patten?" He tried the alternate frequency, but couldn't get through on that, either.

Sturgis and MacLeish tried for twenty minutes to reestablish communication with White Sands, then had to admit defeat. The ionospheric turbulence had increased to the point where nothing would get through. Damn! What was the news about the LWA? He hoped it wasn't the worst — that Van Patten was unable to fix the LWA and had given up trying.

"It was probably bad news, anyway," Dixon said peevishly. "More bad news — that's all we get. We might as well give up. Twenty men, no E-balls . . . I'm getting fed up. It's —"

Sturgis gave Billy a careful look as he rose from the console. It wasn't like the young Southerner to be negative and cavalier. Billy had always been one of the most optimistic, never-say-never men in the Omega Force. But since his torture aboard the *Lenin*, he had been unpredictable, going through abrupt mood changes and saying things that were out of character.

At first, Sturgis had passed it off as a natural boomerang reaction to an extremely stressful experience. But he was beginning to fear that Billy was showing signs of psychological damage. He had suggested to Billy a couple of days before that he should "go skating" for a while. "Go skating" was their term for total escape, complete rest. Billy had blown a fuse at the idea, insisting he was fine, that he wanted more than anything to be active — as much as possible, with his fingers still in casts.

Now Sturgis scrutinized Billy and decided not to respond to the negative remark. The man was entitled to be mad. Sturgis carefully studied the map of New Orleans coming over the computer printer in the Rhino. The printer had begun spewing out a continuous mass of data. The print-head zipped back and forth at two thousand characters per second. Fenton

135

pulled up the sheet and studied the suit-modification plans. It made him knit his brows.

"Aye, this is going to be a problem," he said.

"How so?" asked Sturgis.

"It doesn't look as simple as White Sands claims. I don't know what kind of car mechanics that bastard Gridley was talking about, but I'll need at least a half-dozen men with the best technical and mechanical skills I can find. And the way it looks"—MacLeish pulled up more paper for scrutiny—"is that the Rhino's going to take three or four days. I'd say the suits will take about a day each."

"We'll have to do better than that," grumbled Sturgis. "We have to be in New Orleans inside of three weeks. But we need both modifications, so I don't want to put either of them off. Do the best you can, Fenton."

"Aye, sir. I'll start right away." MacLeish ripped off his printout and climbed up out of the Rhino.

Van Noc, meanwhile, had pulled out an oilskin bag and taken out a handful of roadmaps, the kind travelers used to buy at gas stations. He selected one for the Southeast United States, and spread it out on a small fold-out table.

Sturgis studied routes from the Okefenokee to New Orleans. The fastest, most direct way would be to cut south through the Osceola National Forest—what was left of it—and hook onto Interstate 10, which traversed the Florida panhandle and ran parallel to the Gulf coast, through Pensacola, Mobile, and Biloxi.

But major highways had their drawbacks. They were natural targets for Russian surveillance aircraft and point patrols. They were often clogged with vehicles that had stalled in the nuclear getaway panic, only to turn into mass graveyards. At least by now, rats, bugs, vultures, and other beasts had picked the bones clean of rotting flesh.

"We'll take Interstate 10," said Sturgis, tracing his index finger along the red line from Florida to Louisiana. "Or at least stick close to it. We don't have time to take back-routes inland, and besides, if we stay close to the coast, we may spot the Cargo sub when she surfaces."

His finger trailed off the left side of the map. "If Pinky's recently been in Texas, he'll be coming in from either west or the north—probably the west, through Baton Rouge."

"What do you suppose he's got on this super-tank—nuclear weapons, or just some new armor-piercing shells?" said Van Noc.

Sturgis shrugged. "We'll just have to find out when we get there—and be ready for anything."

CHAPTER NINE

Sergeant Billy Dixon was a man with a problem he would not acknowledge. He insisted he was fine.

He was not; he was a powder keg waiting to blow up.

The physical wounds from his ordeal aboard the *Lenin* were nearly completely healed. The scabs on his cuts were starting to flake off, showing good scar tissue beneath, even though some areas were a little pink and tender. His fingers were out of their casts — they were a little stiff, but they worked. Billy was very lucky, Sheila de Camp told him over and over again.

Yes, given enough time, Billy Dixon's body was going to be just fine.

It was his mind that wasn't healing.

The symptoms did not go unnoticed at the C.A.D.S. camp, but they did go untreated. No one knew exactly what to do, except perhaps to leave Billy alone and let him "snap out of it." Sturgis was preoccupied with the airdrop and the preparations for New Orleans; besides, he seemed a bit moody and withdrawn himself. As a psychologist, de Camp had dealt with many cases of battle fatigue and burnout —

but a man rebounding from torture was not something in her realm of experience. Compounding the problem was the fact that, except for Sturgis, no one really knew what had happened to Billy on the *Lenin*, because he wouldn't talk about it. And Sturgis had been tortured separately.

Billy Dixon had grown up an uncomplicated, straightforward Southern boy. He had the quintessential, all-American hero's look, with his broad shoulders and muscular build, and blond-and-blue-eyed good looks. The words "can't" and "fear" were not in his vocabulary.

He was sharp and clever, but he had played fair his entire life. Long before the war, when his teenaged, hot-blooded fooling around got his girlfriend pregnant, he did the honorable thing—he married her. At age fifteen, they became the parents of a son.

Billy worked hard to support his young family and stay in school at the same time. An expert hunter, he knew guns and rifles, and he began making good money as a gunsmith. The work was ideal—he loved weapons, and gunsmithing enabled him to work odd hours, at night and on weekends.

From his earliest memories, Billy had always wanted to be a military man. As soon as he was old enough, he got on a bus to the nearest Marine recruiting office and signed up. Boot camp for him was a breeze—there was nothing he liked better than testing himself, pushing himself to the limits.

Billy was a natural in the military, the kind of soldier every commanding officer would pay dearly to have more of. His record was clean and superior. When the elite and secret Omega Force was formed, he was a natural for that, too. The C.A.D.S. suit seemed tailor-made for Billy Dixon.

He had only reached his mid-twenties when the war came and irrevocably changed everyone's life. Like everyone else, he suffered enormous loss—his wife and son were dead. They had gone to San Antonio to visit relatives for Christmas, while Billy was on active duty. With its huge military facilities and population, San Antonio was vaporized in a nuclear flash. There was no point in searching for them, because they would not have had time to flee, and there was nothing left of the entire metropolitan area. It was nothing but a hot scar upon the earth, so intensely radioactive that the C.A.D.S. unit had given it wide berth on its cross-country trip to the Southeast.

Billy had gone through the grief cycle, grateful for the fighting to take his mind off his loss, until he finally accepted it.

Or had he? Perhaps he had just stuffed it away inside, a wound left to fester, an imbalance that would not be able to withstand another shock—like torture.

After his return to the Okefenokee, Billy began to go through unpredictable mood swings. He would be his normal self, sunny, joking, and energetic, and then suddenly turn dark with a nasty comment or a thoughtless act. Since Billy had never said an unkind word to anybody, his new razor tongue left bleeding victims who wondered in astonishment, "What the hell is *his* problem?"

Where he used to indulge occasionally in good-natured ribbing of Mickey Rossiter's chubbiness, he became downright vicious. Once, when Mickey was huffing around the Rhino doing some repairs, Dixon snatched the tools out of his hands and yelled, "Listen, fatso, if you weren't such a fucking incompetent blimp, it wouldn't take you so long to get the job done!" A half-hour later, he was slapping "ol' buddy" Rossiter across his beefy shoulders, suggesting a friendly poker game.

When Sturgis requested his input to the New Orleans strategy, Dixon responded with an alarming apathy. "It's a waste of time, Sturg," Dixon said. "The Russians will get there first — and we won't find them anyway." Sturgis gave him a severe reprimand and threatened to throw him in the swamp — without his suit. Dixon screamed back that he was "tired of being sandbagged by a bunch of tight-assed wimps" — a complete non sequitur. Yet soon after that, Sturgis found him analyzing maps and potential battle conditions in the New Orleans area, as though his run-in with the colonel had never happened.

Dean was nonplussed. He was a graduate of the "make or break" school — you either made it or you broke in the process. As an officer, he was compassionate but hard on his men, and on himself as well. He had given countless pep talks to soldiers who had started going to pieces on him. They either pulled themselves together, or they dropped out, or they got killed. It was brutal, but so was war, and Sturgis could not put the lives of his men in jeopardy on account of a weak link.

Usually, the symptoms and behavior of those men were the same: a slide into despair, apathy, isolation, even silence. He had never dealt with a boomerang personality before, one who seemed perfectly normal one minute and not so the next. Was Dixon going *schizo*? Did Sturgis have a Jekyll and Hyde on his hands?

He pulled Billy aside for a private talk inside his hut.

"Look, Billy, about what happened on board the *Lenin*—"

"They're coming along fine, Sturg," said Dixon cheerfully, holding up his fingers. "Still stiff, but they work in all the right ways."

"I don't mean the fingers, Billy, or the whiplashes. I mean, ah . . ." Sturgis, at a loss for words, was flustered. How did one man talk to another about being sexually violated? It was treading on the no-man's land of subjects and humiliations never broached. "Ah . . ." Sturgis fumbled for a cigarette.

"What *do* you mean, Sturg?"

"I was referring to that KGB lieutenant . . ."

"Oh, you mean Revin?" Dixon was nonchalant. How, wondered Sturgis, could he be so cool about it? Dixon added, "I think he's a bastard and scum of the earth, and I'd love to rip out his heart with my bare hands—but so what?"

"Listen, I know you had to endure some pretty brutal things—"

Billy shrugged. "I didn't go through anything that you didn't, Sturg. Except the fingers. Say, what's this talk about, anyway?"

Good God! Didn't Billy have any recollection? Sturgis sat back in his old wooden chair and took a deep drag on his cigarette. Had Dixon completely blocked from his mind what he couldn't cope with?

"You don't remember . . ." Dean's voice trailed

off.

"Remember what?"

"Are you sure you're all right, Billy?"

"Absolutely. Why wouldn't I be?"

"Well, frankly, you've been acting strangely since we got back."

Dixon chuckled. "Cut me some slack, commander. So I've got a few frayed nerves. I'll be fine. Really."

"Really," repeated Sturgis in a flat, unconvinced voice. He debated taking Dixon off the active roster and leaving him behind at the camp while he took the men to New Orleans. Could Dixon be trusted not to go off the deep end?

"If you were worried, why didn't you just ask?" said Billy. "I'm all right."

"Right." Sturgis sighed. "Dismissed, Sergeant." After Billy left the hut, Sturgis sat smoking and thinking. He had a hell of a problem on his hands, and no solution.

The problem finally came to a head when Sheila de Camp barreled up to Sturgis, jabbed a finger in his chest, and said, "Colonel. Billy Dixon has finally gotten out of hand. You've got to do something about him!"

"What's wrong?"

"He's turned into a filthy monster!"

"You'll have to be more specific than that, Doctor."

"He has practically attacked every woman in this place!"

Sturgis could virtually see steam rising from de Camp. This was not the sort of discussion to have out

144

in the open, in front of an audience. He took her by the arm and steered her to his hut. It had seemed lately like his one-room living quarters was becoming a consultation center.

"Calm down," said Sturgis, going through his customary motions of getting out a cigarette and lighting it. "Sit down and start from the beginning."

"I'm too upset to sit down!"

"You're always upset about something, Sheila, but I can see there's a pretty big burr under your saddle. So what is this about Billy turning into a 'filthy monster' and attacking the women? That doesn't sound like him."

"You're damn right it doesn't, because he's not himself anymore. You'd have to be blind not to see it." She glared at Sturgis, arms folded across her chest.

He shrugged uncomfortably. "So he's stressed out. Aren't we all?"

"None of the rest of us are splitting in two. What *really* happened on that Russian submarine to push him over the edge?"

Sturgis evaded the question. "Get to the point, Doctor. I'm a busy man."

De Camp drew in a big breath. "Billy is going around hitting on all the women with the most lewd propositions—"

Sturgis chuckled. "Wait a minute. Billy's always had an eye for the ladies—I certainly can't fault a man for that."

"You *can* fault him for acting like a disgusting swine. Oh! The things he says he wants to do to you! I should know—he had the nerve to hit on *me*!"

Sturgis turned away and looked out his tiny window. He inhaled on his cigarette and flicked ashes on the dirt floor. Hell, despite her brass, de Camp *did* have a luscious figure that could not be hidden by even the most prim clothing. It was difficult to look at her and *not* get a rise. But that wasn't the issue here —

". . . and furthermore," de Camp was saying, "he's violent, full of awful threats if you say no."

Sturgis turned back to look at her. There was an edge in his voice. "Threats such as?"

"Such as . . ." she faltered and put her head in her hands. "Such as you don't want to know."

Sturgis stuck his cigarette between his teeth and went to her, gently guiding her to one of his rickety wooden chairs by his table, and pushing her down onto it. He sat on the edge of the table and kept smoking. Should he tell de Camp what really happened to Billy aboard the *Lenin*? Or was it a dirty secret that should be kept? He didn't know. But he did know he had to do something about Billy — the young man was getting worse.

De Camp composed herself, dry-eyed. She was not the kind of woman to cry, certainly not easily, and seldom under even the most trying circumstances — a trait for which Sturgis was thankful. He couldn't have tolerated a gushing female in his unit. He had seen her cry only once, when one of his bright, promising young soldiers was killed in a tragic accident.

"That's not the whole of it, Colonel," de Camp said. "It doesn't make any sense, neither the sexual come-ons or the threats. In fact, Marla, his girlfriend, came to me and confided he's been . . .

146

impotent ever since he came back."

Sturgis stamped out his cigarette and gritted his teeth. What a mess. He got out another cigarette and lit it. De Camp was so distracted she didn't even give him her usual antismoking lecture.

He stood up and paced a tight little circle around the room. "You're the doctor, de Camp. What do you suggest?"

"This *is* a switch. I'm coming to you because the last time I administered psychological counseling to one of your men, you nearly took my head off. And now you're passing the buck back to me!"

"I asked for your recommendation, doctor," Sturgis said testily.

She sighed. "Sorry. The past is all water under the bridge, isn't it?" She stood up and went to Sturgis. "At the very least, he should be restrained, put under observation, and given counseling."

"Great," said Sturgis sarcastically, waving away her suggestion. "This isn't a mental ward, Sheila. This is the *front*. I've got a sick man on my hands with nowhere to send him, and in less than twenty-four hours, I issue orders to the rest of the men to pull out of here for more combat. I don't have time for *observation and counseling*."

"You can't take him with you! He's dangerously unstable!"

"You're absolutely right. Give the doctor a gold star. But I need Billy. He's going with us."

"Why are you being so hostile? I'm trying to *help* Billy and you're getting mad at me!"

"I'm not mad!" Sturgis shouted. He paused and lowered his voice. "Shit! I'm mad at the whole

147

fucking world."

De Camp put her hands on her hips. "That's not going to do Billy much good is it? Or the rest of us whose welfare is in your hands." Sturgis didn't answer. She went on more calmly, "I would have a better idea of what to do if you told me the truth about the *Lenin*. My instincts tell me you're holding back. Something happened to Billy that pushed him over the edge, didn't it? Perhaps he needs to talk about it."

Sturgis glared down at her. He had decided she, being a woman, couldn't possibly understand. "Listen, Doc, one thing I don't need right now is some Freudian egghead who wants to put a patient on a couch and hold hands in therapy!"

"You've got to do *something*!"

They were interrupted by a frantic thumping on the thatch door of Sturgis's hut.

"What is it!" he shouted. The door opened wide.

It was Marla, a panicked look in her gray eyes. "Oh, Colonel," she cried, you've got to come quickly! It's Billy . . ." The girl with the long sandy hair looked down.

Sturgis tore out the door. "Where? What's happening?"

Marla pointed into the swamp beyond the edge of camp. Sturgis couldn't see anything, but he could hear shouts — Billy's voice rising in anger, and a woman's pleading.

"I don't know what happened," Marla said between sobs. "He just went — *berserk*!"

"Damn," Sturgis muttered under his breath. He ran into the overgrowth toward the voices. Others in the camp were heading the same way.

148

He burst into a small clearing. One of the camp women was cringing, down on her knees on the ground—at least she still had her clothes on—and Dixon was standing in front of her, brandishing an M16. As Sturgis broke through the bushes, Billy raised it to aim at the colonel's chest.

"Come to watch the show or take a turn, Colonel?"

"Billy! Are you out of your fucking mind? Put the gun down and let the girl go!"

Sheila, close behind Sturgis, ran breathlessly into the opening and let out a small scream. "Billeee—don't!"

Sturgis roughly pushed her back. "Back off, Sheila—I'll handle this. Dixon, put the gun down—*now*. That's an order!"

Billy just laughed. The girl on the ground—Sturgis recognized her as the one named Bett—pleaded to Sturgis, "Get Billy away!" Billy lifted the muzzle of the machine gun over Dean's head and pressed the trigger. A hail of bullets went into the cypress and palm trees, causing a cloud of birds to rise shrieking into the air.

"That's my answer to your order," Billy sneered. "Bett said I wasn't a man! She's gonna die!"

Sturgis was enraged, but he didn't get a chance to act, as Billy was already swinging the machine gun back to train it on Bett's prone figure.

"Why, that bloody little bastard," growled Fenton MacLeish, balling his huge hands into fists. "I've had it with him—I'm going to beat his fucking brains out!"

"No," commanded Sturgis. "Stay back. He's liable to shoot that gun off at anything." He jerked his thumb toward the camp. "Get the women out of here. You'll know what else to do." Sturgis knew that MacLeish would be back with armed reinforcements, and would spread them quietly through the bushes around Dixon—just in case force was needed.

While MacLeish herded the worried women out of the danger zone, Sturgis faced Dixon. "What is this, Billy—a standoff? Whatever you had in mind for the lady, you can't do it as long as you're holding a gun. And as soon as you put it down, I'm all over you."

"That's it, don't provoke him—try to talk him down," whispered de Camp.

Sturgis turned to her and said in a low voice, "Stay *out* of this, Sheila. I'll settle it however I have to." He turned back to Dixon. His hot anger at the sergeant's defiance had settled into a cold rage. Gone was his empathy for what Dixon had suffered at the hands of a sadistic Russian. He took a step toward Billy.

Billy swung his M16 down and jabbed the muzzle into Bett's neck. De Camp stifled a gasp. "One more step, Colonel . . ."

Sturgis stopped. Bett whimpered. "Please, Billy, I'll do whatever you want . . ."

"He won't hurt you, Bett," Sturgis said to the terrified young woman. "I promise." He held his hands out from his body. "I'm not armed Dixon, you can see that. I'm going to have a smoke." Slowly, eyes on Billy's trigger finger, he reached into his chest pocket and pulled out a pack of cigarettes and a book of matches. He lit one and stuffed everything else back in the pocket.

"Okay, Dixon, you're the man with the gun, so I guess you're in charge. But let's consider the consequences of what you're doing."

Dixon raised the gun to level it at Sturgis again. "Like what?"

Sturgis shrugged. "Abduction of a civilian with intent to harm . . . disobeying and threatening a superior officer . . . enough to get you court-martialed up one side of the country and down the other."

Billy's laugh sounded nervous. His eyes were steely. "And who's gonna court-martial me in this garbage heap of a country? You playing God now, Colonel?"

Sturgis clenched his jaw. "You're out, Dixon. Off active duty, out of my unit. You're a disgrace to the military and to your country. I don't want you. Take your fucking gun and get out of here!"

Dixon's face twisted in fury. Sturgis looked past him and saw MacLeish in the bushes behind Billy. He knew there were other men sprinkled around, waiting. He shook his head ever so slightly. *Not now*, he thought. He flicked away his cigarette.

Off to the side, de Camp was twisting her hands in anxiety. "No, Dean," she begged mentally, "don't antagonize him! You'll get yourself killed!" Any moment, she expected Dixon to blister Sturgis with lead.

Billy's new anger was just what Sturgis wanted to see. He had gauged correctly, and now, as he stepped forward, he stuck in another needle. "You're a *disgrace*, Dixon," he said, locking eyes with Billy, his peripheral vision noting Dixon's hold on the M16. "You're disgusting."

De Camp groaned. Why couldn't men keep their heads? Bullets were going to start flying any second. She made small, crablike movements toward the protection of the trees and bushes. What would they do without Sturgis? She glanced toward MacLeish and the others in the bushes. Were they going to stand by and watch their commander get slaughtered? Why wouldn't they *do* something?

One of the men snapped a twig. Billy whirled and peppered the bushes with bullets. If anyone was hit, he didn't cry out.

Sturgis lunged at Billy, but not fast enough. Billy whirled back and jammed the muzzle into Dean's ribs. "Get away from me, Colonel," he said. "I swear I'll kill you!"

"Any coward can pull a trigger. Let's see how much of a man you *really* are!" Sturgis pulled back his fist and slammed it into Billy's jaw.

Dixon sprawled backward. He dropped the M16, which went off as it hit the ground, briefly spraying bullets into the air. Sturgis kicked it away and Billy sprang to his feet with a growl and lashed out with his fists. He landed a glancing blow to Dean's jaw and a solid one to his midriff.

Sturgis grunted and stumbled backward, but stayed on his feet. "The gun!" he yelled. "Get the gun!"

De Camp came to her senses and scrambled out to pick up the M16. "For God's sakes, stop it!" It was a fruitless plea. She dodged the fighting men and ran to Bett, quickly undoing her bonds. She pulled the young woman up and scurried back into the bushes, muttering, "Oh! Why do men always have to solve things with their *fists*?"

MacLeish and the other C.A.D.S. men came out of the brush to watch the fight. Sturgis and Dixon were both big and powerful, hard as iron and strong as oxen, and they were both in a fury for blood. Sturgis outweighed Dixon, but Billy was younger and faster.

Dean sank a blow into Billy's solar plexus, knocking the breath from him. Billy coughed and sagged, then kicked out and knocked Sturgis off his feet. He went down on top of Sturgis, gripping him by the throat.

Sturgis put his hands on Billy's chest and pushed, but couldn't dislodge his hold. He rolled and got his knee wedged between them, forcing Dixon off. He grabbed Billy by the legs and pushed him onto his back, but couldn't get in a punch at his face because of the younger man's flying fists. Billy jabbed fingers into Dean's Adam's apple, and, as Sturgis gagged, threw him off.

They rolled over and over in the damp earth clawing at each other, dirt and moldy moss covering their clothes, faces, and hair. At last Sturgis got leverage and pulled both of them to their knees and then to their feet. They were both gasping for breath. Dean grabbed Billy by the shirtfront and gave him a powerful right hook to the face. Blood sprayed out from Billy's nose.

Dixon staggered back, then came at Sturgis, swinging his right fist. Sturgis dodged and he missed. Dean seized the advantage and gave Billy a fast one-two that sent him sprawling onto his back.

He didn't get up. He raised his head momentarily, then his eyes rolled up. "Revin . . ." he said. Then nothing.

The C.A.D.S. men cheered. Sturgis swayed dizzily, chest heaving for air, sweat pouring down his face, his mouth filled with blood. He spat and wiped his brow. "Take him—to camp and—put him—in detention."

"But, Colonel," said MacLeish, "we don't have a detention."

"Make one." Sturgis turned and staggered back to the camp.

Once again, Sturgis's face and body looked like a battlefield. He was sitting in the infirmary hut, shirtless, wincing as de Camp used up a bottle of iodine on his cuts—the new ones courtesy of Dixon, and the old ones that had reopened.

"That's enough," he snapped, as de Camp touched a tender area at his temple. "Later."

"*Now*, Colonel," Sheila said firmly.

He pushed her hand away and stood up. "What's the status on Dixon?"

"A few more cuts and twice as many bruises as you. What the hell were you two trying to prove?"

"You wouldn't begin to understand. Is he conscious?"

"Go see for yourself." It was plain that de Camp did not approve of Sturgis's idea of discipline.

Dean, his muscles aching, put on his shirt and limped to the unused hut where MacLeish had sequestered Billy. He found the young man sitting up on a cot, groggy but coherent, his nose bandaged. It quickly became evident that Billy remembered the fight, but not the reason for it.

"Colonel—God, I'm sorry. Is it true what they said—what I did?"

"I'm afraid so."

"And all the other things they said I did, too?"

"All caused by what happened on the *Lenin*. Do you remember all of that?"

"Every eternal second. Revin—corncobbed me."

Sturgis was relieved. Acknowledgment was halfway to recovery. "Damn, Billy, it wasn't your fault. You're still a man."

Billy cast his eyes down and let out a long sigh. "What are you going to do with me?"

Sturgis hooked the leg of a chair with his foot and pulled it toward him. He turned it around backward and sat down, folding his arms across the top of the back. "I don't have much choice, Billy. You're one of my best men, and I'd hate to lose you. But you've got to pull yourself together. It doesn't matter why. I can't have that."

"I know. A real disgrace, just like you said."

It was the turning point. Sturgis lit a cigarette and picked bits of tobacco from his tongue. "What do *you* want, Billy? How can I help you?"

Dixon's eyes hardened. "I have to have revenge."

Sturgis nodded. "Yeah, we all want revenge. I'd be a fool to deny it. But revenge that gets twisted into acting out is wrong—it'll destroy you." Sturgis rose to his feet. "Keep that in mind in New Orleans."

Billy looked elated. "I'm going?"

"A little revenge, Billy."

CHAPTER TEN

Fenton MacLeish and Mickey Rossiter grunted as they worked on the Rhino, modifying their battered battlewagon for the speed improvements directed by White Sands. The Rhino was their baby, and they had insisted on doing all the work themselves. MacLeish had recruited a team of C.A.D.S. men to modify the suits for VSF, the variable shell firing capability. They had set up a retooling area at the camp site; everyone was working as fast as possible. Even Sturgis was helping. He at least wanted to modify his own suit, to fully understand the new firing mechanism.

The humidity of the swamp added nothing to their comfort. Shirtless, the men were covered in sweat and grease. Conversation was at a minimum; most of it consisted of cursing.

"Hell," muttered Mickey, wedging his beefy hand deep into the Rhino's innards, "who put this thing together in the first place? You have to have a child's hand to get into some of these spaces!"

Fenton, his back at the rear of the machine, only grunted in response.

"Time for a break, boys," called a feminine voice.

Nobody stopped working, but a few of the men looked up. Several of the swamp girls had appeared bearing trays made out of bark, laden with refreshments. The girls were all prettied up, most wore brilliantly colored water lilies and hyacinths in their hair.

"Come on," coaxed the first young woman, a stunning brunette with long, shapely legs and an ample bosom, named Gloria. "You can't do good work on empty stomachs. We're here at the colonel's orders."

"That's right, boys," said Sturgis, setting aside his suit and standing up. "You can keep working if you want, but *I'm* taking ten."

At that, everyone stopped, relieved for a breather. The women set their trays down on the ground and began passing out food and drink. They had used utensils from the men's mess kits. There were cups of fresh palm-root coffee — which packed a better energy punch than caffeine — and chunks of fire-roasted fish caught from the swampwater. The men were hungrier than they realized, and wolfed down the food, polishing off the meal with some oranges that had not yet been affected by the radiation.

The best thing about this damned base, thought Sturgis, is these women. The men have found lovers here, and friends. It gives them a reason not to just shoot themselves, a reason to go on. We're damned lucky we have this place and these women.

The young woman named Gloria served Sturgis, looking at him with wide doe eyes that told him what she though of him as a man. He was by no means immune to the flattery.

"You look like you could use a little more relaxation," she suggested. Her green eyes flashed. She tossed her long blond tresses back over her tanned shoulders. And she winked.

Sturgis let his eyes rove up and down her enticing body, from the swell of her breasts above the low neckline of her tunic, to her perfectly shaped ankles. He was still hungry, but for something other than food. "I think I know what you have in mind," he said.

"Then, let's take a fanboat ride. There are some lovely places in the swamp to see."

Sturgis was sorely tempted to take up her offer right away, but his deeply ingrained sense of duty obliged him to finish modifying his suit. "That sounds like a great idea," he said, his big, rough hand brushing her soft arm. "I'll meet you at the dock in two hours."

He had never worked so fast in his life, finishing his suit. Since the nuke war, there was very little reason to put off till tomorrow . . . or not take a little pleasure.

Shafts of warm sunlight glinted through the canopy of cypresses and palms as Gloria maneuvered the fanboat through the lazy currents of the Okefenokee. Sturgis reclined, his shirt wadded up under his head for a pillow, content to gaze up at the foliage and contemplate what was to come.

Gloria took a series of connecting channels, until they were deep within a part of the swamp unfamiliar to Sturgis. She gently ran up the boat on the shore of one of the many islands dotting the huge swamp. He helped her out of the boat and took her immediately into his embrace, cupping his hands around her firm bottom, pulling her to him, savoring the sweetness of her deep kiss.

Urgent desire ignited between them. Gloria pulled away from him breathlessly and said, "Come, this way." She led him into the cool foliage when the sun did not penetrate, where the thick palm fronds created both an artificial twilight and a curtain between them and the channels. A velvety moss provided a soft blanket.

It was perfect sex. Neither wanted languid caresses or tender words, or to know anything beyond what their bodies told them. As he entered her, he discovered, to his surprise, that she was a virgin. But she seemed to know instinctively what to do to add to his pleasure, and he climaxed in intense ecstasy.

Dean rolled off her and they smoked cigarettes. Then he fell into a drowsy sleep. He awakened to feel the cool touch of her hand caressing his chest. He moaned and propped himself up on his elbows. He fumbled for his clothes and got out his watch. "I hate to say it, but time to get back."

She made a little sound of disappointment. "Can we do this again?"

Sturgis grinned and pulled her to him for a last caress. "That's a question you don't have to ask." He released her and reached for his clothes. Gloria also got dressed.

Dean stood up and stretched. He felt wonderful, the best he had felt in weeks. He turned to go back the path they had come, when a silvery flash caught his eye. He looked toward it, deeper into the foliage in the interior of the island, but it was gone. Was it the low angle of the sun, catching on some bit of exotic flora? He saw the flash again. It looked distinctly metallic.

"What's that?" he said, pointing.

Gloria followed his point. She shrugged. "I don't know."

"Let's find out." Sturgis took her by the hand and led her through a tangle of undergrowth. The silvery flash got larger and brighter until they emerged at a small lake. The silver was a piece of metal jutting from the stagnant water.

"Good God," said Sturgis, squinting at the markings on the metal, "it's the tail fin of an airplane—a *Russian* airplane!"

Sturgis directed the crew of suited C.A.D.S. men who returned to the island to recover the crashed airplane. The craft proved to be a small prop transport. It had evidently crashed long before the C.A.D.S. men set up their base in the Okefenokee, judging from the rust and deterioration and the presence of swamp slime. The Russian crew of two were skeletons, still in their uniforms and strapped into their seats.

The cargo, however, proved to be a gold mine. "It's ammunition, Sturg!" called Fuentes over his radio as he pried open crates in the airplane's cargo hold. "Packed in watertight containers!"

Sturgis hypothesized that the plane had been carrying the ammo from Russian beachheads in Charleston or Washington, D.C., to their Cuban allies in Florida. It had probably had a malfunction. Lousy maintenance. Overuse.

The Americans ferried the ammunition back to their base. There was a wide variety of bullets, grenades, shells, and canisters, some of which the Americans had never seen before, and could only guess at their purpose. But all the shells fit the VSF modifications to the suits.

All the men tested their suits, firing in a makeshift target range on a deserted island. One of the drawbacks of the modifications was that while different ammunition could be loaded in the clips, the VSF "felt" them and *it* alone decided what was fired when. The ammo fell into the firing chamber in a random fashion. A C.A.D.S. Commando raised his arm and directed fire, and hoped that whatever came out did the job.

Sturgis loaded his suit with the unknown shells and prayed. The first shell exploded out with an enormous recoil. It struck the target—a palm tree— and burst into a shower of shrapnel. The second piece, a slim, long shell, ignited a napalm fire that had to be quickly quenched with a blast of flame-retardant from the Rhino. They would have to be careful with that one.

"Check this out, Sturg," said Fuentes, loading one clip with the same type of shell. He blasted one off. It detonated in a cloud of glowing, yellow-green gas, which Dean's suit computer analyzed as a nerve gas that was paralyzing and fatal. "Close visors—quick!" They would have to be damn certain there were no pinhole leaks in their suits. You couldn't tell one shell

162

from another. The marking system was in a cryptic Cyrillic.

A disappointing number of the test ammunition turned out to be duds. Typical Russian technology, thought Dean. The Reds had probably had to fire off two to three times the number of missile warheads necessary to devastate America—but there was small comfort in that thought.

Some of the weapons tubes jammed up. More work would have to be done refining the VSF modifications. Overall, as the smoke cleared from the firing range, Sturgis was pleased. His men were rearmed and their equipment was improved. When they met Pinky Ellis and the Russians in New Orleans, they'd be able to give the Reds some of their own medicine.

While Sturgis plotted engaging the Russians again, life in the "New Society" of Biloxi, Mississippi, was going on as normal. As normal as could be, that is, for a city with radiation a hundred times above normal and populated and run by the former inmates of one of the nation's most prominent sanatariums for the criminally insane. The inmates of Cragmoor were at it again.

These new residents of Biloxi were still quite insane—by conventional standards. But since their escape from their mental-ward prison in Indiana right after the bomb blasts, they had figured—perhaps rightfully so—that *they* were the only sane ones left on the planet. After all, the power brokers of the world had judged them insane because they had murdered a few individuals. But the power brokers

163

had murdered millions, maybe even billions, of innocent human beings.

"So who's really insane?" they insisted to themselves self-righteously. "Who's insane?"

Under the leadership of Carl the King, a former serial murderer from the wrong side of Chicago, the former inmates were busy establishing the New Order of Sane Earthlings — NOSE — which, they had decided by popular vote, would now run the country. From the capital city of Biloxi, of course. Carl's favorite slogan was "Don't blow the NOSE!" Meaning, don't screw up, you jerkheads.

The city was home to several dozen new residents, who ranged from slightly dotty to downright demented — again, by conventional standards. Carl was seeing to it that *new* standards of sanity were established. Most of his group of thirty were new; all that was left of the original gang were eight men and women, including Carl.

The Christmas Eve bomb blasts had set Carl and his cronies free from the Cragmoor Sanatarium for the Criminally Insane in Gary, Indiana. Sixteen of them had gone on a wild, delirious rampage, torturing their former captors — the doctors and nurses and orderlies — and comandeering an old ambulance to race out to freedom.

They'd had an unfortunate run-in with Sturgis and his men — they'd tried to steal the C.A.D.S. suits — that left half of them dead. The survivors were so angry at Carl's bumbling leadership that they tied him up and tortured him magnificently for days.

The chastened Carl was a lot smarter now, but no less an egomaniac. He and his little band had drifted toward the southern part of the United States, which seemed to have fared better radiation-wise than the Midwest. Finally, they landed up in Biloxi, on the warm waters of the Gulf of Mexico, and set up shop.

Biloxi was a still, deserted ghost town when Carl and his group arrived, months after the bombings. The inital fallout had gradually killed all the inhabitants—there wasn't a single person left alive in the resort city. Much of the city was in ruins; evidently the dying had done a fair amount of pillage and looting. The Biloxians had buried their dead as best as they could, until the sheer numbers got out of hand. A great many corpses littered the streets and houses, mostly children, who were unable to bury each other. Fortunately, predatory ravens and locust swarms survived, and had picked the bones clean by the time the inmates arrived. All they had to do was shovel up the bones.

Several factors made Biloxi an ideal site for NOSE. Most important, a shift in the prevailing winds had taken the fallout away to sea. The rad count was so low as to be nonthreatening. The climate was still warm, and the area was isolated. The scientifically gifted among Carl's gang pointed that out. So Carl and his loyal followers set up their regency. For his private living quarters, Carl took over the most luxurious waterfront resort hotel, the Edgwater. He stayed in the Presidential Suite, which took up an entire floor of connecting rooms done in walnut paneling and silk brocade. His closest advisers took up residency in a nearby hotel that was not quite as luxurious, the Silver Breakers.

Among Carl's chief lieutenants was Glue Lady,

who fixed her hair with liberal quantities of Elmer's, making it stand on end one day, or globbing it atop her head and affixing creative decorations the next. She was perfect for public relations. If any of the flock complained, she'd scream them into submission.

Walter the Waxer ran Biloxi's maintenance program. Walter had gotten his nickname at Cragmoor, where he scuffed around with rags beneath his shoes, polishing the floors as he went. He liked thing *clean*. He was entranced by all the bones that needed to be shoved into neat piles and scooped up. After that, well, there was no end of things that needed to be cleaned in this ruined burg.

Helga Hefty, because of her brawn, was a natural for the transportation system. There was plenty of gasoline in the tanks of all the cars, trucks, and buses that once belonged to the deceased inhabitants. She set up a small, conservation-minded transit system. Since most of the vehicles' batteries were dead, Hefty Helga had to push-start them!

The Electrician was frustrated, at first, by the lack of power—there were so many outlets to play with—but kept tinkering, until he was able to get a wind-powered generator going that supplied the city with limited electricity. The changes in the winds, caused by the bombs, kept the generator going almost all the time.

Stella the Axe made an ideal police chief. When Stella laid down the law, that was *it*. She had a mean swing.

The other three of the original band included Doctor Dennis, who believed pain to be the best treatment for any ill—and he was wickedly imaginative in his therapies; Freddy the Fireman—he had been Freddy the Firestarter until Doctor Dennis cured him; and Annie Anytime—well, nuclear war didn't eliminate man's oldest needs, did it?

The other residents of Biloxi had drifted in from around the country, drawn by some sort of psychic homing, perhaps. With few exceptions, they had escaped from asylums, prisons, and mental hospital wards—or had been part of the "street people." As long as they proved useful, and pledged total and undying allegiance to Carl, they were allowed to stay and live in some modest apartments in the center of town—but not out on the Gulf strip. Occasionally a "geek" stumbled in, someone who had managed to get through life without psychoses or neuroses or criminally insane acts. In short, a normal person, now considered to be dangerously insane. And were *they* sorry they ever set foot in Biloxi. Stella the Axe took care of *them*.

At the moment, Carl the King had decreed that Biloxi would now be known as Bagels-n-Lox. He took credit for the idea, though the name had really been proposed by a hotshot from New York, a former criminal-defense lawyer named Louis the Liar who had plea-bargained hundreds of murderers to freedom. Louis, it seemed, missed his morning bagel and was a poet to boot. His scatological verses, which he sent to judges and juries, led to his being incarcerated in a place called Matawan. Until a convenient nuke warhead some miles away blew the wall down. Somehow the crazy survived better than the normals in crazy post-nuke America. He too had wandered south, unmolested.

Carl liked the name Bagels-n-Lox. It had a nice ring to it. "Think of the public relations potential," he said to Glue Lady from the throne he had set up in the old mayor's office in the municipal building. The throne was a huge, high-backed, black leather chair taken from a judge's chamber. "Work up a campaign, will you? Sooner or later, we're bound to be deluged with tourists, and we've got to be prepared." He touched his crown. It was a paper cook's hat taken from a Burger King outlet, a trifle ketchup-smeared but still serviceable.

Glue Lady's head bobbed enthusiastically on her skinny neck. Her first major P.R. effort! Her hair today was a work of art: a Matterhorn decorated with red and blue glitter and dotted with multicolored spangles. She was changing styles less frequently these days because her supply of Elmer's was running low. She had discovered aerosol cans of something called "styling mousse" in many of the households, but that stuff couldn't hold a candle to the staying power of Elmer's.

"Right, Chief." She liked to call Carl "Chief," even though he was officially king.

"But how?" she asked.

Carl's scarred face cracked into a scowl. He had scars all over his body, most of them courtesy of the "treatment" his gang had administered after the debacle with Sturgis. The rest of the scars were the result of his fight to regain leadership of the group. "Don't ask me—*you're* supposed to be the publicity expert, Madam Glue. And it better be good, or I'll send you to Doctor Dennis! He's got a new treatment that he's *dying* to try out!"

"But, Chief," she protested, "we haven't got anything to publicize with. No newspapers. No media."

"Then, *get* them. I want big signs! 'Bagels-n-Lox — Where the NOSE Grows.' Something brilliantly clever like that."

"I've got it!" Glue Lady jumped up and down in her chair. "That new boy from Iowa — he used to publish porn magazines with *wonderful* slogans. 'Best porn in the Corn Belt,' 'Get a Rise in the Bible Belt.' I'll ask him to start a newspaper! Then we can publish articles and advertisements."

"I don't care who or how, just do it, *do* it," said Carl, pounding his fist on the arm of the chair. "I want Bagels-n-Lox on the *map*."

"We don't have a map," said Glue Lady.

"Good God, you're dim. It's a figure of speech! Now get out of here before I change my mind about Doctor Dennis!"

Glue Lady jumped up and dashed out, raining glitter and spangles as she went. She had no desire to see Doctor Dennis. There were people in the city who *loved* to visit him, but she was not one of them.

Glue Lady left the municipal building and headed for Ann's, which was where Uncle Okie, as the porn man liked to be called, could be found almost any time of the day or night. Uncle Okie's only lament about Bagels-n-Lox was that there were no children to pander. He had dedicated himself to working on a solution to that with Annie Anytime, who claimed to be beyond childbearing years. Carl refused to believe it.

As Glue Lady bustled along the streets, she passed

the entrance to Doctor Dennis's "New Age Clinic." She shivered. You definitely were a "new age" when you came out of there—old. "I don't understand it," she clucked to herself. "Just look at all these people, lined up around the block to get in to see him. Why, Carl would beat them up for free!"

Each to his own tastes, she thought, hurrying on. On the other side of the street, she spotted Walter the Waxer absorbed in his bone duty. He was systematically working his way up and down every street in Bagels-n-Lox, scouring out the insides of buildings, brushing bones into neat little piles on the sidewalks. He didn't use a broom or shovel, but still favored his feet as the best tool of all.

When he had a row of little piles, he pushed them into an oversized industrial dustpan and carried them to a big packing carton. When the carton was full, he summoned Helga Hefty, and they carted the bones to Bone Mountain on the edge of town. Walter wasn't sure what he would do with Bone Mountain once he'd swept up all the bones—maybe put a sign on it and charge money to all the tourists who undoubtedly would swarm to Bagels-n-Lox once they heard about NOSE. At any rate, it would be a long time before he had to worry about it. The great Biloxi-Gulfport metropolitan area had once been home to nearly two hundred thousand people, and that made for a lot of bones.

Walter smiled and hummed as he worked. He had gotten to know all the bones by name—Doctor Dennis had lent him an anatomy book scrounged from the ruins—and he had made up a little ditty of them.

Glue Lady stopped. Walter could be very useful in

her campaign. NOSE should have an anthem. She crossed the street and crooked a finger at him. "I have a job for you, Walter."

Walter shook his head and continued sweeping bones with his feet. "I'm busy," he said, glancing up with one good brown eye.

"And *I'm* on the King's business," she shot back. "If you don't do as I say, Carl will see to it that you're busy all right—in *there*." She pointed to Doctor Dennis's clinic.

Walter quickly abandoned his bones. "At your service."

While Glue Lady recruited helpers, Carl remained on his throne and received one of his advisers—Serena the Seer. She was a newcomer, a frail wraith of a girl with long dark hair and mesmerizing green eyes. She claimed to be from 'Frisco, and said she'd left the Bay City long before the bombs hit—because she knew they were coming. Serena had made her living as a psychic, and had drifted in and out of mental clinics. Carl thought she had great potential. Maybe even to be Queen of Bagels-n-Lox.

"Your Highness," she began, "we are getting visitors soon." Carl stared at her pale long face, those black eyes.

"I know," said Carl smugly. "I'm doing a P.R. campaign."

"No, Your Highness, not tourists—astronauts, or beings from another planet. Strange humanoid creatures in black spacesuits. They will come from the east, riding alien vehicles." She said this so calmly it was like she were reporting a fly had landed on the table. Serena was *always* calm.

171

Carl shot up out of his judge's chair. *Strange humanoids in black spacesuits?* Those were no aliens, no siree! Those were the guys who'd humiliated him in front of his own people, and killed several of his followers. So they were headed for Bagels-n-Lox, were they? This was too good to be true. Now he would get revenge!

CHAPTER ELEVEN

No one in the C.A.D.S. camp, if he knew what was good for him, said a word about the incident between Sturgis and Dixon. For Sturgis, the subject was closed. He had decided there was no need to punish Billy for his conduct, as an example of discipline to the rest of the men. It would have been a pointless exercise, depriving the dwindling unit of one more desperately needed man. The fight itself had proved example enough. It had jarred Billy back to sanity.

Sheila de Camp, nevertheless, had to find out the hard way. She broached the subject to Sturgis, only to have him bellow at her to quit meddling in the way he chose to run his unit.

Once again, Sturgis readied his weary men for another mission. It seemed like the last battle had been fought only yesterday, even though weeks had passed. And after New Orleans, he knew, would come another battle and another and another. That was just the way it was. Long ago—lifetimes, it seemed—he had chosen to be a fighter, and he would keep on fighting to his last breath. And so would every single one of his men.

De Camp, the only woman in C.A.D.S., had demonstrated her battle capabilities in the last major encounter, at the Chesapeake Bay Bridge. Sturgis no longer worried about her. She might be a woman, but she was just as tough as the guys when it came to fighting. He did, however, insist that she ride inside the Rhino instead of on a tribike. It was his policy for the medic, regardless of gender. The medic was too important to risk.

Billy Dixon seemed to pull himself back together. The wild behavior and mood swings vanished. There was apology in his deep blue eyes, but no one wanted his contrition; they wanted only for Billy to be and feel himself again. While the old, jovial Billy gradually returned, no one knew for certain what might still be boiling deep below the surface. Only time would tell. His mental wounds were deep.

Sturgis pulled his unit out of the Okefenokee on a carefully planned timetable that would get them to New Orleans about two days before Pinky's planned rendezvous with the Soviets. Sturgis would have preferred more preparation time, but it wasn't possible. They would need at least two days to scout the area and plan their strategy. If Pinky didn't show up until the end of the week—or later—they would just have to lay low.

Sturgis had a feeling Pinky would show up early. The greedy bastard would be anxious to cash in his prizes as fast as possible. C.A.D.S. might, in that case, walk in on a trap.

Dean still had lingering doubts about Billy. He would not entrust him with crucial decisions, but see how well he did under the stress of battle.

Rather than have everyone in the unit on full scan at all times—which would bombard each man with a constant stream of incoming data—Sturgis split the men up into selective scan teams, headed by his Inner Circle, with one exception. "Roberto," he directed, "you and your men take the point. You'll have to be ready for anything, so scan at your discretion. Tranh, you and your guys stay on Geometric Identification. I want every rock and bump, and everything that moves, analyzed. Billy, your assignment is Macro-View. Set it for the full five-mile radius and stay at the head of the column."

Sturgis then divided up the rest of the men. The men on Zoom would sweep their magnified vision onto anything spotted by G.I. or Macro that needed closer examination. Mode Red men would keep constant track of everyone in the unit, and of the Rhino, for there would be times when the entire group would not be visible at once. Mode Blue men would stay ready for instant analysis of enemy troops, should they appear. Sturgis also assigned rotating Infrared Mode duty for nighttime.

Last, but not least, Sturgis selected Joe Fireheels—the Survivor—to monitor atmosphere conditions and radiation levels.

"Everyone will still maintain the modes necessary for personal survival," Sturgis said as a final instruction. "Those include Optimum Attack, Weapons Selection, Trajectory Analysis and Probability of Destruction. And, of course, any analysis screens pertinent to your scanning modes." Finished with that, Dean radioed Rossiter and MacLeish. "How's the Rhino, boys?"

175

"Ready to roll," responded Rossiter. "We won't know for sure until we get on the straightaway if she will do ninety, but Fenton and I would put good drinking money on it."

"All right, men," Sturgis said. "Let's move out."

It was slow going through the swamp, but once they got out on asphalt — and especially once they hooked onto Interstate 10 — they picked up considerable speed. Rossiter indeed pushed the Rhino to ninety, a considerable improvement over its former top speed of seventy miles per hour. They had to make a couple of stops so that MacLeish could make some adjustments, but after that, the Rhino raced smoothly along behind the column of tribikes.

The trip through the Florida panhandle was eerie. Much of the landscape was still thick, lush, and green, but there were signs that the gray death from the north was creeping in. Here and there were clumps of brittle, dead foliage, and fruit trees with mutated fruit. The sky looked mottled from dust and debris swirling in currents high above the earth. The first night, it rained, a sudden torrent that was over in minutes and left a rank smell in the air. The rainwater tested unsafe to drink.

But the oddest thing was the lack of human life. Everything deserted — it was as though everyone had gone out to lunch and never come back. It had *that* feeling. You didn't believe they were all *dead*. Tallahassee was a black, hot crater; they didn't stop to peer in, just skirted the rim wall. To the southwest, along the Gulf Coast, sensor readings showed that the Panama City area was highly radioactive as well. That was no surprise, considering the proximity of

Tyndall Air Force Base. The C.A.D.S. squad by-passed Panama City as well.

Pensacola was another graveyard. A firestorm had leveled it. Not a direct hit — maybe heavy forests further inland hid small bands of survivors, people like the Revengers further north, who were scratching life as best as they could from the land fighting a guerilla war against Red patrols.

At Mobile, Interstate 10 cut south closer to the coastline. In the unlikely little town of Kreole, Louisiana, they picked up sounds on their sensors that led them to human life in a tiny cottage: a wrinkled bean-pole of an old man who was hunched over a portable typewriter with a faded ribbon, pounding furiously away on bits of dirty paper. According to the scans, he was the only living being left in the village. He was suffering the effects of malnutrition, dehydration, and unsafe levels of radiation. His crinkly scalp was dotted with tufts of white hair, and his skin was covered with red, running sores.

He came outside at Sturgis's knock upon his cottage door. Hughes Rutherford, as he introduced himself, was not pleased to be interrupted by a group of bewildered men towering over him in black space-suits. Nor was he impressed with who they were. "Can't help you," he said in a whiny, nasal voice, even though they had not asked for help. "Got to keep working — got a daily minimum, you know." The pale blue eyes surrounded by wrinkles had an odd glaze.

"A daily minimum of what?" asked the puzzled Sturgis.

"Pages, boy, pages! Don't you know who I am? Haven't you ever read any of my books?"

Sturgis confessed that he had not.

Rutherford wheezed a sigh and shook his head, which wobbled on his scrawny neck. "The illiteracy in America is just appalling! Westerns, son—I write bestsellers! Done twenty of 'em. You mean to tell me you never heard of *Sons of the Conestogas* and *The Pride of Abilene*?"

Sturgis shook his head.

"Too bad. You'd see what real fightin' is all about!" He cackled.

"Is that what you're doing—writing a western?"

"The last and the best," said Rutherford. He squinted his watery eyes up at Sturgis. "You say you're soldiers, eh? How come you all in them silly get-ups, driving them kiddie bikes? How come you don't look like real soldiers?" He gestured at the Rhino. "And what's that baked potato on wheels?" His arm dropped as he bent over in a spasm of dry, racking coughing.

"You can't survive here much longer," said Sturgis, side-stepping the writer's questions, which were pointless to answer, anyway. "Don't you have anywhere to go?"

Rutherford shook his head vehemently as he cleared his throat. "Don't want to leave, son. Why, the good Lord let me live for a purpose, to write this book, and He'll see me through to the final page. That's all that matters." He thumped his chest and spat a huge glob of red-laced phlegm onto the dirt. "Now, if you'll excuse me, sonny, I've got to get back to work." He shuffled back into his cottage and closed the door.

"We can't just leave him here," protested de Camp,

178

ever the bleeding-heart humanitarian. "The rad level's too high."

"He's a doomed man," said Sturgis. "Leave him with his dream." He remounted his tribike. "Maybe some future generation will discover his manuscript. The last—and who knows—maybe the *greatest* western!"

The Indian spoke up. "Colonel, sir, I'm noticing something strange."

"What is it, Fireheels?"

"I'm checking my readings here . . . We're only about thirty miles west of Biloxi, and the rad count drops considerably the further west I scan. Biloxi is close enough to Hattiesburg that it should have gotten a pretty good dose of radiation, and should be hotter than it is. It's almost like there's an invisible curtain around Biloxi, protecting it."

Sturgis turned on his own sensors and checked the readout that came across his visor. "Might be another atmospheric aberration, like the Okefenokee. Let's check it out!"

The first evidence that all was not normal in Biloxi—nuclear megadeath notwithstanding—was an enormous sign that proclaimed, "The NOSE Welcomes You to Bagels-n-Lox." The letters were crudely hand-painted on a white sheet, which was draped across a billboard along the interstate, at the eastern city limits.

"What the hell is this shit?" muttered Fuentes.

"It's new," observed Dixon. "The paint looks fresh, and there's no damage to the fabric. This has been put up after the last rain hereabouts."

"Bagels-n-Lox? A restaurant?" joked Van Noc.

"Yeah," said Fuentes, "some 'hot' new cooking."

"G.I. mode, what's the scan?" said Sturgis.

Van Noc read his visor display. "Human life-forms, Colonel. Several dozen!" He paused.

From up ahead, Billy's voice came over the inter-suit radio. "You're not going to believe this, Sturg, but two miles ahead along the perimeter of town is a huge pile that analysis identifies as — *bones*!"

"Everyone on full scan!" Dean ordered. "Forward at low speed!"

The C.A.D.S. men slowly proceeded into Biloxi. They stopped at Walter's Bone Mountain. "My God," said Fuentes. "This is the weirdest graveyard I've ever seen!"

All around were signs of recent human activity — but no people. The computers showed their heat traces. "They've either gone underground to live, or they're in hiding in the buildings," said Sturgis.

They drove through deserted residential areas and on into the commercial heart of the city. They saw Walter's neat little piles of bones on the sidewalks everywhere. They stopped in front of Doctor Dennis's New Age Clinic and read the illuminated sign, "Pain is the Pathway to the Ultimate Cosmic Consciousness. Come in for a free trial session!"

"This place has got electricity!" exclaimed Van Noc, reading his sensors. "How in the hell — ? It's crazy!"

A blurry movement caught the corner of Dean's eye. He snapped his head. What was that? There — again! "I don't believe it," he muttered. "It can't be!"

It was Glue Lady, skittering along in the shadows, her head a stiff beehive with little colored enamel pill-boxes glued into it. "It's crazy, all right," Sturgis said over the radio. "It's those same mental cases who tried to steal our suits, right after the blast. The Insanos!"

Suddenly heavy black wires dropped onto the C.A.D.S. men. They were live electrical wires, cut from trolley lines overhead. Several soldiers screamed as the wires shorted out their suits. Sparks flew into the air. Sturgis raised his right weapons tube, loaded only with 250 machine-gun bullets, and commanded, "Fire!" He aimed at the wires and severed them from their source. The dead sections fell harmlessly to the ground.

Above them in an office building, two heads peeked out of a window and then pulled back. A shriek of laughter drifted down to the street.

"Battle positions!" Sturgis yelled. "Shoot to kill!" The men scattered. "Fuentes, you and Davis get these guys out of here." He pointed to four immobilized and defenseless soldiers who'd been hit and knocked from their bikes. Two were rolling on the street, groaning from the electrical shocks. Two weren't moving at all, and did not respond to Sturgis over the radio. "De Camp," he said, "on the double!" Ineffectual small-arms rounds pinged off his suit."

Sheila sprang out of the Rhino and loped to the casualties in long, well-coordinated strides. She knelt down and flipped open visors and breastplates. "Dead. Dead," she said quickly of the two. She moved on to the other four. "Shock and burns, but it looks like the worst damage is to the suits. They're

181

completely shorted—we'll have to pull the men out of them."

"We'll have to leave them in until we get control of the situation," Fuentes said. "Help me get them into cover."

Sturgis was busting out plate-glass windows at the street level of the building in order to gain access. But just as he stepped through, he heard the maniacal laughter again and looked up. Two figures—one wearing a hamburger cook's hat—were swinging Tarzan-style on long ropes to the roof of another building. They were moving fast.

Colonel Sturgis raised his left arm, loaded with the Russian variable ammunition, and gave the firing command. A shell whistled into the air—but no blast.

"A dud, dammit!" he cursed. He wasted precious seconds popping the dead shell out of the chamber. By the time he could fire again, the men had disappeared into the second building.

Carl the King was beside himself with glee. He and the Electrician had scored a terrific hit. Serena the Seer had been right, even down to the timing. "*This* time, Astro-Fool," he shrieked to no one in particular, but meaning Sturgis, "you won't get away! You're no match for Carl the King!"

They scrambled through the building to the other side, where another set of ropes awaited them. They would swing their way to another part of the city, where Carl had more surprises in store for the C.A.D.S. men. They would make sure they were seen, of course—and followed.

The Electrician felt he had reached nirvana. It was one thing to play with light sockets, another to

182

electrocute people. What a blast! He could do this forever!

"Look, there they go again!" From down on the street, the C.A.D.S. soldiers spotted the two strange figures swinging to the roof of yet another building. As they arced over the street, they hurled two oval objects at the troopers. "Grenades!" someone yelled. The explosions did no damage to the C.A.D.S. suits, but did obscure vision with dust and debris. Meanwhile, the two madmen escaped in one of Helga's vans.

Sturgis spotted the van as it careened away down a side street. "Follow that van but hold your fire," he ordered his men. "Let's see where they're heading." He gauged the width of the streets and decided he would not risk boxing the Rhino in somewhere. "Mickey, keep the Rhino here and look after the wounded."

Sturgis and the rest peeled off on their tribikes. But the van had disappeared. Dean switched on his Infrared mode and picked up the vehicle's heat trail. It led around a corner and stopped; the size of the glow indicated other vehicles. He waved to his men to follow him and sped toward the glow on the grid map in his visor.

As the tribikes roared around a corner, they were greeted by a street-wide phalanx of city buses coming at them head-on. Except, these weren't ordinary city buses — the fronts had been modified with highway construction equipment, and sported claws, jaws, and scoop shovels. Helga Hefty, driving the middle bus, led the charge with a war whoop. Her transportation system at its finest!

The C.A.D.S. men brought their tribikes to a screeching halt. "Open fire!" roared Sturgis as the buses bore down upon them. A hail of ammunition launched through the air. Machine-gun bullets tore through the metal and split windows and windshields. A shrapnel shell ripped off the entire roof of one bus, the screams indicating there were people hidden on board. The bus crashed into a lamp post.

The other buses roared on, and behind the front line was another line of buses. Helga had mobilized a good portion of the city's entire fleet. When the buses got close enough, side windows opened and Stella the Axe's recruits shoved out the muzzles of their police weapons—shotguns and automatic machine guns— and opened fire.

The bullets bounced harmlessly off the C.A.D.S. suits. One of Dean's men fired off a canister that proved to be a smoke shell, and the air filled with a stinging, acrid smoke that made the attackers cough and choke. It also obscured vision, so that no one could see much of anything, and the buses began careening wildly all over the street and sidewalks. One soldier was struck and knocked off his bike. The bike was destroyed, but the man was saved by his suit.

Sturgis switched from visual to Geometric Identification and ordered Billy to do likewise. They focused on a bus and fired from the VSF sleeve. The bus erupted into a wall of flames.

From his vantage point above the street, Carl watched the scene with mounting fury. Those imbeciles in the buses! The enemy was demolishing them.

Helga had assured him that nothing could stop her "monster buses." He turned to the Electrician. "Go tell the Second Force to launch their attack."

Minutes later, as the last blasted bus was sighing to the ground on flat tires, the C.A.D.S. men were attacked from the opposite direction — by fire trucks.

The huge hook-and-ladders raced toward them, sirens wailing, red and white lights flashing. A frail figure clung to the top of one of the trucks, gripping the nozzle of the big hose. It was Glue Lady, dressed in a fireman's rubber coat and trousers, her hair still filled with pillboxes. She pointed the hose at the black suits and pulled a lever to a tank of XN-3 Experimental Epoxy Glue she had dragged from a warehouse on Alton Street.

A thick gray liquid sprayed out over the C.A.D.S. men as they opened fire on the trucks. It wasn't water. It was — *glue*! Epoxy glue, the kind that instantly binds any two materials together. Stuff that got into any joints or openings.

Suddenly the C.A.D.S. men were frozen in position, unable to bend their joints, their feet stuck to the pavement. One man, who had brushed his hand across his visor to clear it of the liquid, couldn't get his hand unstuck. Sure, increasing power could break the hold — but the suits they knew, would be damaged. Specs said *no epoxy*!

Above, Carl howled with laughter. Now they were his prisoners, stuck in place until he decided what to do with them! He turned from the window and scurried down the stairwell to the street level, brandishing his own shotgun. Ha! The bastards could starve and suffocate right in their own suits. Then he would figure out a way to pry them open and dissolve the glue so that he could use the suits.

Sturgis was furious. Goddammit, glued to the street by a bunch of insane maniacs! It was more humiliating than anything else. His arms stuck in position, he had to wait for the fire trucks to get into his line of sight before he could fire. A Russian shell whizzed out of his sleeve and knocked Glue Lady off the truck, but did not explode. Another fucking dud!

Billy, coated with a frosting of epoxy, did what he always did in a pinch—fired up his jetpacks. The jet roared, trying to lift him off the ground, while the epoxy held him firmly in place. He increased the jets, which threatened to overheat. Then, with a loud ripping sound, the pavement around his feet tore loose and he rose up into the air.

With huge, bounding leaps, Dixon sailed to the fire trucks, blasting away with whatever from his weapons tubes, then using his entire body as a battering ram to demolish the trucks. Other C.A.D.S. men followed his example. Many of them could move their hip and knee joints, since the glue had landed mostly on their upper bodies and feet. They stumped awkwardly about, turning at all sorts of crazy angles to get their frozen arms into firing positions.

The former mental patients began scattering like rats—those who survived, that is. Bodies littered the street and sidewalks.

As he broke out to the street, Carl was first horrified, then dismayed, to see his victory turn into defeat. Once again, he'd been outsmarted. This was no time for self-sacrifice! He turned and fled down an alley to a van parked several blocks away, its engine running. It was his getaway vehicle—just in case.

Serena the Seer was at the wheel, and as soon as Carl jumped in, she put the van in gear and tore off, heading out of town. Carl, his Burger King crown long gone and his face streaked with dirt and sweat, screamed at her. "You didn't tell me it was going to turn out like this!"

"You didn't ask," she said, barreling through the streets. Ahead, she spotted a group of Carl's subjects, waving frantically at the van. "Look, there are some of the others." Serena slammed on the brakes. Glue Lady, Doctor Dennis, Uncle Okie, and Ann piled in, along with five of the recent newcomers to Biloxi.

Further down the street, she stopped for a bewildered Walter the Waxer, who was limply hanging onto an enormous femur. "I never got a chance to use my club," he wailed as they pulled him inside.

"No more!" screeched Carl. "Let's get out of here!"

Glue Lady was in hysterics, crying over Stella, the Electrician, and Helga, who had apparently met their ends in the street fight—along with the greater percentage of the city's small population.

"Shut up!" said Carl. "Or I'll glue your mouth shut for good!"

Back at the scene, the fight was over, and the C.A.D.S. men were clumping around assessing damages in the smoke-filled air. Van Noc's voice came over the suit channel: "Colonel, there's a vehicle heading out of town on the interstate at high speed!"

"Let 'em go, the bastards," said Sturgis. "We've got suit problems enough."

"How in the hell are we going to get these suits

cleaned up?" asked Fuentes.

"There's bound to be some industrial solvents somewhere in this city," Sturgis said. He raised the Rhino on his radio. "Fenton, we need a computer search on formulas for dissolving epoxy glue. Pronto!" Sturgis was disgusted. A bunch of Insanos had again succeeded where armies of Soviet troops failed. It was a good thing the Reds hadn't caught on to the effect of epoxy on C.A.D.S. suits. But all the Reds ever thought of was firepower and *more* firepower!

CHAPTER TWELVE

"Bloody muck-up," muttered Fenton MacLeish as he watched the bizarre army of stiff C.A.D.S. suits clomp back to the Rhino. "What an attack! Did any troopers die?"

"Never mind that," said Sturgis. "Just get the solution to the glue. We're stuck in these things until we can dissolve the stuff."

"Mickey and I are still analyzing the computer data," Fenton said. "Do you know how many hundreds of epoxy glue formulas there are?"

"That," said Sturgis, "is the least of my concerns."

"Right-o, sir." Fenton disappeared back into the Rhino to manipulate the computer data.

De Camp came up to Sturgis. "Two men are dead, Colonel. The other two who were hit by the electrical wires received bad shocks, but are doing well."

"At least that's some comfort," the colonel frowned. With his movable right arm, he was dabbing a sticky left shoulder with a solvent-soaked rag. The Insanos killed two good men, he thought.

Hordes of Reds have done less. What kind of luck keeps putting them in our way? Maybe they are right—this post-nuke world belongs to the crazies. It seems to belong to *that* branch of psychos, anyway!

Rossiter's voice interrupted his broodings. "Colonel, sorry, but the suits of the men who were killed are beyond repair—we simply don't have the parts. The others I think I can fix."

"Make it quick," said Sturgis. "We'll destroy the two that are beyond salvage." He looked around for someone who would get his double meaning, and found him. "Fireheels, go do it."

Sturgis looked around at the rest of his men, who stood awkwardly on the chunks of asphalt glued to their feet. Fireheels hadn't been touched by the glue. He went off to burn the dead men.

Presently MacLeish emerged from the Rhino with a computer printout. "I think I've got it, Colonel—a solvent formula we can make from some common industrial chemicals."

"You and Rossiter scout the docks and the warehouses. There's bound to be chemical supplies around somewhere."

After several hours of searching sections of Biloxi, Rossiter and MacLeish returned with four drums of chemicals, which they carefully mixed together. The fumes were potent, and they wore their suits for protection.

"I feel like a mad scientist," said Rossiter.

"You'll be something else if this doesn't work," responded MacLeish. "The colonel's as mad as a wet cat."

They tested the solvent on one of the suits that was

190

minimally impaired. It worked. The cleanup of all the suits was long and slow. One suit — Davis's — was not repairable. Fireheels stated that Davis could use his suit. He said he *had to* be out in the air. Sturgis said, "Okay. For *now*, Fireheels."

Sturgis was uneasy. They were behind schedule, but nothing could be done. He hoped the Russians didn't show up early in New Orleans. Nor Pinky.

The hot, humid air lay over New Orleans like a thick blanket. It was the kind of dog day, if this had been before the war, that would have made anybody work up a sweat in half a dozen steps. But no one moved through the streets of New Orleans because no one was left alive. Radiation had killed everyone. Or, rather, everyone that had used to live there.

The Russians had spared the Crescent City from serious structural damage, figuring the port facilities could prove to be valuable at some point in the future. No missiles had been sent there for direct hits. Marshal Veloshnikov thought the city itself to be nothing but a den of iniquity, whose population would self-destruct if left to its own devices.

Which it did. When the clouds of lethal radiation wafted over from Houston, those who hadn't already fled the city still did nothing but party away their lives. One last grand Mardi Gras. Then the winds shifted and the radiation blew out to sea, leaving New Orleans as safe as Biloxi, eighty miles to the east. Give or take a few rads . . .

Now, a strange caravan rolled in from the north-west, led by a black Rolls Royce limo reinforced with armor and bristling with antennae. Pinky Ellis, the world's most powerful military-industrial contractor, was blowing into town, cruising past skeletons still wearing party hats and holding noisemakers from their *Final* Mardi Gras.

The Rolls was followed by a string of trucks and cars that were filled with his new army of followers — men and women he had picked up here and there, desperate and vicious creatures who would do anything and kill anybody to stay alive. In Pinky, they saw their New Messiah. He promised them life. He promised them riches. He was still immensely powerful, and he promised them a share of it.

In the middle of the caravan rolled a flatbed semi, surrounded by cars full of armed guards. The semi carried Pinky's golden payload, the supertank that would gain him transport to the Pacific Nuclear Free Zone. The caravan's rear was brought up by two conventional U.S. Army tanks that Pinky had stolen from abandoned military bases in the West. The tanks were beauts — M1 Abramses, loaded with 105mm main guns.

Pinky had plenty of ammo for his bazookas and submachine guns, and didn't hesitate to use it. Like he did in that town called De Quincy, on their way to New Orleans, where they'd blasted that pathetic group of starving beggar boys. Imagine the nerve the boys had had, to approach his shiny, spotlessly maintained white Rolls Royce, to touch it, beg for food!

None of his followers knew it, but the fat man planned on getting out of New Orleans *alone*, abandoning his army and even his loyal circle of close advisers. Pinky smiled. Soon they'd be ragged and starving too—without his genius for leadership to help them along!

He perused the town for suitable quarters and found them. Soon, Pinky wallowed his obese bulk on the pile of mattresses in the main bedchamber of the Ursuline Convent, located in New Orleans' French Quarter. Beneath him, nearly swallowed in the mattresses, was a young girl he'd kidnapped in Texas, shortly after Morgana Pinter had escaped. Her name was Martha.

Pinky grunted and sweated buckets with the exertion of releasing his sexual tension. His rigid member—which, considering his bulk, was not all that big—jabbed in and out of the girl. She was too terrified to cry out in shame and disgust—Pinky had described for her in lurid detail what he would do to her if she didn't submit to his every whim. She was pretty, but he missed Morgana. Oh, how he missed her. Someday, if she lived, he'd find her. Thinking of Morgana, he satisfied his lust and rolled his hoglike body away. Around the mattresses, a bevy of nubile beauties leaped into action with towels to swab the man down as Martha wept silently.

"Is that one still any good?" sneered the greasy man who sat in a nearby chair, watching. His name was Blaze Lewik—Lewd Lewik, as he was known—and he was Pinky's top thug. "You've about damn near wore her out."

Pinky wheezed and propped himself up in the pillows. His flesh hung in folds around his middle, and on the insides of his thighs. "Damn sight better than any pussy *you're* getting," he growled. He knew Lewik was licking his chops just waiting for Pinky to

193

get tired of little Martha and cast her off among the rest of the men.

He liked young ones—especially platinum blond and small.

He reached over to Martha and grabbed the kidnapped girl roughly by the arm. "You, out! The rest of you stay!"

The Texas blonde ran cowering and whimpering from the room. Pinky settled into his pillowy seat and accepted a towel to drape across his loins. He pointed to one of the remaining girls. "Okay, darlin', now you can fetch me some of that wine we found in the cellar. Bring a glass for Lewik here."

The Ursuline Convent, built in the mid-eighteenth century, was the oldest French colonial building in New Orleans. It was on Chartres Street in the French Quarter, just minutes off of Interstate 10, and close to the Mississippi River. Pinky got a big thrill out of using it as a temporary headquarters and desecrating its holy ground. He didn't think the nuns had been any too pious, anyhow; why, all that wine they found in the cellar would last for communions until the year 3000. Nope, he bet those nuns had tied one on every night—and probably invited over a bunch of priests as well. He couldn't believe *anyone* had pious motives.

While Pinky took over the bedchamber that once belonged to the Mother Superior, the rest of his gang spread out through the convent, disporting themselves as they pleased while they waited for the Russians.

The naked girl returned with a jug of wine, a communion cup, and a mug. She gave the communion cup to Pinky and poured out the burgundy. She kept her eyes always downcast, as Pinky demanded. He liked submission. Naked submission.

"So, when you think them Reds are gonna show, hunh?" said Lewik between gulps of wine. He drained the mug and held it out for more. His free hand roamed all over the girl while she refilled the mug. She tried not to grimace.

Pinky shrugged and belched. "Any day now. That was the deal I made over the radio with that Supreme Marshal Veloshnikov cat. Be in New Or-leens, he said, between yesterday and five days from today, and he would send some of his boys by sub to meet us and take the prize."

"What if they stiff us?"

"They won't," said Pinky with the confidence of a man who holds a good hand of cards. "I told 'em enough about the Bandersnatch to whet their mean little appetites. They won't pass up *that* baby, no sir." He slurped wine from the silver cup. "And on top of that, I've got the technology blueprints for the Black Commando suits. The Russians have a version that stinks. They'd *love* to have the improvements. Some ain't on paper—only in my head, see?"

Lewik grunted. "They'd better move their asses. This joint's pretty dull—the whole fucking city is empty!"

"It's only empty of people, dumbshit," Pinky said peevishly. "All you got to do is walk down the streets of the Quarter and you can get yourself a drink from any bar, or watch any skin flick you want. All that stuff is here—it's fine here. We got our own women. What the hell more do you want? Paradise? Well, we're shipping out for the nuke-free zone in a few days. That's *real* paradise. Palm trees, low rad. The Reds got 'em cowed down there — We'll be sitting pretty. Ain't *that* great?"

Lewik answered by shrugging and gulping his wine.

"Who's on duty on the roof tonight, looking for the sub's signal flare?" Pinky said.

"Garrity," mumbled Lewik. "Got so much haze out there most of the time, he'll be lucky to see anything. *Shit!* I just thought of something — what if the Russians signal us and we can't see the flare because of all the haze in the air? What if we miss it? They'll *leave!*"

"I don't know what I keep you around for. It sure ain't your brains. Of *course* there's a fallback, dolt. Two, in fact. If we don't answer the first flare, they'll send another, and if we fail that, they'll send a radio blast on a special frequency. Besides, we ain't going nowhere — we're sittin' right here, aren't we? We'll *get* the signal." Pinky shook his jowls and muttered, *"Balls."*

"I know, I know," said Lewik. "I'm anxious to get outta this godforsaken country. I keep dreaming of them warm Pacific beaches and brown-skinned girls."

Pinky smiled to himself. Poor Lewik. He wasn't going to anywhere outside of the good ole U.S. of A.

"You sure there aren't any Americans around who might try to stop us?" asked Lewik, still paranoid and nervous about the whole setup. "Like those guys in the black suits that got the gold?"

"Those wimps? Probably dead. Even if they're not, the odds of them showing up are one in a zillion. And even if they *did* show, the Bandersnatch would take care of them in nothing flat. They'd be *gone*, baby, wiped out. Blotto." Pinky snapped his fingers at one of the girls. "Honey, how about a massage? And do my nails while you're at it."

While she ministered to him, delicate hands kneading his corpulence, his thoughts turned to Morgana Pinter. Damn, he still had the hots for her, even though she'd humiliated him by escaping. He couldn't get her out of his mind.

At least he'd had his revenge on her, that tight-assed high-society bitch. She might have snubbed his advances back in Philly, but after the war came—and she wanted to survive at all costs—Pinky had offered her survival. At a price, of course, and he had seen to it that Morgana paid *big*. Even so, he'd loved her in his own way. Then she'd had the *nerve* to split.

It was small consolation to Pinky that Morgana was probably dead by now, done in by the New Mexican desert, or by bands of thugs, or even by radiation. He still had it bad for her, and none of these juicy young girls was a decent substitute.

Thinking about Morgana made Pinky madder and madder. "Bitch!" he screamed, lashing out with his fat foot, catching his masseuse in the face. She fell backward with a yelp, then got down on her knees and apologized.

"I'm sorry, master, sorry," she whimpered.

"Get out of here!" he shouted, waving her away with his ham-sized arm. The sniffling girl got up and hurried out of the chamber.

Lewik helped himself to more wine. "Serves her right for putting her face in the way. You let her off too easy. There's only two kinds of discipline women understand. This"—he made a fist—"and this." He

197

grabbed his balls.

Pinky reached out his pudgy hands, and the three girls who were left tugged him up out of the pile of mattresses. He snatched a robe that one offered and shrugged it on.

"Go relieve Garrity on lookout," he snapped. "Tell him to run down to the garage and check on the Bandersnatch tank. He'd damn well better be ready to drive that thing at a moment's notice."

Lewik thought for a moment, then said, "Sure, you're the boss. But why should Garrity drive the tank? — How about me? Garrity can't even drive a damn *truck*. Think about it, boss."

When Lewik had shut the door behind him and Pinky had shooed out the rest of the girls, Pinky went to the leaded-glass windows of the chamber and pushed them open. The view looked out toward the river. A gray, humid haze still hung in the air, obscuring the river and giving the French Quarter an even shabbier look than usual. Wisps of fog clung to the pavement, wafting in and out of the wrought-iron lace balconies of the old buildings.

Soon he would turn over to the Russians the flawed but powerful Bandersnatch Float-Tank. Never mind that the research had been funded by the Pentagon and that the tank rightfully belonged to the United States. To the winner go the spoils, and the Russians were the winners. That attitude dovetailed nicely with Pinky's overall philosophy toward life: *he who has the most when he dies, wins*! Pinky was determined to have the most things, and the Russians were going to help him.

Soon he would be on his way to clean air, warm

beaches, lots of food and plenty of brown-skinned women in the Pacific Nuclear Free Zone — the next stop in accumulating more things and more power. *No one* was going to stop him.

CHAPTER THIRTEEN

Sturgis and his unit approached the outskirts of
New Orleans at eleven P.M. He stopped his men at an
abandoned Roy Rogers restaurant that still had its
walls and doors intact, and kept them out of sight.
He did not want to enter the city and risk detection
until he knew the *exact* location of Pinky Ellis—
assuming the bastard had gotten to town ahead of
them.

Tranh volunteered to scout ahead. He went to the
top of a ten-story building just a mile from the
harbor. A building two blocks away had lights in it,
on all five floors. His computer ID'ed it as an old
convent in the French Quarter.

He scanned the darkness. This time using Infrared
mode. This mode could pick up any living thing in
the dark. Tranh searched up and down the streets
methodically in an arc from the convent. Then he
spotted something. Several shapes, twenty in all, on a
dark cobblestone road approaching a warehouse. It
was a slow procession. The men were on foot; the
glowing images bobbed up and down as they walked.
The way they kept winking in and out indicated that
some large object was between them. A large trailer
truck, according to his computer analysis. Increasing
the I.R. to maximum, Tranh saw more clearly.

There *was* a large truck with them, all right. And in Zoom mode, Tranh could see a fat man waving the creeping truck on with his flashlight. The scene was suddenly flooded with light as the huge doors of the garage opened. The nineteen men clad in khaki uniforms escorted the truck in. They were armed with submachine guns, according to G.I. mode. The load the truck was carrying was covered with tarps. Tranh watched the G.I. readout at the bottom of his visor. SHAPE — SAUCER. SIZE — 50 FEET IN DIAMETER. WEIGHT — 50 TONS. IDENTITY — UNKNOWN. The truck disappeared into the garage as the doors shut behind it. It was dark again. Computer mapping indicated it was on Hester Street.

"I couldn't see all of it — it's under tarps — but it looks more like a big saucer than a tank," Van Noc reported.

"A saucer?" Sturgis asked. "You sure you found his tank and not something else? A float for the Mardi Gras?"

Van Noc shrugged. "It was under heavy guard — that's why I couldn't get closer. G.I. mode confirmed it was heavy enough, and fifty feet in diameter. I couldn't get a complete readout, because I was so far away. I thought it best to keep back and not be spotted."

Dean called his small band together for a briefing before heading into the Crescent City. They sat at the small orange and brown tables and chairs bolted into the floor. Sturgis stood in front of the order counter. Behind him, a sign listed the outlet's selection of fast food — Chicken Nuggets, Bar-B-Q Sandwiches.

He had Van Noc deliver a summary of his reconnaissance, then addressed the men. "Okay, men" — he still used the masculine gender when addressing his command, even though it now included one woman — "Pinky has hundreds of men, according to White Sands. Tranh saw just nineteen, but there's a lit-up building too. More must be in there. The traitors have a tank — we don't know what kind. That tank has unknown capabilities. We expect a small group of Russians by diesel sub, soon. We'll take Pinky *before* then."

After additional discussion of routes and logistics, Sturgis assigned his men to small groups for the last leg into New Orleans. "Anybody else have any questions before we get down to details?" he finished.

Billy Dixon stood up. Running his fingers through his unkempt platinum blond hair, he said, "Why aren't we going to wait for the Russians to show before we attack? Why not take the Reds at the same time we take Pinky and his artillery? I, for one, would like to get a sub for the U.S.!"

"Because our primary objective is keeping technology out of Soviet hands. If we withdraw before the Soviets land, we can save ourselves for strategic missions *we* choose. A diesel sub isn't worth losing one man over."

"One more thing, men," Dean looked around at the faces before him. "Some of these traitors may try to thrown themselves on your mercy, once they see they cannot win. *We will take no prisoners.* There will be no exceptions. Do I make myself clear?" The men murmured their assent. "That goes for medical assistance, too, Dr. de Camp," Sturgis added. "We will give no aid to the enemy."

"Affirmative, Colonel," she said stiffly.

As the men dispersed to get ready, Sturgis pulled Joe Fireheels aside. "I wish you'd reconsider using a suit, Fireheels, for your own protection. You're more competent than Davis with the modes and VSF. He can assist in the Rhino—"

Fireheels shook his head. "Davis can use the suit. My—intuition—Colonel, tells me that it must be so. You must trust me on this. My people have lived and fought by Nature, and the forces that exist in the unseen universe. I will be as useful, I promise you, without the C.A.D.S. suit."

"I have a great respect for your culture," Dean replied. "If the white man possessed the native American's reverence for nature, perhaps we wouldn't be in this mess. But we're up against some very sophisticated weaponry, Joe. I don't want to lose you—you're too important."

The Indian bowed his head slightly in humble acknowledgment of the compliment. Then he raised his eyes. "You honor me, Colonel. Please, you must trust me. I shall be more effective for you as your Invisible Warrior, without a suit."

Sturgis responded largely on intuition. "Oh, hell." He shrugged his shoulders. "All right. I'll grant your request on the basis of this 'intuition' of yours. I hope I'm doing right."

Slowly, in the dead of night and with engines on low, the C.A.D.S. Force entered New Orleans by different routes and convened in Louis Armstrong Park, just north of Chartres Street. The trees and bushes in the park provided an ideal camouflage for the Rhino and the tribikes. Sturgis set up watch shifts, and ordered the men to rest up in the Maison Dauphine Hotel across the street from the park. Rossiter and MacLeish would bunk in the Rhino, as usual. The colonel also dispatched a two-man watch to the Presbytere and Cathedral church, where they could have a high lookout for the signal from the Russian sub.

Sturgis—thinking of Billy—had modified the plan. They'd get Pinky and at the same time get the sub. Billy was right. It was a prize worth a risk. Besides— and maybe this had changed Sturgis's mind—Billy saw taking the sub as some sort of revenge on his part. If it helped Billy's stability to exact revenge, so be it. For now, then, it was a waiting game.

The Maison Dauphine was full of old-world grace and charm, and was in excellent condition, awaiting countless guests who would never arrive. It sported pink marble floors, staircases, and pillars, black wrought-iron railings, huge crystal chandeliers, and rose-colored velvet and brocade curtains and swags.

The rooms were similarly appointed, with soft, wide beds, comfortable wing chairs, fully stocked wet bars, and sybaritic bathrooms of marble and gilded fixtures. Sturgis allowed every man to take his own room instead of doubling up. They spread out quietly through the second and third floors. There would be no wild parties at the Maison Dauphine to give away their presence.

Sturgis took a large suite on the second floor, near the main staircase. He got out of his suit, his tired body thankful to be free. He unbuttoned his shirt and stretched. Then he went to the bar. It was well stocked, and his portable dosimeter showed the bottles to be nonradioactive. "Thank God," he said to himself. "I could use a stiff one."

The liquor came in little individual serving bottles. He took out a tumbler and half a dozen bottles of bourbon, and went to the bed, where he reclined against the headboard and poured the booze.

He drained the first drink in one pull, and the hit went straight to his head. For a man who could drink just about anyone under the table, it was a bad sign of the extent of his fatigue. Hell, he didn't give a damn at the moment. He poured another.

His thoughts turned to Robin, as they always did in free moments. He wondered where she was; if she was safe. If they would be reunited. No, Dean, he told himself, not if — *when*. He tried to remember their life together before the war. It was getting harder and harder to recall those times, when life was not full of hardship and fighting.

The second bourbon put a pleasant buzz in his head. He poured a third, and drank it more slowly. Sometimes, he thought, he could truly understand the temptation of Faust. Faust sold his soul to the Devil to get what he desperately wanted — youth, knowledge, and magical power. Sturgis desperately wanted something more basic — to be reunited with his woman, and to have the freedom to pursue life, liberty, and happiness. Both of those desires were being denied to him.

Through the windows, he could see that a quarter-moon had risen over the city. It ducked in and out of fast-moving black clouds. It was running and going nowhere. Sturgis yawned. He hoped to get at least a few hours' sleep before dawn but he was on edge. Perhaps a drink . . .

Dean was into his fifth little bottle of bourbon when a knock came on the door. "Yeah?" he grunted.

Sheila de Camp opened it and stood tentatively in the doorway. Her auburn shoulder-length hair was down. She looked very unofficial. "Busy?" she asked.

Sturgis had expected anyone but her. What the hell was it now? He was in no mood for problems. "Don't stand there with the door open—you're either in or out," he said. "What's it going to be?"

She slid further into the room and shut the door behind her. Sturgis flicked his eyes over her. After four shots of bourbon, she was not so much medic as she was Sheila de Camp, woman. *Attractive* woman. She was dressed in regulation khaki shirt and trousers which showed off her curves quite nicely.

Dean put his mind back on business, and spoke gruffly to cover up his distraction. "Well? Is someone sick? What's the problem?" He reached for his pack of cigarettes on the nightstand beside the bed, and lit one.

"Nothing," she began hesitantly. "I—I just felt like talking to someone."

Sturgis nodded. He was no stranger to the feeling—the sudden loneliness that welled up inside. He was feeling that way himself. "Sit down. Have a drink."

207

"I'm not disturbing you?"

"That's a question you should never ask me, Doc. Go on—sit down, put your feet up. Have a drink from the bar—it's all rad-free." He hoisted his tumbler full of bourbon.

Sheila smiled tentatively and smoothed her long hair. "Thanks, Colonel. I don't mind if I do. A gin and tonic would taste pretty good, and I hate to drink alone."

"That's a habit you should break," said Sturgis. "A soldier has to spend plenty of time alone." He swung his legs off the bed. "Gin and tonic?"

"I'll get it."

Sturgis waved her aside. "I don't get a chance to be civilized much these days. The least a man can do is get a lady her drink." While Sturgis went to his "bar" and poured a gin and tonic, de Camp sat in the wing chair near the side of the bed. She lowered herself gingerly, as though the chair might collapse from under her.

He handed her the drink, pleasantly noticing how her shirt was unbuttoned more than usual, to the top of her braless bosom. Interesting, he thought, mentally taking off the shirt. That fantasy was as far as things would go—as an officer in his command, she was "off limits."

"Thank you, Colonel," she said, trying not to stare at his muscular chest exposed by his open shirt.

He took a deep breath and turned away. "Cut the formality, Sheila. There are times when it's not necessary, and this is one of them."

She smiled. "Okay, Dean."

He settled back onto the bed, crossed his ankles,

and crooked one arm behind his head. It was damn distracting having a woman here in his bedroom. "So, what's on your mind?"

She shrugged, sipping on her drink. "Nothing specific. I just—"

"—wanted some company," he finished for her. "Right?"

"Yes, but—actually, there *is* something specific . . ."

"Which is? . . ."

She sighed a long, slow sigh, as though something had been weighing on her mind. "Is there any hope for . . . us?" Even in the growing darkness, Sturgis could see the red flush spreading on her cheeks. "For *America*, I mean."

Good God, she wanted to have a philosophical discussion while he was only concerned with the basics in life. "You're asking a man who's only a soldier. I fight the fights, regardless of the odds. I don't try to analyze the broad picture every time I pick up a weapon." He finished his bourbon and opened the last bottle. If he kept on drinking, he would have to move on to scotch. "But answer your question, yes, there is hope. There has to be—otherwise none of us could go on." He eyed her. "You're not *losing* hope, are you?"

She sighed. "No. I'm weary, I suppose. I want to go back to life before the war."

He smiled. "Wouldn't we all? Unfortunately, time only goes forward."

Sheila rose from the chair and went to one of the floor-to-ceiling French windows. She pulled back the heavy draperies and looked out. "It's nothing but a dark, dead city out there. No lights, no neon signs, no people out for a night on the town — we've become a nation of death, Dean."

"Not as long as there are a few of us left alive. Somehow we'll survive, build again, rise from the ashes."

"Even nuclear ashes?"

He was silent a moment. "It all comes down to hope. Determination. Will. And *that's it* for tonight's discussion of the current human condition. My sole goal is to relax and forget for a few hours."

She turned and smiled. "Sorry, I'll lighten up. And you can freshen my drink." She held out her nearly empty glass, and he rose and took it and went to the bar.

He returned it to her, reaching it around her from behind. As she took it, he was seized with an impulsive desire to slip his arms around her waist. It suddenly didn't matter that she was his subordinate, that most of the time they disagreed on nearly everything, that occasionally they went at each other hammer and tong. The bourbon had loosened him, and he had an acute need for human warmth. There was so little pleasure to be had in this hellhole of a world — you had to take what you could get when you could get it.

Sturgis felt Sheila tense, then relax. She wanted his touch. She leaned into his body, moaning as he caressed her breasts. He took her drink glass from her hand and set it down on a table at their side. He turned her around and pulled her tight against his chest. She felt even better this way.

Sheila hesitantly slipped her hands up around his

neck.

"God, you feel good," he said, feeling a rush of desire knock down what remained of his constraint.

Sheila blushed self-consciously. "So do you — Colonel." She let one of her hands roam slowly down his chest as she looked into his eyes. The light outside was quite dim now, but he was able to see the desire in her wide pupils, feel it in the pounding of her heart — matched by the racing of his own blood. The universe had narrowed to the two of them, and the only thing that mattered was becoming one. He brushed her silky hair back from her face, then lowered his lips to cover her mouth in a kiss that was long and hard, surpassed only by exquisite caressing. By the time he drew back, breathless, the pale moonlight had spilled across the bed. In its light Sheila looked like the most beautiful woman in the world.

Sheila said, "I've wanted you for a long time, Dean."

"I know."

Her hand drifted below his waist to caress the bulge beneath his belt. He groaned with pleasure.

"I thought you'd feel the same way," she said. "I hoped — someday it would be like this."

Sturgis cast a glance to the bed. He was a man of action, not words. And right now, he had nothing to say but plenty to do.

211

CHAPTER FOURTEEN

Dean took Sheila by the and hand led her to the wide bed, barely able to contain his arousal. He yanked back the covers and they tumbled down into the soft bed, pulling at each other's clothing. They were stripped naked in nothing flat. Volcanoes long simmering erupt spectacularly.

Sheila came on like a wildcat. It shouldn't have been any surprise to Sturgis. She was one hell of an aggressive woman on the job—what had ever made him think she wouldn't be aggressive in bed? She quickly demonstrated her skill as a lover. Dean had met his match.

Sheila teased him unmercifully, bringing him to erotic heights until he thought he could no longer stand the buildup—only to make him back off and slow down—and do it all over again, each time to a more exquisite peak. She guided his hands and tongue to do the same for her. And when the moment came at last for him to enter her, they both cried out in ecstasy.

"Hard!" she gasped. "Give it to me hard! Oh, yes! Like that!"

He lost count of the number of times he brought her to climax, but when his own came, it obliterated everything in a searing, white-hot flash.

When he regained his senses, Sturgis found he'd managed to flop back onto one side of the bed. He was covered with sweat. Did he have a prick left? Did he have any brains left? If he could find his cigarettes in the dark, he'd smoke one . . .

Dean came awake to dawn's light coming through the huge windows, and to Sheila's expert touch, arousing him when he didn't think there was anything left to arouse. He reached for her and they made love again, this time slowly and gently, savoring the act.

Afterward, he smoked one of his cigarettes, feeling terrific. She had the look of a satisfied cat. While he blew near-perfect smoke rings, she ran a finger down his chest, tracing old scars, skirting the newer ones.

The perfect peace of the moment was shattered when Sheila turned her large blue eyes on him and said, "Can we talk?"

Sturgis practically choked. Why did women always want to turn sex into an encounter session on "the meaning of our relationship"? Why couldn't they be content to leave some things unsaid. Wasn't it in his body, his movements, that the truth lay. What was there to say?

It dawned on him that perhaps he should have kept her off limits. As his medic, she was under his nose twenty-four hours a day—hardly a fling he could get up and walk away from. And he certainly couldn't get *involved* with Sheila, for a number of reasons, not the least of which were duty and wife. Well, too late for those thoughts.

"Talk about what?" he grunted, staring up at the ceiling. He'd never noticed the rococo frieze around the chandelier before. It was fascinating.

"I'm not sure how this . . . changes things."

"It doesn't, Sheila. You ought to know the rules. No explanations are required." He gave her a businesslike smile, but saw she wasn't buying it.

"I'd hate to think this would never happen again." She stroked his chest and belly.

"We'll see," he mumbled.

We'll see. To Sheila, that translated to the old escape line, *I'll call you.* "What do you mean, 'We'll see'?" she said anxiously.

"Nothing more, nothing less," Sturgis answered testily.

They were at it again. At loggerheads. Why, oh why, she thought, do opposites attract?

Sheila was frustrated. Why were men so damned hard to talk to ? Why did they say such passionate things during sex, and then clam up afterward? You'd think they were on a witness stand! You'd think they were amnesiacs! Dammit, she wanted to know how to *relate* to Dean from now on. A terrible thought seized her: Maybe he'd *hated* it. Maybe he thought she was *lousy* in bed, when she'd cut loose with everything she knew.

She tried a different tack, and put sugar in her voice. "Didn't I please you?"

"Wasn't it obvious?" He gave her a playful cuff on the chin. She was relieved.

She hesitated, not knowing quite how to proceed.

215

What de Camp wanted more than anything was to be The Woman in the life of Colonel Dean Sturgis. Okay, so he had a wife who was allegedly alive somewhere. Out of sight, out of mind — no competition. Dieter, of whom Sheila had been *insanely* jealous, was gone. Now finally, after months of longing, she had succeeded in bedding him — and had happily discovered that he was every inch the stud that she expected. Sheila wanted to keep her ground, not become another of his one-night-stand statistics. But the situation didn't look promising.

"I think we need each other, Dean . . ."

Sturgis gritted his teeth as she talked. She was busy setting up emotional housekeeping while he was preoccupied with a battle that could start any minute. He should have guessed de Camp would make his life complicated. Unfortunately, reason never prevailed in the face of passion. He chain-smoked another cigarette, lighting it with the still-burning butt, half-listening to what Sheila was saying.

". . . last night, when you said you've wanted me ever since you first saw me . . ."

Holy Smoke — was she going to hold him to whatever escaped his mouth in a moment of madness? She ought to know men had no control over that. Hell, he couldn't even *remember* what he said. This was getting out of hand.

He sat up, his gray eyes blazing. He took her by the hand. "Stop it, Sheila, and listen to me. Last night was good. Nothing more, nothing less. It might happen again. In the meantime, we've got a war to fight. I demand the same of you that I do of myself and every man in this unit — that you give your all to duty. Anything else that comes along is a bonus."

"Does that mean I was just a convenience—*sir*?"

He softened. "I think you're a hell of a woman."
She looked so forlorn that he put his cigarette down
in the ashtray. "Come here," he said, and reached out
to embrace her.

Ten minutes after de Camp left him, Sturgis was
smoking his last cigarette when Joe Fireheels came to
his suite and asked to see him.

"I request permission, Colonel, to act as a spy and
attempt to get to this strange tank the enemy has," he
said, once ushered inside.

"Explain your rationale."

"Simple, Colonel. Your Lieutenant Van Noc reported it to be under heavy guard. With all due
respect, sir, none of your men have the ability to
sneak up close to it without detection. I do. I am the
Invisible Warrior. It would be to our advantage to
find out what we can about this vehicle before it
could be turned against us."

"And how do you propose to execute this mission?"
Sturgis sat down on the edge of his bed to put on
his boots.

"I will handle it my own way. I can get by a man in
the blink of an eye. I have many techniques for that.
Once I'm in, I'll find out all I can, maybe *steal it*."
His dark eyes flashed.

"I see . . . I appreciate your initiative, Joe, though
it sounds like a long shot. If you got caught, it would
tip our hand—as I said yesterday, I want to get them
all at once." Sturgis stood up. "But I believe you can

do it, Fireheels. Okay, go spying for me. Eavesdrop on the guards. Just don't get caught."

"I will wear only my hunting clothes. I won't be apprehended, but even if I'm caught they will think me a civilian survivor, nosing around."

Sturgis nodded. "Then, leave at once."

Minutes later, Fireheels was padding silently through the streets of the French Quarter. He was dressed in his customary rawhide outfit, a loose-fitting tunic over wide slacks, both the color of sand. His shoes were nylon running shoes with thick rubber soles, the next best thing to moccasins for silence. He was an experienced chameleon, knowing how to blend in with the scenery, to slip along unnoticed.

There was one lookout guard stationed at the outside of the garage where Pinky was storing his tank. The man looked clearly bored and thoroughly convinced that there was nothing to guard against but occasional rats — New Orleans was a ghost town. He paced back and forth with glazed eyes that looked unseeing into the haze. Sliding past him into the garage was effortless for Fireheels. He ducked down between parked cars and inched his way further in.

Deeper inside the garage, security was a different story. Four guards with stubby submachine guns patrolled the ground floor around a huge tarpaulin-covered object. Joe spotted another roaming the parking level above. He receded into the dark shadows along the walls, tucked himself into a crouch where he had a good view, and settled down to wait. The discipline for remaining motionless and keeping his sharp eyes tuned to the softest sounds came naturally. He could stay like this for hours — all day and night, if necessary.

The guards inside were just as bored as the man outside. "The fucking Reds better get their act together and show up today—I'm fucking tired of waiting," grumbled one man, whom Fireheels labeled Flat Top because of his haircut.

"It's a bitch," agreed another. Fireheels labeled him Ox because of his size. "Maybe the bastards are going to stiff us."

Flat Top shook his head. "I doubt it. When Pinky told that honcho officer what this baby could do, you could practically hear him drooling over the radio."

"It probably gets their goat that they have to buy it," chimed in a third man with a mouth full of jagged teeth—Razor Teeth, Joe decided. "The Russians are used to just stealing whatever they want of Western technology."

"Yeah," said Flat Top. "But *this* baby's got a price. Ain't nowhere else to get one—it's the only one in the world. Yep—we're all gonna be sitting pretty sooner than you know it."

Razor Teeth looked at the lump under the tarp. "Can it really do everything Pinky claims? I never seen it in action."

Ox grinned. "It ain't called the Float Tank for nothing, Zips around like a regular flying saucer from Mars." He thunked his fist on the covered tank. "Made of super-thick armored titanium—it'd take a nuke to punch a hole in *that* skin. The best part is the laser guns—they can vaporize men, tanks—practically everything."

"Jesus," murmured Razor Teeth in awe. "No wonder the Reds want it."

Flat Top picked at his teeth with a nail. "Except, it's got some drawbacks—for one, it uses up a hell of a lot of fuel doing all these fancy things, so it don't go far at one time. But we ain't telling the Russkies that—let 'em find out for themselves!" He guffawed, "We'll be living free and easy in the South Pacific!"

The conversation went on, drifting to other topics—mostly women and fantasies about what the men were going to do in the sunny Pacific Nuclear Free Zone—but Fireheels kept listening. Occasionally another nugget of information about the Float Tank was dropped, and he absorbed it and filed it away. He remained impassive, emotionless—a receptor of information.

After fifteen minutes, there were noises out front, and the men responded. Someone was visiting—a very important person, judging from the way the men snapped to attention.

An enormously fat man, accompanied by a tall wiry fellow and six khaki-clad men carrying Uzis, lumbered into the garage. The fat one must be Pinky Ellis, Fireheels thought. And he was in a hurry.

"Get the Bandersnatch ready!" Pinky commanded. "We've gotten the signal—the Russian submarine is here!"

"Lewik here," Pinky pointed to his wiry companion, "will take the controls. Show him how to bring her to the docks. I have some negotiating to do at dockside."

The fat man turned to the wiry one. "Wait for my okay, Lewik, then bring the Float Tank."

Lewik nodded.

Pinky left with five of the troops, leaving one of

the soldiers with Lewik. Pinky, damn him, had increased the security!

"Unfasten the ropes and roll back the tarp!" Lewik snapped. The guards scurried to obey. The ropes holding the heavy tarp in place were unfastened. Other ropes attached to pulleys were pulled, slowly drawing the tarp up and back. At first, all Fireheels could see was the cab of a truck driven headfirst into the garage. As the tarp was drawn further back, Fireheels could make out the huge shape behind the cab, bearing the sign OVERSIZED LOAD. Fireheels inched in the shadows toward a better vantage point. Balanced on the back of the oversized flatbed truck was a hulk about sixty feet in diameter. It looked more like two saucers placed face to face. He noted the name "Bandersnatch-1" on the underside of the craft. It seemed to be made of a seamless silvery metal.

Fireheels' hawk eyes took in every detail. A machine of shiny silver metal, ringed with gun slots — now closed tight. Between the slots were small glass dots. Perhaps lenses. At last the tarp was off. He could see several hoses now leading from three places at the top of the thing down to a generator-type machine to the side.

"Detach the system-charging cables!" Lewik barked. The short guard climbed up a ladder and passed the hoses down to the soldier. As each cable was detached from the Bandersnatch, the man closed a hatch door.

Fireheels thought for an instant that he could rush Lewik and the guards. But before he could long contemplate the probable suicidal attempt, four more men in flight coveralls wearing odd blue helmets and carrying deadly looking submachine guns came through the garage door.

The Blue Helmet in the lead asked, "Who's Lewik?" Lewik waved. The Blue Helmet went to Lewik and saluted smartly. "Mission Control Officers here. I'm Gunnery Officer Dennis Museti, reporting for duty. This is Communications Officer Jenkins, Antigravity Officer Mackensie, and Hydraulics Officer Smith—he's the guy who keeps the pressure up and keeps us level." Each of the men nodded in turn. "Are we ready to board?"

"Having trouble with one of the cables," the short guard called down.

"You and you," said Lewik pointing to Flat Top and Razor Teeth, "get up there and help him."

Museti ordered his men, "Spread out. Stay alert!" Instantly they surrounded the truck. These men were sharp. Fireheels had thought he could slip unnoticed past the original guards. But now his chance was lost. Fireheels hung back in the darkness, wondering how he'd get out.

Lewik turned to Museti. "Pinky just left to do some bargaining with the Russians at the dock. The tank goes down to the dock as soon as Pinky tells us over the communications system." At this point their voices lowered. Fireheels got as close as he dared, inching behind a parked Toyota pickup near the garage entrance.

"Tell me about the tank. Why the name?" Lewik asked.

"The *Bandersnatch-1*," said Museti, "is the first antigrav-drive tank ever built. The next step in tank warfare. Don't worry, Lewik, it's a snap to drive. Even for a nontechnical man."

"Antigravity—isn't that revolutionary?"

"Well, it's not *true* antigrav. It can't get more than fifty feet off the ground. It's really an anti-*magnetic* drive field that acts against magnetic particles in the soil, concrete, ground—anything that's underneath. It repels the Bandersnatch into the air like a kid's magnet. We *called it* an antigrav to sell it to Congress. The U.S. government wanted Exrell Corp.—Pinky's outfit—to build a super-tank that could fly, and shoot light beams, and yet be operated by a single inexperienced soldier. Exrell Corp. had already gone five billion over estimates when the war came. The Bandersnatch was set to be delivered years ago but it failed government check-out. Confidentially, Lewik, the Harrier Jump Jet costs one-hundredth of the price and could do the same thing—if it had the lasers." Museti smiled. "I'll coach you. I've been on the Bandersnatch test team for years.

"Piloting and shooting in the Bandersnatch is easy, but there is the need for four systems officers on every flight—that's us."

"How can I see out? I don't see any windows."

Museti smiled. "No windows—better than that! See the small lenses between the gunports?" Proudly he pointed to the upper part of the craft. "Those are camera eyes made of super-hard reinforced glass. Because they're so small, they make the skin of this thing virtually unbreakable. There are no windows to break."

"You men," Lewik called up to the guards on top of the craft, "have you found the problem?"

"It was a little tricky, sir. But we think we have it in hand. It'll only be a few minutes more."

"Hurry it up!" Lewik said impatiently. "We haven't got all day." Turning to Museti, Lewik said, "You guys are lucky Pinky needs you. He ain't taking all of the men on the sub," he said in a low voice.

"Yeah, we expected that. Our skill buys us our ticket." Museti winked. "I figured we'll all stay inside the thing until we're in the Pacific."

"Well, at least until we're well on our way," Lewik agreed. "Pinky says the sub should be capable of getting this tank in its cargo hold, safe and dry. We're the luckiest men in America. Soon we'll be out of this hellhole. We'll just bring this baby down to the sub and park her in and the hold, and then we're off."

The last of the hoses had been detached. The three guards dismounted. "Hatches closed," said the short guard.

"Lower ramp!" At this point Lewik's voice was beginning to betray excitement as he paced anxiously on the concrete. Museti went and pushed a button recessed in the hull. A hatch door on the tank opened, and a built-in ramp slid out and down to the garage floor. Neat! The Indian watched Lewik board the ramp leading directly into the Float Tank. Lewik had to bow over to get through the hatchway. He was followed closely by the four blue-helmeted men. The others covered their rear, waving their submachine guns around as if the expected trouble. They were very cautious. Then Flat Top pressed the same button and the ramp slid in the hatchway door closed tight. Bright red letters lit up above the door said, LOCKED. The Bandersnatch was sealed.

Fireheels looked now for his chance to escape. But Flat Top and Razor Teeth positioned themselves just inside the garage entrance. Unlike before, they were alert. Fireheels would have to wait it out in the shadows just a little while longer.

Inside the vessel, Lewik sat down at the controls. He was right where he wanted to be—in the driver's seat. He had demanded the right to pilot, reasoning he couldn't trust Pinky. Pinky might leave him behind. But now that he was in the tank, he wondered, despite the assuredness of Museti, about driving her. *No.* Somehow he would load the damned tank aboard the sub as planned! He was going to the Pacific Islands, and that was that.

His seat was right in the center of the boomerang-shaped plastic control panel which was something like a bent luncheonette counter. There were five seats in all, each placed equidistant along its inside arc. The twelve-foot oval room was dominated by its five curved vision screens. The flashing array of colored lights and function buttons on the console panels reminded him of the bridge deck of a TV spaceship.

While the blue-helmeted systems managers checked through system after system to his right and left, he examined the controls. The weapons officer had been right. The controls resembled that of a car—only this baby could also ascend and descend, so the steering wheel pulled in and out too.

"Here," said Dennis Museti. "You can check this out while we wait. He handed Lewik a blue helmet. "You'll note there's a small light in the center of it.

That's a laser beam. You aim it at your target on any of the screens. For firing, there's two cannon controls." He pointed to two switches on the console before Lewik. "If we were in battle, you just turn your head at a target, the laser on your helmet lights it, and you press these do-hickeys. It's all computer-controlled. Just aim with your eyes, squeeze the trigger!"

"It's just like a video game or something out of *Star Trek*," Lewik snickered.

"Except you're not the only Captain Kirk," Dennis explained. "All of these seats have some controls. This button opens the camera-view shields to look at the ground below," Museti said, pushing the green button. Instantly the entire left screen lit up with a technicolor picture of the concrete. "The same goes for all the cameras to the side and aft." Suddenly the craft vibrated with an audible hum.

"What's that?" asked Lewik nervously.

"That means the antigrav is ready."

Museti looked over to Mackensie, who said, "AG systems up. We're floatable now."

"This thing is virtually invulnerable, right?" asked Lewik.

"Right! Don't worry about banging into things."

"What's this thing?" Lewik asked, jiggling a switch.

"Don't!" Museti yelled, too late.

Flat Top and Razor Teeth had been guarding the doorway. They turned their heads when the humming noise rose, just in time to see the craft rise quickly above the truck bed. Both of them, alarmed, moved instinctively out of the doorway and pressed their backs against the garage wall. Suddenly the Float Tank nosed upward and wobbled dangerously close to the roof of the garage. The two guards ran like hell as a howling wind started throwing around tires and other loose objects.

Museti managed to set the craft down again.

"Sorry," said Lewik.

"*Yeah*. Well, let's *wait* for Pinky's signal, okay?"

Fireheels had seen his chance and made a run for it, beating a fast path back to the C.A.D.S. troopers. Fireheels found them already mobilizing in Louis Armstrong Park—the flare from the docks had been spotted. The Indian located Sturgis, who was firing off a series of orders.

"Colonel," he said, "the tank—it flies!"

He filled Sturgis in on what he had seen.

"We'd better hurry our attack before the tank gets into it. Hit and then *get the hell out*."

CHAPTER FIFTEEN

"Is the cargo bay on the sub as wide as I requested?" Pinky wheezed, mopping the sweat off his brow with a huge white handkerchief. He had just begun taking the official tour of the sub. He'd had to squeeze through spaces too narrow for his bulk. Now the Russian commander and Pinky had come topside, to his relief, and were standing on the deck.

"See for yourself, Mr. Ellis," said Captain Machev. The cargo bay whirred open slowly revealing a large circular area. "That is over twenty-five meters in diameter . . . but where is your Bandersnitsky? Where are the cranes to lift it into my sub?"

"You won't need cranes. When I give the signal it'll be flown here and land in the cargo hold. Though it weighs fifty tons, *it flies*." Pinky grabbed onto the railing to support his weak knees. God, how he hated explaining things to morons like this one.

"That I will believe, when I see it," said Machev suspiciously.

"You will see." Pinky stared vacantly, longingly, to the firm shore. What he saw made Pinky roll his eyes around with sheer terror coursing through his clogged arteries. Blacksuits!

The C.A.D.S. men hit the dock with all the fury of a horde of barbarians. Bullets came whizzing from all directions. From one side a set of whistling shells fell on the big dock near the sub's deck. The attack caught the Russian sailors on the dock unprepared. Dozens died instantly in the hail of bullets and exploding shrapnel of shells. The rest scattered for cover, firing back haphazardly in all directions.

Pinky grabbed Machev by the sleeve, demanding to be taken inside for his safety. The officer pushed Pinky down as he tore himself away. He ran to the hatch, leapt inside, and sealed it. Pinky Ellis scrambled to his swollen feet, running along the deck as fast as his short legs would carry him. The Bandersnatch! He had to signal the Bandersnatch!

As he ran across the deck, bullets whizzing about his head, Pinky Ellis realized that he was now depending for his survival on a machine he had swindled the U.S. government on. The Bandersnatch would be more aptly named the Albatross—Pinky knew that the Float Tank had a hundred faults. Still, they wouldn't matter in a short battle. It *did* have great weaponry—the red lasers and its cannons. The $20-billion Exrell Corporation's joke on Uncle Sam might save his ass anyway!

Just before he jumped onto the dock, Pinky felt the sub move beneath him. The sub was already gliding out and lowering itself in the water! He braced himself for the leap across an ever-widening gap between the sub and the dock. He made it—

narrowly, belly-flopping on the dock. Amid the sound of bullets and the panicky screams of the sailors awash on the sub's deck, Pinky yelled to his guardsmen to radio for the Bandersnatch to come to the rescue.

Before one guard lifted the mobile phone a bullet bored into his head. As he slumped, Pinky grabbed the receiver and yelled: "The Blacksuits—they're here! Do something quick! Bring the Float Tank! Lewik, shoot the lasers!"

"Coming, boss," Lewik's voice crackled over the radio. Pinky let go the receiver when he saw a Blacksuit riding a tribike was bearing down on him. The Blacksuit raised his right sleeve and fired a blast of machine-gun bullets. Pinky grabbed the dead guard and thrust him in front to take the bullets. The man was shot to pieces. Pinky shoved him away and dove for cover behind some crates.

Inside the huge garage the Float Tank shuddered and glowed. Antigrav Mission Specialist Mackensie pressed a complex series of buttons and turned dials. A humming sound vibrated the craft and then a shudder commenced. After thirty seconds a howling windstorm erupted around the craft, blowing tarp around the garage, overturning empty barrels. He turned to Lewik, nodded.

"Now take her out *easy*. Just pull the wheel forward *slowly*," Museti instructed Lewik. "*Easy* does it, not like before."

The craft rose slowly ten feet above the truck. "Put your foot gently on the accelerator and drive straight

231

forward out the garage door." The tank lurched forward. "Don't turn the wheel until I tell you. Remember, the controls are very delicate, something like power steering." The craft wobbled slightly and made it through the open doorway. "Now turn!"

As Lewik moved the wheel to the right he lost altitude. Instead of braking, he put his foot down hard on the accelerator. The craft pitched forward. Suddenly a building loomed up on the screen.

"Pull and turn!" Museti instructed, trying to remain calm. Lewik pulled up gently and then turned hard to the right. The craft banked straight into the garage taking half the side wall of the brick building with it. He let up on the accelerator and the craft stopped in midair.

"Did I do any damage?" Lewik yelled. "Are we okay?"

"It's hard to damage this thing. But for heaven's sake try to *steer straight*. Now ascend a few more feet and slow down."

Soon, it was moving down the avenue toward the dock. It shuddered and leaned as Lewik gained skill at the controls. They were still barely fifteen feet off the ground and glided slightly off course. Museti screamed, *"Slow down! Rise!"* The Bandersnatch's magnetic field tossed several parked cars into the air.

Blacksuits storming the docks filled the screens. "Get on the guns."

"Guns?" Lewik froze. "What guns?"

"The *guns*—the laser right trigger and left—remember? Just point your eyes at the target and squeeze the trigger slowly—like I showed you."

"Maybe you'd better take it," Lewik suggested.

"Can't! This machine requires *us* to keep it stable. *You*, the pilot, have to shoot and steer!"

"Great. Well, here goes." Lewik leaned back. On each of the five screens before him appeared battle-views. "Line up the target with your helmet's laser pointer and squeeze the trigger." Lewik aimed at one of the Blacksuits riding down the dock and squeezed the trigger. The man flared into fire, his melting Blacksuit sending up sparks like a Fourth of July sparkler.

"Damn! I did it!"

"You got it—now keep shooting."

A Blacksuit let loose a barrage of shells—armor-piercing stuff from his arms. Lewik was afraid. Pinky had told him of these super-troopers. But it was quite another thing to see one of these guys firing at you. He winced, preparing himself for impact. The shells exploded directly on the screen. When the smoke cleared—"*Nothing* happened!" he yelled exultantly.

"Now keep firing. They can't touch us with anything. This thing can be one thousand feet from a nuke and still survive. Keep *firing*," shouted Museti. He was beginning to believe in the invincibility of the Bandersnatch, himself. "Just remember to keep away from the damned water. A big splash would wipe out half our systems. Otherwise, just remain calm, work the lasers. We can't lose!"

Lewik went after the Blacksuit who'd fired at the craft. He glided straight for the dock. Suddenly Pinky appeared in his sights. He was sticking his porky head out from behind some oil drums on the dock. The sight of Pinky being in danger, in contrast to Lewik's position safe inside the Bandersnatch, made Lewik giggle. For a moment he thought of wiping him off the map. "Save Pinky," said Museti. The Blacksuit was turning toward him. Lewik sighed. Maybe killing Pinky would nix the deal for the trip on the Soviet sub. So Lewik tilted the ship right and left, up and down. He sighted his second target. The red laser beam shot out, turning the next Blacksuit into burning flesh and fused metal melting on the concrete of the dockway.

Pinky gave the thumbs-up. On his porta-phone he shouted, "Good!"

"Yeah, I did good," Lewik muttered. "But to save my *own* ass, nor yours, Pinky."

Sturgis saw Grimes cut in half by the red light-beam. Jesus, he'd never seen anything like it. A tank that flew — with a laser killer-beam! The tank banked and came back for another strafe. Sturgis and a half-dozen of his men took aim and fired, sending off a stream of different sized ammunition. Shells and bullets alike bounced harmlessly off the tank's hull. Grenades and Liquid-Plastic Fire did no damage, either. Fireheels had heard right — the damned thing was near invulnerable — and had no tank treads to blow off!

The tank's gunports opened. With a thunderous *boom*, shells rained from the sky, scoring direct hits on two of his men, who were blown into tiny fragments.

The Float Tank was hovering over the dock, firing from all ports. "Take cover," Sturgis hollered over the radio. "Use Jump mode, keep moving. Fenton, can you get a bead on that thing?"

"Affirmative, Colonel," said Fenton from the Rhino. "We're in position now. We will put some dents in it."

"Then, fire!" Sturgis watched the Rhino, half-hidden behind a warehouse, open up with its big guns, with no results.

"Fuck this!" Sturgis heard Billy yell, and watched the heroic Southerner try for the Float Tank's roof via Jump mode.

The blinking red light on screen five drew Lewik's attention to a hurtling C.A.D.S. trooper shooting his body up on jets toward the Bandersnatch. Before Lewik could line up his sights and fire, the figure had passed above the ship. "What do I do now?" Lewik yelled.

"See the red button marked *deflector*?" Museti replied. "Hit it. He'll quickly be magnetically repelled from the ship—Do it fast! Someone topside could do damage. There's a lot of exposed systems in the maintenance hatches up there."

Lewik squeezed the red button. There was a crackling sound as a dull blue glow erupted and coated the skin. The blue mist of the magnetic force field misted the camera eyes of the screen for a second. Lewik smiled as he saw on the screens the flailing C.A.D.S. figure, some distance away, tumble end over end and slam against a building wall like a swat fly. *"Got him!"*

"You just keep them off this thing," said the gunnery officer nervously. "If one of them gets topside, he might pry open a maintenance hatch. That's one of the flaws of the Bandersnatch."

"That's *dumb*!" said Lewik.

"Yeah, we were working on modifying that, but never got around to it before N-day."

Sturgis saw Billy fall, repelled by some force on the tank. From where he stood he could see a deep dent in the middle of Billy's breastplate. Billy might still be alive—his suit had apparently withstood penetration.

Sturgis raced to the fallen Billy, dragged him off to the side. He nearly froze in shock when he saw his visor was cracked in filaments. The young man's ashen face showed through his visor. Pink foam welled through his lips, possibly a punctured lung. Then Sturgis saw the overload readout blinking just inside the helmet. Billy's life-support systems had been out for over two minutes.

"Oh, my God," Dean whispered. Not Billy. Not after all he'd been through.

Another shell hit the dock and splintered wood. Sturgis jumped and grabbed Billy, pulling him out of the direct fire. A crackling stream of red laser fire melted a C.A.D.S. man to the left. The C.A.D.S. armor suit was impervious to nearly everything, but the laser had pierced through like a knife through butter!

De Camp arrived on the run, carrying her medical satchel. When she saw who the victim was, she murmured, "Oh, no—not him of all people." She opened his visor and then rummaged through her bag. "His lung is punctured, Colonel, and God knows what else. I can't do much without getting him out of his suit."

"Get a bear hug on him," Sheila," Sturgis snapped, "and Jump-mode out of here. That's an order." She obeyed, managing to reach a warehouse with thick walls a few hundred yards away. As soon as the two figures were safe behind the building, Sturgis returned to the battle.

Damn it, thought Sturgis. Pinky's responsible for this. I'm going to crush the fat man, tear him up—wipe the docks with his blood. He leapt onto his tribike and roared down the dock looking for Pinky. When he found that blubberman he was going to blow him into little pieces of traitorous gelatin. Sturgis radioed, "Spread out, keep shooting."

Back at Pinky's commandeered convent headquarters, the slave-women saw their chance to get away. The guards had all run off toward the raging battle that had commenced at the waterfront. The women didn't know who or what was going on, but they knew they'd never get a chance like this again.

"Quick," whispered Martha. The young Texas blonde had led six of the girls out of the building through a door left open. "Keep to the shadows," she told the terrified girls. "Slip over to the white brick building up the hill one at a time. I'll go back and get the others." Martha shivered. She was dressed only in a thin silk bikini. The chill misty morning air wasn't inviting.

"Please! Don't leave us, Martha," pleaded Betty, a sixteen-year-old Pinky had held for the past two months, ever since he had shot her parents in the big Oldsmobile diesel sedan that they were trying to reach California in.

"I have to," said Martha. "Now be quiet. Wait for me and the other girls at the white building. If we don't come in five minutes, head up the hill further. Find some clothes, weapons if possible."

"But shouldn't we wait to see if the others win against Pinky." Betty asked. "Maybe—"

Martha said, "We don't know who they are. They might just enslave us in Pinky's place. We've got to get away."

Martha disappeared into the convent and the girls began running one at a time up the street. They waited for just two minutes. Then, to their great joy, Martha appeared with the four other girls. "Let's go," the Texas teenager said.

The freed girls disappeared into the night.

When Fireheels saw Billy repelled from the tank by the blue force, his proud heart sank. Nothing seemed to penetrate the tank's thick skin. Even if the C.A.D.S. unit had E-balls, it didn't stand a chance against the Bandersnatch. They were doomed.

Something *had* to be done. Billy shouldn't lose his life in vain. He tried to quell his emotions. They were getting in his way. He had to *think*. Fireheels had to remember . . . When he'd spied upon the Bandersnatch, he'd seen the maintenance men uncouple the hoses and close the hinged doors manually.

That was it! Important connections, having to do with the Bandersnatch's power supply, were sealed in those hatches and could be opened from the *outside* of the craft. Fireheels thought it might be the Bandersnatch's Achilles heel. Billy had had the right idea, but he'd gotten repelled by something. Bandersnatch operated on—what was it?—antimagnetic drive? Magnetic! That's it! Billy's *suit* got in the way. The Bandersnatch could repel *metal*. Could he get on top of the tank without a suit? He knew he couldn't jump that high.

Fireheels watched the tank. It wobbled past a building. It was unstable, making sharp turns. It reeled as it veered. To compensate, it slowed down. Now it rose slightly and hovered near the top of the building for a second, before continuing the turn. He decided to try a jump. Keeping always in the shadows of the crates and barrels, he headed off—running for the stairwell of the building. Clad only in his rawhide outfit, Fireheels stripped off his watch and tossed away his knife. He ran up the stairs to the top of the three-story warehouse. Taking the stairs two at a time, he reached the roof just as the Bandersnatch careened that way again. As before, it rose nearly to the height of the roof and then hovered, sending out red streams of laser death at Fireheels's friends.

Seeing his chance, Fireheels leaped to the top of the saucer-tank, having barely enough time to establish a fingerhold on a hatch.

The tank banked from the building, nearly throwing him off. As the tank leveled, he pulled with all his strength to open the hatch door. Besides giving him a better hold, the door exposed a set of switches and the charging-cable connectors. A volley of rockets seared past him, shells exploding in midair as the

C.A.D.S. team valiantly defended themselves against the strafing tank. As the smoke cleared, he could see the oily words "Main Deactivate switch — weapons systems four and five." Fireheels flicked them to "Off."

The sound of the strafing suddenly stopped. Within seconds the top of the craft was enveloped in a blue crackling mist. Fireheels's jet black hair stood on end. A prickly sensation passed through his body. But he was still there — unrepelled. Now to get to the next hatch to do more mischief! And if he could hang on long enough — deactivate the tank's flight systems.

The blue mist faded as he braced his feet against the open hatch and inched his way toward the next small door. He hooked his fingers along the edge of the next hatch. The crackling repel system again set his long black hair straight. Someone inside the tank was trying again and again to repel him!

As before, he pulled open the hatch door. He had just flicked one of the switches when suddenly the Float Tank tilted wildly, throwing his grip loose. He slid like a fallen skater over the tank's smooth surface, Fireheels grabbing for dear life. He lifted his head and saw that worse was to come, for the Bandersnatch was flying full tilt at the warehouse building.

A booming was heard inside the saucer as the tank collided broadside with the warehouse building. "Did it work?" Lewik yelled. "Did I shake the mother off?"

"*Shhhh!* Everybody quiet!" Museti commanded as Lewik struggled wildly to gain control of the tank.

"The scratching's stopped!"

"I guess we shook him off. But the damage is done; the laser is out," Lewik said. He squeezed the trigger twice to demonstrate. "What do we do now? We're out of action."

"I'll tell you what *else* we're out of," added MacKensie, "—time."

Lewik paled. "What do you mean? Something else is wrong?"

Museti responded. "This thing can only fly twenty minutes out of any twenty-four-hour period. We've only got a few minutes left before we have to land, back at the garage, or in the sub cargo bay."

"Why can't we just land on the ground?" said Lewik. "We may be out of weapons, but the skin of this thing is invulnerable, isn't it?"

"I forgot to tell you. The Bandersnatch needs a *landing cradle*. We have no landing gear."

"Forget the garage," Lewik said frantically. "I want the sub! I want to get out of here *now*. Somebody get on the com, call the sub!"

No sooner had the laser stopped firing its deadly red beam than a new danger arose. Pinky's hundred-plus reinforcements arrived, firing not only armor-piercing bullets, but lobbing grenades, and firing bazookas. It was a poorly planned frontal assault, but still formidible.

The Rhino, no longer concerned with the Bandersnatch, turned heavy guns on the army of traitors, and greatly helped the efforts of the surviving C.A.D.S. troopers.

Tranh tried to find Fireheels in the smoke and debris. The last he saw of the Indian, he had been hanging on the edge of the floating tank. Then Tranh had watched in horror as the tank careened into a building, attempting to dislodge the fighter. Fireheels was nowhere to be seen after that terrible collision, which sent a wall of crumbled bricks down onto the pavement.

Tranh thought Fireheels was a goner for sure, crushed to bloody pulp against the side of the building. The fighting Indian, without a single weapon, without the C.A.D.S. suit, nevertheless had accomplished his mission. Incredible. "What a loss . . . "

The sound of splashing waves behind him caught Tranh's attention. The sub was resurfacing further away from the dock, its huge cargo bay already opening wide to receive the Bandersnatch. Tranh mounted his tribike and raced to the dock, hoping against hope to outrace the rendezvous. The Bandersnatch headed for the water. It missed the sub on its first try, but the second time around just made it, lowering quickly into the cargo bay. Then the sub fired two torpedoes; both were aimed for the dock. The sub started submerging. Most of the C.A.D.S. troopers still alive were tied up exchanging fire with Pinky's private army. Too busy to do anything else. Tranh, using the last ten percent of his jump-pack fuel, propelled himself up fifty feet as the dock exploded beneath him. Tranh fired both weapons tubes at a computer-calculated angle. His explosive shells roared out toward the Soviet cargo sub, hit the

242

sail portion of the sub, blowing it open. The sub continued to dive for a second, trailing a plume of cherry and black smoke.

Then there was an explosion, sending up oily towers of steam and flame, followed closely by a secondary blast. Then the water geysered up in plumes of fire. A titantic eruption of oil, metal, and bodies occurred in the frothing, boiling harbor. The Bandersnatch was going to the bottom with the sub!

Tranh's rockets cut out as he just made it to shore. He looked around at the continuing battle. He saw Fireheels emerge, dusty and clothes torn, from the stairwell of the warehouse building. The Indian gave the thumbs-up sign. Tranh's suit was hit by some Soviet slugs, and he became busy returning fire. The twelve C.A.D.S. members who still survived went on the offensive, cutting down Pinky's soldiers and advancing on a remaining pocket of traitors.

Pinky had seen his hope of escape by sea die with the sub. But from his hiding place in a fat barrel, he could see a tribike parked less than twenty feet away, its rider dead on the ground beside the slick low-slung speed cycle. He ran for it, grabbed the idling bike and sped off, up the hill past the warehouse. Before almost anyone noticed, he had turned the corner and was up to 130 mph, heading north!

Colonel Sturgis cut down two of Pinky's men who were running back up the hill. One had been yelling, "No, Pinky, don't leave us . . ."

CHAPTER SIXTEEN

A series of breakneck turns brought Pinky and his pursuers through the winding waterfront-area streets to a broad stretch of Canal Street bordering the French Quarter. Sturgis and Roberto were on the arch-villain like musk on a pole cat, Roberto having caught up to Sturgis.

"I want that maggot juiced," Sturgis hissed through clenched teeth.

Roberto was at his heels, their tribikes gunning up to 165 mph even as they dodged the clutter of cars and desiccated skeletons littering the boulevard. Pinky was a mere three hundred yards ahead. Surprisingly, he handled the tri like a pro, the fruit of a penchant for collecting expensive cycles. The commander drew a bead on him, but his prey fishtailed around a corner just as the spray of hollow-tipped shells bit into the stone buildings crowding the street.

Sturgis signaled Roberto ahead with a brief wave of his arm. "I'll cut him off. Keep me on your visor. You stay with him. We should be able to squeeze him."

Roberto pulled ahead and onto the wide sidewalk to gain an open lane, as the street was filled with abandoned cars, while Dean screamed around the corner, his wheels spinning in a slick of spilled diesel oil. He gained traction and thrust forward just as Pinky's coattails flapped out of sight again. What the hell!

"No good, 'berto. He's doubled back."

"Comprende, Colonel. Coming about. Got him on my screen."

They zigged through quaint stone courtyards and zagged up blind alleys overhung with iron-railed balconies facing French doors. Sturgis was starting to feel like a stunt man in a Hollywood chase scene, except that the ivory grins from sun-baked skeletons cluttering the streets weren't the product of the special-effects lab, they were real. Skeletons picked clean by seagulls and ravens in the months since the apocalypse. Many still wore tattered costumes—pirate outfits, outlandish boas and dresses, and party hats of bright colors.

Sturgis had heard the story of New Orleans' last hours from a Revenger at the crystal caves who had managed to escape the area by boat. Areas west and north of New Orleans had been devastated by nuclear blasts, cutting off all land escape routes. After the few boats left, the rest of the inhabitants partied. Intense fallout was coming; they had just hours to live.

As word of the end of the world vibrated through the jazz capital, the denizens confronted their fate with typical New Orleans verve and panache.

Mardi Gras, Fat Tuesday, the day before Lent, would have to be celebrated *early*! The whole idea of the Mardi Gras was to have as much fun as humanly possible before embarking on the solemn Lenten season of fasting and penance.

It would be a long Lent of death they had concluded. The majority had donned costumes, had broken out "the good stuff." Some who could escaped in boats via the Gulf, but the vast majority of residents, feeling flight a senseless undertaking, crammed the French Quarter for one last blast. A Mardi Gras to end all Mardi Gras.

As the massive dose of radiation from the near-hit neutron bombs engulfed the city, its victims were caught in their drinking and reveling. The bars had been thrown open, musicians had grabbed their instruments and taken to the streets, costumes were pulled from closets, even a float or two had been improvised. Now, Sturgis and Roberto hounded the rogue Pinky in a wild chase through this macabre party's aftermath.

In many places the piles of dead were so thick they had to be skirted by the tribikers. Elsewhere the corpses assumed solitary poses, a bleach-white form draped over a gate or balcony rail. The rad levels had been high even for rats and flys, but birds flitted from safer areas, to eat, dying later, far away.

One massive float dragged out for the final celebration rose dramatically from an iron trailer in front of Preservation Hall. Even in his stalwart pursuit, Sturgis had to briefly glance at the sight. The float's form suggested a giant wedding cake—a mass wedding had perhaps occurred here, judging by the many bodies wearing tuxedos and white wedding dresses that formed a mound around the tall float. Atop the white-papier-mâché structure two wooden thrones

247

had been placed. A crown lay on each seat, awaiting claimants, a king and queen of the wedding . . . and death. But the thrones remained empty, the gesture unfinished.

Without a protective C.A.D.S. suit, the traitorous Pinky Ellis was being exposed to whatever germs were in the area. Maybe, thought the colonel, Ellis would catch something. But he wasn't counting on it!

The treacherous wharf rat had escaped doom before. It seemed as if he'd made a pact with the devil and, becoming evil incarnate, actually flourished in the post-nuke-world's deadly atmosphere. This time he'd make sure Pinky wouldn't survive! The fat man wouldn't disappear down an alley, or crash through a building and escape.

Sturgis's arm cannon swelled with heat as he coughed thick waves of heavy shot, chewing up the quaint New Orleans scenery but somehow leaving Pinky unscathed. They had worked their way through the Quarter and to within a mile or so of the Huey Long Bridge, one of the two spans crossing the mighty Mississippi along the levees south of the city. The colonel hoped for a clear shot there.

"I'm gettin' a tad aggravated with this guttersnipe," Sturgis spat as Roberto pulled up to join him. They watched their visors as the red dot marking Pinky's movements darted to and fro. Lacking the C.A.D.S. suit map-guidance system, he was operating blind, moving erratically but heading in the general direction of the bridge. The Commandos pursued. They had their Mode Red sensors, showing the tri's location, superimposed on their area computer-map screen. The result showed the path of the vehicle against a background of a gridwork map of that sector of the city. When the dot finally worked its way onto a ramp leading onto the bridge, Sturgis and Roberto agreed that was the place.

Their engines roared as they converged on their prey. An elevated highway carried them toward the span. It was relatively free of obstructions and they accelerated to 150 mph, sensing the kill.

"Watch him . . ." Sturgis warned as Roberto pulled even. "Remember, he's as slimy as a rat, and as long as a rat lives, it can still bite." They swerved around a pile of tuxedoed skeletons.

"Don't worry about Roberto Fuentes. The weapon ain't been made that'll take me out when I'm on. And I'm *on* right now, Colonel. Cool your rods, lay back. I'm taking this fish." Roberto pulled ahead at an even-more-reckless speed.

Roberto raised his right arm and six steel darts clicked into quick-fire position. Then he switched hands on the tri's control bar, and six more clicked into place on the left. Pinky was 300 yards ahead, weaving wildly.

"I'm gonna skewer that meat like a shish kebab," he boasted. "Two of us going on that bridge, Colonel. Only one of us coming off."

"No good," barked Sturgis. "We both cross. *You* can have first shot. I'm stayin' close. Just in case."

They sped onward, Roberto straining to hold the lead. Sturgis was a bit worried. Roberto's bike was wobbling madly.

"*Easy*, Fuentes," he called. "We got him. Don't press. You savvy?"

"Comprende, Colonel." Still, Fuentes surged

ahead. "No problem, Sturg. Cool your jets. I'm closing for a good shot."

"Don't lose control. You've got him."

A short laugh crackled through Sturgis's radio. "Here, piggy, piggy . . ."

Pinky was in the crosshairs of Roberto's firing system. The suit-computer directed the Puerto Rican's right weapons tube, following the erratic target. If only Pinky would go straight up the middle! Sturgis accessed his Trajectory Analysis Mode. The T.A. made a determination based on speed and direction of target. The readout said OPTIMUM SYSTEM FOR DESTRUCTION IS VSF.

Roberto released a first salvo of steel spikes in an even pattern from beam to beam crosswise just as Pinky reached the midpoint of the bridge. One dart penetrated the tough rear fender of the tri and sank harmlessly into the tri's storage compartment. The other five missed entirely.

Roberto cussed in disgust. "Couldn't skewer the pig!"

"Use your damned VSF!" barked Sturgis. "Quit hot-doggin' with this clown. T.A. says ice him with a *shell*!"

Computer . . . Laser aim . . . Variable shells system."

He raised his right arm and moved his lips to form the order to fire.

Roberto never got the word "Fire" out!

Pinky did the unexpected. The traitor dropped three trench-digger grenades. In a fraction of a second, they exploded, breaking up the concrete, leaving a gaping web of steel beams and reinforcement bars

250

across a sixteen-foot chasm.

The impending horror was all to clear to Sturgis. He started to blurt out a warning.

"Roberto!"

It was no use. Sturgis knew that. Before his eyes, the tri roared into the breach, flipping over a mangled girder at 160-plus mph and catapulting Roberto violently forward. The Latin called out the intelligent command, "Fire grappling dart." But Roberto's suit malfunctioned.

As he flipped, the dart released toward Sturgis. It flew up, sinking deep into the right shoulder of his suit and penetrating a full inch of shoulder muscle to the bone. He winced in pain and wrestled his Tri to a skidding halt, pulling to within inches of the opening. Big Muddy coursed lazily below.

Roberto had fired correctly, but his targeting system had been damaged, and another malfunction at just the wrong time set off his back jets, spinning him wildly down toward torn bridge-support girders. Roberto slammed into steel reinforcement bars protruding from the concrete. One narrow round shaft found the joint where his helmet fixed onto the suit. Two more rods penetrated just above each steel glove. A bizarre happenstance. A half-inch higher or lower at Roberto's neck, and he might have had a chance. In any case, it was academic now. Sturgis saw that Roberto hung dead, impaled at neck and wrists. *Crucified.*

Sturgis paused for a moment. The thought of Pinky winging his way to freedom, and the feel of warm blood trickling down his side, were cast away. He could only mourn his devoted brother in arms.

Roberto had been with him from the start, a fellow rebel whose restless energy and disdain for unqualified authority had hurt him as well as helped him. *Roberto* . . .

Sturgis clasped the steel dart protruding from his right shoulder and yanked it out with the powerful claw of his left hand. The puncture was painful and bleeding. His suit was still operative, though the right-side servomechanisms were out because of the dart-hit.

After a brief grieving moment of silence, he did what Roberto would have wanted: he returned to the chase.

First, he'd have to get his tri across the crevass.

He fired the tribike's line of steel cable from the vehicle's front tube, snapped a quick-release connector onto the frame, and jetted upward to secure the other end around one of the bridge's crossbeams about halfway over the hole. Then he descended, took a seat, started the engine, and rammed it into gear. As he hit the edge, he hunched over the handlebars and fired his jets, sending the bike swinging across the chasm to the other side. He released the cable as he swung, and hit the other side with squealing tires. The suit-computer showed Pinky had made good time with the fatal diversion. He had gained almost twenty miles as he sped westward on the Route 90 bypass loop south of the river, then picked up Route 45 heading south toward the Baratarian shore and bayou country. Once he reached the flooded plains of the delta, he could ditch the tri and disappear into the wilderness.

The pressure was on Sturgis now. He could rationalize and tell himself Pinky had been exposed to a fatal dose of microbes. But who knew for sure. Sturgis wanted Pinky to suffer before death took him. He was, the colonel vowed, going to die by Sturgis's own hands. For there was too much blood, too many evil acts of slaughter, too many scores to settle, between him and Sturgis now. Not the least of which was Roberto. Never before had a C.A.D.S. warrior been snuffed in anything even close to a one-on-one encounter. They had lost men before, but always in general action, usually with the odds overwhelmingly against them. Here, Pinky had taken on two C.A.D.S. troopers, and had already disposed of one. Added to that was the fact that Roberto was the first loss from among the outfit's inner circle of officers. *No.* There was too much at stake. He had to stay with him, personally kill the bastard, *see* him die.

Pinky covered a twisting twenty-mile stretch on Route 45 in less than ten minutes, while Sturgis, pushing his bike to the maximum, managed to gain less than five miles on him. Pinky's tri moved fast without the weight of a C.A.D.S. suit. The red dot marking his adversary's progress froze on Sturgis's visor. A full minute passed, then two. He had abandoned the bike. Five minutes at top speed brought the C.A.D.S. commander to the discarded tri. There, the highway split, near a northeast finger of Little Lake. Beyond lay a backwoods water route to the Gulf via Barataria Bay, historic stomping grounds of Lafitte the pirate. Sturgis sat in the middle of the road; he had to decide.

Sturgis sprang skyward and hovered at about

thirty-five feet. "Macro view," he croaked, fearing the swine had switched to another vehicle. His probes scanned a five-mile circular perimeter, picking up and sorting out a barrage of images. Life-forms, not vehicles. Animals. He ordered "Scan discrete for humans." To Sturgis's surprise, dozens of dots littered his visor. The bayou was teeming with refugees who had fled the city and environs, perhaps. Who knew who they were. But Sturgis knew that one dot was Pinky. He watched the viewer intently. The closest dot, and the most separate, attracted his eye as a good candidate. It moved down the sluggish bayou as if in a motorboat. Pinky. He had probably found a boat nearby — or had one stashed there all along.

Sturgis snapped, "G.I. mode, boat moving thirty-two degrees northwest." It was identified as a twin-engine Chris-Craft cabin cruiser. The boat was making 25 knots down the waterway.

CHAPTER SEVENTEEN

Pinky hummed "America the Beautiful" as he sped down the bayou at the helm of his craft. He had already ditched his rad-contaminated pants and jacket for a tropical Hawaiian sport shirt and clam diggers; washed off in the waters; and swallowed a handful of antibiotic capsules—just in case! Pinky Ellis planned to live a long, long time, still. But first he had to lose the pursuer!

Swinging a set of binoculars up to his eyes he peered eastward, he chuckled over the way he'd tripped up the C.A.D.S. commando. No sign of pursuit. He chuckled again, leaned back in the comfortable pilot's seat and rummaged through a fat bag of provisions at his feet. Good thing he had prepared this little escape plan. He *always* had a fall-back plan. He was a *survivor*. The boat was fully fueled and it was stocked with "gifts" for the bayou men upstream. They would be eager to help their old pal Pinky. The stupid illiterates thought Pinky was a representative of the U.S. government, after all. He'd convinced them of that the last time he'd come by their way! Pleased with himself, the fat man spread a smear of blue cheese across a Ritz cracker and stuck a pearl onion into the center. He would soon be among friends!

"Above the fruited plain . . ." he sang, cramming the hors d'oeuvre down his throat and starting to work immediately on another.

America, America, God shed blue cheese on thee,
And drown thy food, with Cordon Bleu,
From sea to shining sea . . . HA HA HA!"

The lyric struck a chord and he reached for the bottle of cognac he'd found handy, uncorked it, and quaffed a three-finger dose. "Here's to my damned good planning!"

"Ahhhh," he smiled, slicing a dollop of cheese and plopping it onto his tongue, smacking his lips with satisfaction. Then he popped a trio of pearl onions for good measure and began singing again in a booming basso. The twin engines of his Chris-cruiser rushed him along the bounding main.

"Oh, beautiful for spacious skies,
For amber waves of GAIN . . . HA HA HA!"

Fien Jolie stood at the prow of his canoe, beaver pelt layering his body, his eagle-beak nose sniffing at the wind, ears perked. He'd heard—and smelled—something.

"Smells like . . . cheese! Blue cheese, to be sure! Sacre bleu! It's *heem*! The government minister!"

"Leesen, mon capitan," said Longshanks, his mate, from the stern of the six-man craft. The tall crewman rubbed his raw and reddened eyes, then listened with added intensity. His huge ears festoned with earrings heard off-key warbling emanating from the middle of the channel, just across from where they lay in hiding among the reeds.

"*Leesen!*" Longshanks repeated emphatically. He flicked on a flashlight, waved it in the darkness.

"Jolie!" Pinky called loudly, cutting his engine to an idle and coming around. "Longshanks?"

"It's *heem*, it's *heem*!" the men called, striking out from the enclave, their canoes gliding across the crystal bay to the sound of Pinky's voice. "He brings the supplies!"

"Call out, Monsieur Minister!" Jolie hollered. "We come!"

"Ahoy, poor unfortunates," Pinky lamented loudly, then broke into a moving chorus of "Old Man River" while the company of night navigators came along-side, groping for the rail of the cabin cruiser. Jolie and Longshanks tumbled aboard, eager for the prom-ised goods.

"Have you brought us our relief packages?" Jolie asked after foundering his way to Pinky guided by his flashlight.

"Of course, of course, my children. Do you think that I would not return as promised?" He lit the cabin lights and pointed. "There, beaver traps!" he called, dangling a handful of them overboard to the grasping men below. "And here! Chocolate bars!" he ex-claimed, stuffing several in Longshanks's pockets and handing him a box full. "And here! Soda pop!" he called, twisting off a top and passing it along. "Ciga-rettes! Beef jerky! Potato chips! Fish hooks! Gifts from the American government that I, the disaster minister of the bayou country, give to you freely, completely unencumbered and tax free without lean nor mortgage attached thereto, as promised when I had passed through here but days ago!"

Pinky had stumbled on them weeks ago, and duped them into thinking he was a government agent sent to help them. Now, for periodic doles of supplies, they did his bidding. He had "deputized" them as a local police force and set them to work collecting loot from the bodies of irradiated refugees who had died in flight through the wilderness of the bayou, usually laden with their valuables. At first the band of locals had satisfied themselves with picking the pockets of the already dead. But with Pinky's orders in mind, they began killing anyone who crossed their path. Pinky encouraged their savagery and rewarded them for it, driving their sickened minds to new heights of criminality. Lately they hadn't heard from him, as he had planned to leave them to their folly while he sailed away.

The men shuffled through the odd lot of goods, feeling and sniffing the items to identify them, then stuffing them into pockets or lashing them to their belts. Only Jolie himself stood detached, waiting impatiently.

"Ahh, Jolie, my pet," said Pinky, noticing his disconsolate confederate, "how could I forget?" He rewrapped the remains of the cheese block he'd been nibbling and handed the foil pack to the rad-wracked shadowy figure.

He grasped it with trembling hands and lifted the tiny parcel reverently to his nose, inhaling deeply.

"Ahhhh, mon dieu. Cheese! Oh, merci merci *merci*, Monsieur!" he cried, falling to Pinky's feet and showering them with kisses.

"Enough. *Enough!*" shouted the imposter. "Get ahold of yourself, Jolie. We have work to do!"

"Work? Of course! Anything, Monsieur Minister! We shall do our part to save the nation."

"Let's get back to your camp," Pinky said, looking suspiciously up the bayou, the wheels of his sinister brain spinning. "I'll explain there." Pinky soon started up his craft, and led the tiny flotilla at a leisurely pace through the reed beds into Turtle Bay. The camp was little more than a clearing on the shoreline where half a dozen large canvas tents stood. He anchored his cruiser and stepped into one of the larger canoes which ferried him the last thirty yards to land. Four other bayou men attended the outpost, gathered around a smoldering campfire in the middle.

"First, let's see what you've collected," Pinky said.

Jolie and Longshanks led him to one of the tents where several steamer trunks were lined up in a row. The hapless pirates felt their way along and pulled one of the trunks forward. "We followed your orders to search for valuables. This is what we've claimed since we saw you last," Jolie said, inserting a key into the iron latch, releasing the lock, and hoisting the heavy lid.

Pinky's eyes twinkled as he approached the cache. The large box was over half-filled with gold and gems of all sorts, bracelets, rings, cufflinks, watches, necklaces, and earrings. He scooped the booty up in his pudgy hands, plopped a jeweler's lens into an eye, and examined several of the more spectacular baubles before pocketing them.

"Excellent, *excellent*. The President will be grateful

to you men for your efforts. Believe me, they will hear of this in Washington!"

"Tell us the news," said Jolie, still holding his precious package of cheese. "Is the war still on?"

"Oh, yes, yes. The devastation rages, the suffering is almost intolerable," Pinky said sadly. "Most unfortunate. And that's exactly what I need your help with."

"Anything, Monsieur Minister. You know you can count on our loyalty!" said Longshanks and Jolie in unison.

"Good, good," Pinky chuckled, "for I must inform you that there is a Russian colonel chasing me. We must destroy him."

"One lousy Russian?" Longshanks cried, grasping his cutlass. "I will run heem through for Uncle Sam!"

"Easy, Longshanks. No ordinary man. He's equipped with very special equipment—a strange metal suit that protects him from radiation and all but the most potent weapons. He's part of the communist invasion forces. There's an entire army of these commandos, and they're stalking the country, terrorizing citizens, destroying everything, just as they've always done. And they're clever! They'll stoop to anything to destroy!" Pinky's jowls reddened with the lie.

"What can we do?" asked Jolie.

"We must trap him. That's where you men come in. He's followed me. I'm sure of it. I can tell you he's very determined! When he arrives, you will make it look as if I'm your prisoner. He'll try to convince you he's an American, that I'm the criminal. You must let him think you believe him. Gain his confidence. You must get him out of his armor. Then, we can take him."

Meanwhile, back at the highway, Sturgis had set the remote homing device on his tri to alert the C.A.D.S. squad of his location. He had spotted a small outboard hidden in the reed thicket along the shore, and, deciding it would make better time than his bike, tried to start it up. But it was out of fuel. He'd use his tribike. It was slow in water, but its big wheels moved it along resolutely.

The wound in his shoulder had swollen badly. All C.A.D.S. warriors were inoculated against the deadly poison that coated the darts, but they were still susceptible to some of the symptoms, including severe nausea and fever. Sturgis piloted the outboard down the bayou, monitoring Pinky's movements on his visor. He had watched as the dots representing other boats appeared on his screen in little rows of six. Now they dashed from the shore, surrounded the cabin cruiser, and moved off with it after a moment. *What the hell?*

The narrow bayou reached a confluence with another channel and stretched into a wide westward bulging gulf before narrowing again at the mouth of Little Lake. Just south, indicated the computer, on the eastern shore, lay Turtle Bay. Sturgis approached the opening to the lake slowly, swooping along the far crescent of the bay and coming up through a maze of tupelo trees which creeped off the shore well into the waters of the bog. It was now easier to see without I.R. mode—a half moon shone through cloudcover.

261

He cleared the narrows and fronted the wide vista of Little Lake. Colorful bands of strontium and cesium clouds streaked the horizon. Ahead, beyond a cluster of channel islands overgrown with live oak and cypress, lay the broad waters of Barataria Bay and the Gulf. He veered easterly, skimming through a vast field of water lilies and reeds. Here the thick vegetation began to entwine his big tribike tires, so he propped the engine and drifted onto the confines of Turtle Bay, aided by an occasional power burst. With his suit's sensors to guide him, he had no trouble finding Pinky's cruiser anchored in a hidden cove.

He knew Pinky still had the grenade launcher and watched his Trajectory Analysis screen, anticipating an incoming bogey any second, jets lit and ready.

"Zoom, G.I.," he ordered, scanning the shore. Six canoes were beached with their crews milling about the tents, a dozen men apparently oblivious to his presence. After scouting the cabin cruiser and finding it empty, he switched on his voice amplification and addressed the camp.

"You men! Listen to me! I am Colonel Dean Sturgis, U.S. Omega special forces. I'm seaching for a traitor—a fat man! I'm coming ashore. Hold your fire!"

Sturgis checked systems, swallowed against the nausea gagging him, and coaxed up his overworked air conditioner to cool his fever. The hole caused by Roberto's dart had taxed his environmental controls to their limits.

The Bayou marauders waited silently, alertly, gathered on the short stretch of mud beach. At the end of the cove the "Russian" approached. Pinky wasn't anywhere to be seen. He had told them what to do. They stood up, waved. "Hey, friend, over here."

"Where's the pilot of that boat?" Sturgis demanded as soon as he came up to them. The men were not at all surprised by his suit. That should have tipped him off at once that something was peculiar. But Sturgis was tired.

"We got 'im. Why?" responded Longshanks abruptly.

"I want him."

"And who might you be?"

"An American—my name's Sturgis, Colonel Dean Sturgis, U.S. Omega Force. I'm tracking a traitor, a fat man. Don't be alarmed by my armor suit."

"C'mon along, Colonel. I'm Longshanks. The leader here." Longshanks had taken the lead role since Jolie was in a fit of reverie over his cheese. "This here's Tom, 'n Jack, 'n the rest of our clan. "We've got your man all trussed up and ready for you."

"Obliged," said Sturgis, wincing in pain with every word. He quizzed his computer on his vital functions.

BODY TEMPERATURE, 104; PULSE, 120; BLOOD PRESSURE, 205 OVER 101.

Sturgis frowned. He was a human pressure cooker!

The band of locals led the C.A.D.S. colonel to a wooden cage. Pinky stood inside it holding the thick bars.

"Colonel Sturgis, you bastard!" Pinky cried from the cage. "Tell these maniacs to let me go! They said they were gonna burn me alive! You've got to stop them!"

263

"Oh, really?" Sturgis replied. "Maybe I'll let them burn you."

"No! You can't Sturgis. It's an atrocity! You wouldn't let them have me — would you, Colonel? Be civilized!"

Longshanks reached over and leveled a slap in the direction of Pinky's head, catching the man on the hand instead. Sturgis opened his visor.

"Easy, Longshanks," said Sturgis. "I'll take care of him. It does me good to see him all wrapped up in a nice little package for me, just like a sausage on the supermarket counter, ready to fry. But he's got to come with me, stand trial."

"Aye, Colonel," answered Longshanks, playing his role like a first-rate thespian. "It's no surprise to us he's wanted by the federals. He's robbed us before and no doubt was looking for seconds. But we outfoxed him this time. But, say — you know, you don't sound too good, Colonel. Could we get you something? A cup of coffee? Something to eat maybe?"

"No . . . no thanks. Have to get back, really. Thanks. My squad's . . . waiting back in the city."

"Maybe a quick shot of whiskey? It's quite a piece back."

Sturgis paused. "No . . . no thanks. Well . . . all right. Maybe a little coffee *would* help."

"Fine! Excellent! Tramp, prepare fresh coffee for the colonel. Tramp brews an excellent cup, Colonel. Adds a touch of chicory to take the edge off. Come on out in the open air. Stuffy enough here!"

They gathered in the midst of the camp along some wooden benches padded with beaver pelts. Sturgis and the men seated themselves around a small campfire. With some concern he checked the rad level of the clearing. *Not bad.* The bayou men had picked a good location.

Tramp filled a coffee pot with ground beans and put it on a grill over the flames. The enticing aroma soon drifted Sturgis's way.

"Can you give us news of what's been happening?" Longshanks asked. "We have a million questions."

"I'm sure you have," replied Sturgis, almost nonchalantly releasing the vacuum seals on his helmet and lifting it off. He peered down at the wound opening. His shoulder was swollen so badly it pressed against the walls of his C.A.D.S. suit. He would have to treat it.

The series of popping seals put a start into the men.

"Sorry," said Sturgis. "Seals make noise."

"That's some mean gas you're passing," said Longshanks. "I see army chow ain't changed much from my days in the service." He laughed at his own vulgar joke, joined by the others.

Sturgis smiled through a grimace as he peeled back his blood-soaked fatigues from the wound. "No, not passing gas — Just some e — quipment — I'm wearing. Ouch!"

"What's the matter, Colonel?"

"Nothing, really. Just . . . a little flesh wound . . . that's all . . ." He took the aluminum cup of hot coffee from Longshanks. It tasted divine. Aromatic and rich, lightly sweetened with sugar cane.

Slowly the symptoms overtook him. He was flushed, then warm and dizzy, finally delirious. The surrounding woods spun. He thought he saw a weird collection of skulls spread about on a nearby knoll. Then he hit the deck.

Longshanks heard the thud and reached over to shake him. "Colonel? Colonel?" He paused for a moment. "Tell Pinky and Jolie it's all clear. He's out like a light."

Sturgis awoke in a burning sweat, his head pounding. It was daylight — early light. He shook the sweat from his eyes and strained to focus. Less than twenty feet away, at the water's edge, Pinky stood leaning over a canoe. He was alone. All alone. Pinky appeared to be laughing. He thought he saw a C.A.D.S. helmet jutting from the canoe. Then, Pinky turned and started walking toward Sturgis. The colonel squinted up in disbelief. It seemed like his head was at ground level, yet he felt like he was standing up. What kind of position was he in?

Pinky was nearly upon him. Sturgis shook his head again. He tried to pull his hands to his eyes but they wouldn't move; maybe they'd been lashed. He tried to move but his legs were like iron weights. A fly lighted on his nose and he puffed at it. It flew away. The coffee! It must have been drugged. "Pinky—"

"A fitting end, Sturgis," said Pinky solemnly, standing before him. Sturgis looked up from the man's shoes, peering at the shadowy underside of his vast belly.

"Oh, my God!" Sturgis gasped, suddenly cognizant of his position. He was buried to his neck in a huge ant knoll. There were pieces of bone near his head.

They had all been picked clean. *Fire ants!* Poisonous, painful death!

Pinky bellowed in a brief fit of uncontrollable laughter. " 'Oh, my God'? Priceless! Sturgis, the look on your face is just priceless. I wish I had a Kodak!"

Sturgis struggled uselessly; his entire body was immobile. He mustered his last vestige of dusty saliva and spat at Pinky's patent-leather loafers.

"Tch, tch," said Pinky, wiping his shoe on Sturgis's cheeks. "Pity. We might have made a good team, Sturgis. I'll tell you something, though—you and your fellow black robots are *terribly* overrated. A bunch of fancy-ass washing machines. I guess it just goes to show, brain over brawn, every time. Ha ha! Ah, this is rich. Well, I wish I could hang around for the show. Gotta run, though, good friend. And don't depend on your buddies to find you. You've been asleep for ten hours! They must be way off course. Sorry, pal! Not your fault, though. You have to get up pretty early in the morning to fool Pinky!"

He kicked sand in the C.A.D.S. leader's face as he turned to leave. "Oh, and by the way," he added, stopping short, "they tell me it takes a good two, maybe three days to die. Hope you enjoy your stay with the fire ants. The other men have left already— so you can scream, but no one will hear you. I just *had* to see you wake up!"

Pinky waddled to the shore and boarded the canoe along with Sturgis's pilfered C.A.D.S. suit.

"I'm gonna give it a try," he called to Sturgis, holding the helmet up, "once I turn it over to the Soviets. Who knows? With my brain, this thing might prove useful. I know it must be booby-trapped.

I'll let the Reds figure out how to disarm it! Bye, Colonel."

Sturgis looked about at the excited red ants scurrying toward him, and swallowed hard. He heard Pinky's paddle start splashing in the water. As Pinky rowed, he yelled back, "You can *eat* the ants, Sturgis. One guy lived a week doing that. But then, the ants ate *him*!"

Sturgis tried desperately to remember one of the prayers his mother had taught him. When none came to his feverish brain, he mouthed a more practical incantation.

"C'mon, Billy, ole pal," he prayed.

Pinky couldn't find Sturgis's tribike parked in the reeds fifty yards south. Nor the homing device leading one *damned determined* Billy Dixon after his commander.

As Pinky paddled away, breaking into a refrain of song again, there was another sound on the waters—the sound of Billy's tribike eating up the narrow lily-pad-choked passage.

Pinky stopped singing when he heard the churning of Billy's big wheels. He twisted his neck to see the Southerner lining him up with his right arm.

"Fire gas shell—one second," Billy commanded. He did his order over Audio mode, so that the fat man in the canoe could hear. The fat man had gotten half up out of the canoe when the captured Soviet ammo screamed out of Billy's under-the-sleeve weapons tube.

It was a sleep-gas shell. The shell took only a

fraction of a second to reach Pinky Ellis and much, much less than that to explode.

"Please," Pinky begged, "please don't leave me here. You're an American. Please don't." Tears streamed down Pinky's reddened jowls and soaked into the sand of the ant hill. All around him, a few advance scouts of the hordes of local fire ants tentatively approached the traitor's blubbery face.

Billy smiled, wiped a muddy boot across Pinky's face. "Oh, I don't know, Pinky. Maybe you'll get along with these *red* ants. You're a bit *Red* yourself aren't you? And don't be expecting your friends back — they aren't coming back for you," Billy sneered.

"Please, I'll do anything. Let me live." Pinky began kissing Billy's boots, running his tongue over the filthy muck. "See? See? I'll do anything. *Anything.*"

Billy moved his foot back. "I believe you would. But I was listening when you told my commander what he could do to stay alive, and I suggest the same for you. *Eat the ants!* Eat 'em until you can't eat no more. Then they eat you!"

As Pinky screamed and screamed, Billy walked slowly back to the canoe where Sturgis lay with a fever, weak and unable to stop his junior officer from committing this torture.

Billy had tied the canoe to his tribike. Now he mounted his vehicle, started it up, and moved away from shore. The canoe with Sturgis lying in it drifted along behind the tribike. It eased down the murky waters of the bayou back toward New Orleans. There the survivors of the C.A.D.S. unit awaited news of their commander.

Billy tuned out the blood-curdling screaming of the traitor, and in the air-conditioned silence of his metal armor suit contemplated the happy sounds of the others when he brought the colonel back alive. He knew what he had done to Pinky was sick. But, after all, it was a sick world now. The beginning of a new Dark Age.

THE SURVIVALIST SERIES
by Jerry Ahern

DOOMSDAY WARRIOR
by Ryder Stacy

After the nuclear devastation of World War III, America is no more than a brutalized colony of the Soviet master. But only until Ted Rockson, soldier of survival, leads a rebellion against the hated conquerers . . .

DOOMSDAY WARRIOR   (1356, $2.95)

#2: RED AMERICA   (1419, $2.50)

#5: AMERICA'S LAST DECLARATION   (1608, $2.50)

#6: AMERICAN REBELLION   (1659, $2.50)

#7: AMERICAN DEFIANCE   (1745, $2.50)

#8: AMERICAN GLORY   (1812, $2.50)

#9: AMERICA'S ZERO HOUR   (1929, $2.50)

Available wherever paperbacks are sold, or order direct from the Publisher. Send cover price plus 50¢ per copy for mailing and handling to Zebra Books, Dept. 1993, 475 Park Avenue South, New York, N.Y. 10016. Residents of New York, New Jersey and Pennsylvania must include sales tax. DO NOT SEND CASH.